For My Mother

WHEN A TREE
FALLS
IN-A
FOREST

CHRIS BENTLEY

ISBN 979-8-9850664-5-6
Library of Congress Control Number: 9798985066456

Cover and interior design by Tamara Cribley, The Deliberate Page

Printed in the United States of America

Email: Connect@ChrisBentleyInc.com
Visit www.ChrisBentleyInc.com
Facebook: @cbentley1160, Instagram: @christoph.w.bentley

THE PINE DIDN'T HAVE ANY CLEAR CONCEPTION OF BEGINNINGS OR END-
ings. Its germination was something lost to itself and spanned so many
human lifetimes that none of the shorter-lived animals, like deer or the
occasional hiker that strayed off the Middle Fork Trail, had any idea
what life meant to a tree.

The pine was alive with billions of cells bursting onto the scene for
their short season only to be replaced by others. The pine was aware of
all of them as they existed in a collective of time and space and growth
and death. When the ponderosa pine looked back at its growth rings
to those early years, its origin story seemed more of an emerging than
a birth. No one was there to teach it how to be a tree—its parent tree
being unknown and lacking the necessary vocabulary to describe such
concepts as maternal care or love or history.

All those centuries, the pine stood on the ridge until it crashed down
the hillside in one rushing moment. Not having eyes, which had photo-
receptors, the pine experienced the change in geography in other ways.
The new ground was felt and soils tasted for just a few seconds as its
roots lifted from their moorings, leaving the greater portion fixed deep
in the bedrock. Its trunk creaked, gradually bending closer to the earth
until gravity won out and roots lost hold, finally setting the tree free.
Then the massive pine, weighing in at many tons, had nothing but loose
gravel and unstable soil to slow it down.

The pine gained momentum in the extreme, steep grade of its fall, gouging a rutted path that would remain visible for a couple of seasons. It slid off a lower ridge thirty feet above the Middle Fork of the Salmon River, tumbling end to end once, and with nothing more to stop it, plunged branch first into the river, making waves that splashed high on the canyon walls.

The river was low by that time of year, so the pine's branches held the tree in place with its root wad partially exposed. Its roots, not knowing what to do other than what millions of years of evolution had taught them to do, drank deeply from the newfound source of water, the river providing a lifetime's worth of precious moisture with every passing second.

The pine felt something strange tangled in its branches. The drag of polyvinyl blocked water in unnatural patterns. The branches holding that foreign material were soon swept downstream. But the branches supported something more delicate—a woman with life gone, suspended in the surrounding water and pierced by branches. It wasn't right, as far as the pine knew, for human life to be held that way, but the pine, too, was losing sense of itself with each passing moment. The river was washing its trunk and roots and branches clean of memory.

But the pine had enough clarity to hold on to a few last thoughts—signaled through its cells and shimmering through its remaining needles. It had been a tall ponderosa pine—*Pinus ponderosa*—that had seen many fires before. But, this time, it experienced just the right combination of a weakened root system, gravity-fed earthflow, bug infestation, age, and a gentle nudge from the wind to start the series of events that led to its descent to the river.

The pine's iconic veins that dripped down its trunk had been earned after enough years of life to produce them. Most ponderosa pine seeds failed. The pine was one of the exquisitely lucky ones to not only germinate but to go through a tree's full life cycle. The right combination of soil moisture, pH, sunlight, and darkness had to work together to even signal seeds that they should break free of their shells. When analyzing the success-to-failure rates of the billions of seeds a forest full of ponderosa pines might litter the understory with, the ones that grew were the exception not the rule.

The pine knew that. It also knew that any number of hungry creatures or fungi or diseases could spell a seed's ruin long before it grew roots and bright needles. As it fell down from the ridge as if in a timelapse, the pine felt a three-dimension profile of its roots searching for nutrients and the branches multiplying under countless sunrises. Each growth ring stood as a remarkable achievement. One more year of beating the odds.

And in harsher climates, those growth rings spread out in very thin rims, some portions of the pines' life rings having melted together into imperceptible years equivalent to the tree gritting its teeth—biding its time for years of plenty when the growth rings would be more pronounced.

The pine had withstood hundreds of winters. Its roots digging deep into its familiar acidic soil, far deeper than the mere loamy duff that collected under its base, clinging steadfastly to the unseen boulders and scree that always slowly churned underneath, falling at a geologically scaled slow motion. Micro root tendrils had intertwined with ancient bedrock and clay and funneled water from the ground hundreds of feet below ridgetops where the proud tree had leaned out to welcome the scanty, slanted sunlight that canyon-life had afforded for so many years.

On that ridgetop, the pine had experienced thousands of days and thousands of rafts float below it. It had felt eagles raise fledglings in the tops of its branches. It stood witness to the deaths and births of small woodland creatures that became food to produce the next generation of wolverines and weasels. It had made silent note of ticks leaping with hope on a mountain goat's back and recognized the passing of an ant that was crushed underfoot by the goat's hooves, ground into the soil that eventually became a part of the pine's vast pool of nutrients pulled into its phloem.

The pine had used every survival tactic in its arsenal. Its bark was several feet thick, designed to withstand wildfires. Rather than viewing fire as an enemy, the pine had adapted to embrace fire as an element of *germination and its eventual uplift into the canopy—one more sapling to brave the frantic, harsh realities of life.*

The pine didn't do well in crowds where it would be forced to fight for resources like sunlight, water, and helpful root microorganisms. Since the pine was mainly left to its own devices, it grew three times as fast. And fire had kept the crowd of eager seedlings down as well as anything. Stout saplings and particularly mature trees might get their bark blackened in some areas by fire, but because of the thickened bark, the critical processes that took place at the most intimate portions of the trees didn't get disrupted and they survived just as the pine had done for hundreds of years.

It was a paradox—the pine had spent so much of its energy producing cones to proliferate its genes into future generations, but for the tree to survive, it had to experience the death of most of its offspring, especially those planted nearest it. Not that seeds planted under their parents' shadows had much of a shot at germinating anyway, but under natural conditions, where fires went through drier forest stands at regular intervals, those that managed to break soil at their parents' feet would be swept off in the heat of the flame.

Only high-severity fires posed real risk to the pine, so long as fires crept under the canopy. Ladder fuels like lower branches, bunched-up saplings, and overgrown bushes were kept down by frequent low-severity fires. The burns helped to clear the ground.

The pine had lost its lower branches naturally while transitioning into a mature tree. Its understory, and that of its few neighbors, had been kept clean of undergrowth by the stately sentinels towering over anything needing photosynthesis. The constant rhythm of the fire regime had done the rest.

But the pine knew high-severity fires could kill even the best-prepared ponderosas. Fires that burned too hot or too high could burn through centuries of bark and jump high enough to reach the branches and needles, leading to crown fires where flames could jump from the tops of trees, leaving moonscapes of blackened soil and ash.

But fire wasn't the only concern of resilient trees like the pine. Along the ridgelines following the Middle Fork, temperatures could be extreme enough to take down the less hearty. Unusual hot spells could last for weeks, drying the arid soil, causing trees to lose needles and branches in an attempt to slow photosynthesis and preserve what reserves remained. And cold snaps could lead to temperatures dipping well below zero. Ponderosas' thick coats of bark helped to insulate the trees, but cold that extreme could find its way past even the best-laid bark.

That's why the pine marshalled another defense. During the drier falls, the pine naturally lowered its water circulation so there was less water to freeze come the more frigid winter months. And if that wasn't enough, the pine also used a natural antifreeze that flowed in its soft, moist, vulnerable inner core.

But every tree had its temperature threshold. The pine knew of trees that had been taken beyond that threshold, whether by absorbing too much sun in the summer, causing the loss of moisture and needles, or through life-ending events of violent explosions that caused fractured trunks in severe winters. The very things that kept a tree alive—water and sunlight—when joined with severe temperatures could, in turn, be its end.

Any of the pine's neighbors could have been the one to fall that day. The pine considered it a miracle, in some ways, that any tree stood as long as it had. Every tree in a forest would eventually fall.

The pine wished for pleasant climates, sufficient water sources, and ample sunlight to warm its frigid needles. But it had no way to compare its lot against any of the millions of other ponderosa pines throughout the forests of America. It recognized its good fortune to have some models of resilience in its neighbors that had seen a few more winters than it had. Though it had no words to describe the feeling of its constant awareness of an upwell of fluids, a swelling energy from a particularly sunny afternoon, or the playful interaction with microorganisms at its roots, it somehow sensed that the challenges it faced hardened it against future turmoil. And for that, it was grateful.

VALERIE JAMISON HAD BEEN A PARENT LONG ENOUGH TO KNOW that if she wanted a relationship with her kids, she had to do more than feed and clothe them. In some of her more sentimental moments, usually in the early mornings when she opened her two kids' doors a crack to reassure herself that they were still breathing and to muster whatever maternal superpowers she hoped she had to send good thoughts into her sleeping babes' dreams, she longed for the days when her primary job was to keep her kids clean and fed and slumbering with soft songs and gentle rocking. Those days were long past.

The job description now required her to know enough about clothing brand names so as to not embarrass her eleven-year-old daughter and so her daughter could fit in at school; provide enough support without hovering; and possess the mystic's touch in knowing her kids' moods long enough before they did to sooth their hurt, share their rage, and stay out of their way.

In her darker moments, she weighed the value of staying in the arena at all. *Do all mom's face such decisions? Why be beat-up and bruised to stay close to our children? What if I revert back to just biological needs?* There would always be food enough for the children to survive. And though they didn't notice how much work it was to keep it up and pay for it, they would always have a roof over their heads and beds to sleep in.

Of course, that wasn't enough. And Valerie would never want it to be enough. Now that she knew the difference between being a mom and not being a mom, she couldn't imagine life without that title. It was a part of who she was—viscerally infused into her like being a woman or a wife or a sister. She never talked to her husband, David, about it directly, but she sensed that he understood that the title of mother held a higher place in her heart than others. Maybe even higher than being a woman.

Being a woman wasn't such a clear-cut role these days, and she was glad for that, in most respects, too. She certainly wouldn't be happy as nothing more than a little wife living in a small suburban home, cooking and keeping house and looking pretty for her husband.

Valerie picked up a stray sock from the gently stained dark-green carpet and thought, as she always did anytime she noticed yet another stain on the carpet, how incredible laminate flooring must be. She tossed the sock into the hamper in the small closet where they kept the organized chaos of towels. She folded every towel, but through some cruel magic, after going through so many towels in a single day, the stacks fell, and the neat folds were undone by the time she reached for a washcloth to remove her eyeliner and mascara at night.

She clung to a few vanities, like never leaving the house without makeup, but had let most others go as a young mom. Most days, she wore oversized T-shirts that smelled faintly of sour milk, yoga pants that weren't as flattering as they'd once been, and New Balance shoes because they were so completely broken in that she could slip them on without bothering to untie the laces. That is to say she tried to cherish the good days and gritted her teeth through the less good ones.

She heard the creaking of the bed Evelyn insisted on keeping even though she was too big for it. Valerie's alone time was over. She took a deep breath to savor the silence a few more seconds.

Evelyn burst out her room in a flurry of dark-brown curls and passion for each day. "Mom! What're we doing today!"

With Evelyn, answers like *I don't know.* or *We'll have to see.* never satisfied.

"Good morning, sweetheart. How did you sleep?"

"Fine. But, Mom, it's the weekend. We need to do something!"

"Like what?"

"I don't know. You're the mom. Aren't you supposed to make plans?" Evelyn accused while opening the fridge and scanning for snacks.

"Eat something real. There's cereal in the cupboard."

"I was looking for the leftover pizza. You didn't eat all of it, did you?"

Valerie glanced behind her shoulder and saw the two pizza boxes stacked on the top shelf in the fridge. Did Evelyn think she had that much of an appetite?

"I guess cold pizza is a real food of sorts. It's right there on the top shelf."

Valerie brought out one of the boxes for Evelyn and pulled out a small plate to put the pizza on.

"Keep the pizza on the plate please. We don't need any more stains on the couches."

"Fine. Thanks, Mom," Evelyn said as she ran out the room with two slices of cheese pizza in one hand and the plate in the other, leaving the pizza box wide open.

Valerie tucked the top of the pizza box back in and put the box away in the fridge. When she walked into the living room a few minutes later, she found Evelyn intently chewing her pizza while engrossed by a robin that was hopping about the front lawn and pecking at the wet grass.

"What're you looking at?"

"A bird, obviously," Evelyn said with a mouth full of pizza.

"What's it doing?"

"Looking for worms. It got one! Ew!" Evelyn turned around with her second piece of pizza locked in her teeth. The plate discarded on the couch. "So what are we going to do today?" Evelyn asked, remembering her previous question and still chewing a mouthful of pizza.

Valerie tried a new tactic. "I thought you could decide what you want to do. You could call it a *Choose Your Own Adventure* sort of day."

Evelyn looked skeptically at her mom at first, but then her face instantly lit up.

"I know exactly what I'll do!" And with that, Evelyn ran to her room.

Valerie heard rummaging from behind the closed door and after about thirty seconds, Evelyn burst out her room, wearing a rain jacket and hiking boots over her pajamas and toting three books.

"This looks promising," Valerie said as Evelyn plopped the books down on the dining room table, she debating whether it was worth the fight and effort to get Evelyn to change into regular clothes.

"Yeah. I think I should be set," Evelyn said, digging out three granola bars and a can of diet Sprite from the kitchen cupboard.

"It looks like you've chosen your adventure. Do you mind filling me in?"

"I'm going to climb the big maple tree and spend all day reading up there!" Evelyn announced with every bit as much enthusiasm and solemnity as if she were announcing the end of a world war.

"That sounds like an excellent plan. Reading is a very good thing."

"I know. So I'll just be outside."

"I'll come by to check on you in a little while, okay, honey?"

Evelyn was already out the door and didn't respond. Valerie stepped outside and shut the screen door that led out to the carport and watched from a good distance as Evelyn disappeared around the corner on her way to the maple tree. Only when Valerie could tell—by peering through a knot hole in the fence—that Evelyn was well situated on a not-too-high branch of the tree, did her mind race back to that disorganized muddle of towels.

There was something comforting in folding towels. They came in the hamper jumbled with socks and underwear, but when they were pulled out, every single bath towel visibly lowered the load in the hamper. And then the folding process was so much simpler. Step one, fold the long side. Step two, tuck it into thirds, folding both short sides in. Done.

Valerie was having a good morning. Not that she had clear measures to indicate a good or bad morning. It depended on how many tasks she could knock out before lunch. Somehow, by the time lunch rolled around, her day felt already over, for practical purposes anyway. David would suggest they do something as a family. *No wonder Evelyn is obsessed with doing things to mark the day.* Or, on school days, she would need to pick Thomas up, maybe run an errand or two, and then time to make it back so that she or David could be there when Evelyn got home from school. That way, they could feel comfortable with her walking home from school on her own.

She folded all the towels in the towel closet again as well as a hamper-full that she'd set aside for just such a situation—a time before Thomas woke up and Evelyn was miraculously occupied in a wholesome activity and David wasn't quite suggesting they do something away from the house. She knew he meant well by suggesting they leave the house. He probably assumed that since so much of her time was caught up in the house, she would relish leaving it, with an extra parent to keep track of their two kids to boot.

But she loved her home. It never resembled a prison to her. She had intentionally chosen to downsize her technical-writing career for the time being, and David would support her if she ever wanted to ramp things back up professionally. No, the few freelance projects she took kept her skills sharp enough and provided some sense of professional achievement, particularly important when her kids were unusually ungrateful. Plus, it was fun to have a bit of extra play money to surprise the kids with something fun from time to time, like Evelyn's bike from last Christmas.

She liked the house best on summer mornings. The sun rose over the mountains and filtered through the trees in the backyard. An area Evelyn had dubbed Mosquito Forest years before. The house was situated in a small bowl at the base of the mountains, so it took until midmorning, even at the height of summer, for the sun to reach it fully. That kept things cool without the harsh, bright light of direct sun.

Valerie put the empty hamper back in the dirty clothes closet and swept back her hair that still retained its black and glossy veneer, though she did have some suspicions that, now that she'd reached her mid-thirties, when her hairstylist, Abigail, talked about adding highlights, she actually meant touching up a few invading gray strands. Valerie never asked for clarification.

She heard David starting up the exercise bike in their bedroom, which reminded her that she didn't say good morning to him when she left the room that morning. She was trying to decide whether making some peanut butter toast to take in right as he finished his ride would be worth the effort and had just brought out the jar of peanut butter from the cupboard when she heard the scream.

Valerie dropped the peanut butter jar. The lid burst open on impact, shooting a line of the jar's contents up the side of the lower cupboards. Her heartrate instantly climbed, and her peripheral vision blurred as she focused on what she needed to do. She knew that scream instinctively, even if Evelyn had never before let out a guttural scream like the one Valerie had just heard. Yet, some primal evolutionary tract inside Valerie knew it was her daughter. And she knew Evie needed her right then. Valerie was out the door before she could assess what she would do. She sprinted around the fence to find Evelyn crouching on the ground, tenderly holding her right arm, her wrist bent at a sickening angle.

Valerie dropped to the ground next to Evelyn and pulled her face close.

"Are you okay? What happened?"

"I was climbing down, and I slipped—"

"Oh, Evie, I'm so sorry! Let me take a look at that arm, okay? Is anything else hurt? How's your head?" Valerie searched frantically for any blood in Evelyn's hair.

"Fine. I didn't hit my head."

"That's good." Valerie inspected Evelyn's wrist, which was already swollen to twice its normal size. It was during those moments when a user manual for raising kids would be helpful. *Broken Bones, Chapter 11…*

"I can't tell for sure, but you might have broken your wrist. Can you walk, honey? Let's keep your hand stable."

Valerie helped Evelyn to her feet and helped slip on the boots Evie had discarded under the tree, then the two of them slowly made their way to the door that had been left open. Valerie supported Evelyn's arm, carrying most of the weight. Just then, a new wave of sobs bubbled out of Evelyn as the shock wore off and the pain sank in again.

As the two entered the kitchen, Valerie yelled to her husband. "David!"

David appeared from the bedroom with a towel over his shoulders and a concerned look.

"We need to run Evie to urgent care, oh and grab a towel. We'll need to make some sort of sling."

David took one look at Valerie and then at his daughter's hand and swung open the towel closet, then rushed to Evelyn with a pink-and-yellow-striped beach towel.

"Not a beach towel! How big do you think her arm is?"

"Sorry you just said a towel. Sorry. Got what's going on here." David dashed back to the closet and stopped midway, opening it when he realized he still had a towel draped over his shoulders. David returned to Valerie and draped one end of the towel over Evelyn's left shoulder. "Here, Evie, hold your arm bent like this with your good hand. Yes! Exactly like that. Good."

Valerie took a breath to admire how adept her husband was while he tucked the rest of the towel underneath Evie's cradled arm and wrapped it around the forearm and over her right shoulder, tying the two ends using a variety of knots that she had no idea the names of. But they held.

David took a step back and both adults inspected the makeshift sling.

"Can the sling hold your arm up, honey?" Valerie asked.

Evelyn gingerly let go of her right arm and nodded, instinctively trying to wipe her eyes with her right hand but remembering and awkwardly doing it with her left instead, then bursting into a new round of tears.

"I guess all those years of scouting paid off for something after all," David said, giving Evie a goofy look that momentarily made her smile before she shifted back to whimpers.

"Evie, we'll get you fixed up!" Valerie turned to David. "Go grab some protein bars and snacks and start the car. I'm going to get

Evie in some different shoes." Just as she was saying that, Valerie heard Thomas's bedroom door open. "And you'll have to stay here with Thomas—"

"Let's just take him with. I need to be there—"

"We don't know how long we'll be at the clinic. It might be hours. It makes no sense to take Thomas, so you'll have to stay with him," Valerie said.

"Okay. It's a plan. I'll still pack the go bag and start the car." David squeezed Valerie's hand and pulled her face closer to his. "We've got this," he said before dashing to the kitchen to load up snacks.

That's why I married you, she thought as she kicked back into high gear, remembering what she was doing.

"What's going on, Mama?"

"Nothing, honey, good morning. Dad's going to stay with you for a while so I can run your sister to the doctor," Valerie said, rummaging through Evelyn's closet for a pair of matching shoes.

"How could she have so many blasted shoes that don't match!" Valerie yelled to herself.

"Are you mad, Mama?" Thomas asked, hiding halfway behind the door frame.

"No, honey. I'm not mad. What am I? Scared? Frustrated? Maybe. I guess scared. But everything will be okay. Go see Daddy. He'll get you some breakfast," Valerie said with her head still in the closet.

"Come on, Thomas. Do you want some Lucky Charms, maybe?" David said just as he came back from starting the car. He took Thomas's hand and led him to the kitchen table.

Valerie ran through the house, scanning for anything else she might need during the unknown length of time it would take for Evelyn's arm to be checked and hopefully fixed.

"A book? Should I bring a book? I might be there a long time," she muttered to herself. Valerie picked a book from the murder mystery collection she was into, but it was the book after the one she was currently reading. She quickly put it back down. "Evie will need me to distract her the whole time I'm there. The whole time…" Her thought drifted to all the things she had been hoping to knock out that day. Saturdays were so precious—having two parents working in tandem to run errands while keeping track of the kids. She focused on her contingency plan that she formulated as she went along.

"On to Plan B, or is this really more Plan C?" She dashed back into the living room, her right arm draped with a change of clothes for Evie and three reusable canvas grocery bags strung over her left shoulder. Her hands were full of assorted changes of shoes, snacks, books, and a tablet in case she got too desperate trying to entertain Evie by herself. She sent up a silent prayer that the clinic had Wi-Fi.

"I could go with Evie. I could blow up some surgical gloves, and she could draw a face on them or something," David said, carrying a large tote bag with the exact things she needed. Even the book in the murder mystery series she was actually reading. "Just kidding," he added as she gave him the *look*. "Anything else I can grab? I threw in a few dark chocolate squares. You deserve it today. You just aced the advanced-parenting course." David stuffed the change of clothes and shoes in the tote bag and took the canvas bags off Valerie's shoulder.

"Let's wait to call that until Evie's wrist is in a cast and back at home. But we were a good team this morning. Thanks." She landed a grateful kiss on his cheek.

David handed Valerie her keys before she had to search for them like she always did, even though she almost always put them on the counter in a ceramic tray by the KitchenAid mixer. She took one more look at Thomas trying his best to get a spoonful of cereal in his mouth. Milk was dribbling down his chin and spilling down his shirt.

"I've got things covered here," David said, turning to dry the spilled milk and help Thomas get more of the cereal into his mouth.

Valerie mouthed a silent *thank you* and ran out the side door toward the whimpering sounds coming from Evie, who waited inside the parked Subaru Outback in the carport. And then she remembered a previous thought. She ran back inside.

"Do you mind helping me find—"

"A sweater? Got you covered," David said, helping her into her favorite gray wool sweater that he'd grabbed from the back of one of the kitchen chairs. "Anything else? Are you good?" He gave Valerie a hug from behind.

"Ready or not. New adventures in child-rearing" Valerie waited a moment, enjoying the warmth of David's arms around her. Then she summoned extra energy with a deep breath and a sigh out, and with that, Valerie was out the door and on her way to experience yet another new experience with her child—at the medical clinic. Choose your own adventure be damned.

The pine didn't know exactly what it felt like to be in its neighbors' xylem, but it had as much of a sense as nearly any organism could. The same desperate need for moisture, the desire for sunlight, the hunger for protection from the biting cold of winter, and the hope of new growth and easier days in late spring all drove it too. That meant there was more than a big hole to fill when a tree fell from the ridge. The pine felt the loss in the hollow wind at its branches and the emptiness at its roots.

VALERIE LACED UP HER SNEAKERS TO VISIT THE FARMERS MARKET. Even though she usually only purchased produce or a small item from promising artists, the existence of farmers markets struck her as rather miraculous. As far as she could tell, none of the vendors got rich selling handicrafts or small-volume produce, yet they set up their booths week after week and welcomed customers with a smile. That built such a connection to community.

And perhaps the bigger miracle in Valerie's eyes that morning was that Evelyn decided to join the family when Valerie announced she was headed to check out the market. Valerie was pretty certain Evelyn had ulterior motives that had nothing to do with family time, but she'd take what she could get. It was important to Evie that she be one of the smart kids at her high school, and by the copy of *Crime and Punishment* that was way too thick for Evie to easily hide in her messenger bag, Valerie guessed that attending local events like the farmers market was a part of that crafted image.

"That's some pretty light summer reading there, Evie." Valerie nodded to the book bulging inside Evie's bag.

"I'm trying to read real books about real things rather than just reading for entertainment," Evie said, tapping her fingers on the cover of one of Valerie's books, which was definitely for entertainment.

Valerie helped Thomas put on his bright-blue rain boots that he loved. "I admire that. Books can do both though. Entertain and enlighten. I personally prefer Tolstoy to Dostoevsky." Valerie enjoyed watching Evie process that. *Yes, I am very well read, and I read books that are fun too*, she thought.

Evie's mouth drifted shut, and she started fiddling with her phone.

Valerie sighed while helping Thomas into his jacket. The thing that never got discussed in biological anthropology classes was that kernels of wisdom and knowledge weren't just endowments of instinct, like how foals innately know how to stand and run within minutes of birth. With humans, the younger generation needed to want to improve and learn from the older generation. Like how she was determined to coax Thomas into wearing shoes with shoelaces—eventually.

Valerie remembered feeling much the same as Evie appeared to, with the same urge to be valued and seen as special, based on a good reputation and recognition of her intelligence and potential. But she also knew that gnawing anxiety that bubbled up—based on the fear of being seen for who she really was. As a teenager, that anxiety had filled her headspace anytime she had to face herself alone.

Being a woman and expected to learn how to navigate the social landscape carried familiar burdens that Evie might like help with. And Valerie had gone through them. But Evie would need to want that help because the whole eye roll–and-ignore routine wouldn't get Evie anywhere good. It was maddening and strangely fascinating to see all that latent progression stymied by youthful insecurity and pride.

The family walked the few blocks to the market, which was centered around a small plaza off Main Street. The gravel block was where customers could buy wooden tokens they could use instead of cash, in case any of the sellers didn't have a way to receive credit cards. Valerie usually bought twenty dollars' worth because she loved the feel of the wooden coins in her hands.

Evie dashed off right away.

"Text me occasionally, okay? And we'll be leaving in an hour," Valerie yelled in Evie's direction—a force of habit—though Evie was already around the corner, probably looking for that artisan coffee place that would fit with the thick tome in her bag, finishing off her desired sophisticated look.

"Did you see? She has *Crime and Punishment* in her bag?" Valerie asked her husband with each of them taking one of Thomas's hands and, together, swinging their arms in step with their strides, which threw Thomas into a fit of giggles.

"No. Seriously? Poor girl. I didn't read that until college. Russian literature is such a slog."

"Yeah, like the long Russian winter." She smiled.

"It's a shame that our Evie is too cool and smart to realize that her mother is about the best-read person she's likely to meet in her life," David said admiringly.

"You can hold your own on discussions about *War and Peace* with the best of them too."

"Maybe. But not willingly." David smirked. "I think I've finally gotten past the need to read what I'm supposed to read. I'll gladly admit that these days I prefer a good Dan Brown thriller."

"Your Dan Brown is the equivalent of my murder mysteries."

"Yeah! Exactly! Except Dan Brown novels are set in major cities like Rome or Paris where a murder or two wouldn't make too much of a dent. Those poor coastal towns where those books you read are set would be murder capitals of the world, for sure."

David and Valerie took a slow turn round all the booths and then circled back to the few that warranted a second look. David took Thomas to play on the playground by the performance riser, and Valerie took a closer look at a few artists' booths. She started thumbing through postcard-sized prints of landscape photos. Most of them were familiar mountain-skyline shots. As she scanned through the prints, she was amazed at the clear beauty of the landscapes, and she felt a rising guilt that she had ever complained about the deficiencies in her current town. How could she complain about the price of groceries or that she had to use an interlibrary loan to get the most recent book in a series or two when she lived in a place like McCall?

The back half of the photos were of a place where a river cut through canyons with staggeringly high canyon walls and craggy rock formations mingled with forest trees that defied the cliffs.

"You like those ones, eh?"

Valerie visibly jumped as the photographer came up from behind her.

"Sorry! Didn't mean to startle you like that."

"It's fine. These are gorgeous. Where were they taken?"

"I had to earn those ones, for sure. I took most of these on a rafting trip down the Middle Fork."

"The Middle Fork of the Salmon River?"

"That's the one. Quite the adventure actually. It was a miracle that my camera survived the journey. Those are three for twenty dollars, just in case."

In case of what? Valerie thought. But the photographer went back to his lawn chair, and Valerie took a better look at the river scenes. Could it be coincidence that the photographer would talk about miracles? The very theme she had been musing about all morning. The miracle that was the farmers market. The miracle that humans learn anything from their parents. The miracle that her daughter had decided to come along that morning.

She was definitely not a superstitious person, but she'd seen how her life sometimes aligned with some kind of serendipity. If she said yes to the opportunities that presented themselves, good things generally came.

Not always pleasant things. Like her decision to cut down her work hours and be home with the kids after Thomas was born. David left that decision to her to make and that decision had felt right. The next logical step in her life's progression. And being a full-time caretaker of two kids had its bright moments but plenty of dark ones too. And she had known that when she made the decision to resign from her marketing firm, logically at least. Same with the things that made the morning at the farmers market feel that way too. Similarly serendipitous. Full of possible opportunity and growth.

The problem was she didn't really know what decision she was being asked to say yes to this time. "Excuse me, do you mind if I ask you how you rafted down the Middle Fork?"

"Don't mind you asking at all. I did it with a rafting company, but you don't need to if you have a raft, some experience, and a permit. The permit is the real kicker."

"I don't have any of those, so I guess I'd better go with a rafting company," Valerie said, surprising herself even as she said it.

I can't take my family rafting. That's crazy. "I mean, if I were to go. It would probably make the most sense to do it that way rather than doing it ourselves."

"That's probably for the best. For your first time, for sure. There are companies that'll take care of everything, so you just have to show up with a change of clothes, basically."

"Thanks. That's really helpful."

"So you're really looking into doing it?" the photographer asked, looking at her with some curiosity for the first time. The man lifted his hat above his eyebrows and sat forward, rather than his former laid-back stance with legs outstretched and resting on a cardboard box.

"Yeah, I think I really am. Looking at least. No harm in that, right?"

"None at all. One of the most beautiful places I've had the chance to take photos. Just gorgeous. You won't regret it."

"Thanks," Valerie said, gathering three postcard prints. "I'll take three of these too." Valerie handed the man her four wooden market-tokens, each equaling five dollars, and the man took the postcards from Valerie and put them in a small paper bag.

"If you end up going, don't forget a real camera. Those darn phone cameras are decent, but it sucks the joy out of the photography experience. Nothing like hearing that shutter close around that perfect scene. But be prepared to get wet. I'd suggest the oar boat rather than the paddleboat for photography."

"I'm sure I'm not good enough of a photographer to know, but I can imagine where you're coming from. Thanks again," she said, filled with questions like what he'd meant by *the oar boat*. Don't all rafting trips require people to paddle?

Valerie stepped out from under the man's canopy and shielded her eyes from the bright sun bearing down on her. She dropped her sunglasses from the top of her head to her nose. The truth was, Valerie was good enough of a photographer. By most accounts, she was an amazing photographer. She'd been told by a number of friends that she had a wonderful eye. And in that moment, she felt a hunger to be able to show those friends places she'd captured. Places she'd been and experienced for herself. Places like the Middle Fork of the Salmon River. She loved her home. But that didn't change the fact that she needed an adventure. A real adventure.

And then there was Evie. She wasn't sure if she was actually remembering a conversation or just the concept of one, but she was certain that somewhere in her thoughts and reading and studying she had discovered that outdoor adventures were really good for kids. Especially for teenagers. She was almost certain she had read that somewhere. She admitted that she might be recalling an ad in a magazine for an outdoor adventure company, but it still thrilled her.

"You didn't make it far."

Valerie turned around to see David with Thomas, who was licking a melting chocolate ice cream cone. She was so excited to talk to her husband about the prospect of the rafting trip that she didn't even think to give him an unapproving look for jumping to sugar to keep Thomas happy. "No, I didn't, but I think I may have found our next family vacation!"

Valerie tried to convey not just the concept but also the feelings stirring inside her as she explained the rafting trip. She didn't describe it in a very coherent way. She had no idea what went into planning a rafting trip. No concept of what rafting companies offered as packages, how much a trip cost, or even if there were slots available in a rafting tour. But she was confident in at least a couple of things—a rafting trip would do her and her family a world of good, and the Middle Fork was the spot for that trip.

"Whoa! Okay, I got you. A rafting trip down the Salmon River—"

"The Middle Fork of the Salmon River."

"Excuse me. The Middle Fork of the Salmon River. Thanks for specifying, Miss River Expert," David said with an amused look.

"Sorry. I don't know what's happening to me, but just the thought of taking this trip. It really just… I don't know…"

"Excites you. I can tell. It makes me excited just seeing you so excited. I haven't seen that for a while."

Valerie's enthusiasm was deflated a bit at that.

"Not in a bad way! Sorry. No, I think both of us have gotten comfortable with a certain routine that kind of lacks what would you say? *Pizzazz*, maybe?"

"Yes! Exactly! We need some pizzazz, David! I think we really do!"

"I agree. Let's look into it when we get home."

"Oh, don't worry. I have my phone right here, and me being an early millennial, I know how to look things up on it, using a cool thing called the World Wide Web," Valerie said, holding up her phone like it was a newly found artifact.

"I don't know about all of that newfangled technology. It'll just rot your brain," David said with a chuckle.

"I'll take Thomas if you can track down Evie."

"Sounds like a plan. See you in a few."

David wandered off in search of their daughter, and Valerie pulled up a browser on her phone to do some quick searches for rafting companies.

"I'm ready to go, Mom," Thomas said, looking up and grabbing Valerie's free hand with his sticky ice cream–caked one.

"Oh, son. Let's get you cleaned up."

Later that day, Valerie stopped at Scott's Grocery, where the prices were easily 40 percent higher than in Boise and whose aisles were always too narrow. Especially when they set up those random pull-out displays to feature certain items that never seemed to go with the other items on that aisle. Price of living in a rural mountain town she supposed. She shrugged. Maybe it also didn't make sense for anybody to care as much as Valerie suddenly cared about such things.

"Excuse me."

Valerie looked up with a start. An older gentleman in an over-coat and tweed derby hat smiled at her once she saw she was blocking his way down the aisle. "I'm so sorry," Valerie said, sliding her yet-empty cart out of the man's way.

"No bother. These aisles are far too narrow," the man said, tipping his hat in Valerie's direction. She halfway recognized the man, she thought, staring at the well-pressed back of his beige overcoat. Or maybe the effect came more from him basically being the stereo-type character of every Masterpiece drama, which she had seen far too many times of late, instead of getting to bed at a reasonable hour.

She tried to focus on what she was there to do: getting some Alka-Seltzer for David to deal with his indigestion, which was a new experience for him now that he wasn't running marathons anymore. That and some soap, ginger ale, and a gallon of milk. Alka-Selzer, soap, and a gallon of milk. That was it. No, wait! And ginger ale. She couldn't forget the ginger ale. Did she really need to write a shopping list for four items? No. She was a smart woman, and she could keep track of more than a couple of things at a time.

Thomas! She couldn't forget to take Thomas to the dentist next week! He hated the dentist, and he would be miserable. Maybe she should plan on having a special dinner next Thursday so he could have something to look forward to once his mouth was less numb. That vein of thought seemed vaguely familiar though. Had she already planned that special meal? It wouldn't hurt to stock up on a few of the things she would need, just in case, right? Then again, Scott's was just down the road, so there was nothing stopping her from returning to the charming, overpriced mountain-shopper's paradise with too-narrow aisles.

She snapped out of her thoughts. She'd just put a six-pack of Canada Dry Ginger Ale back on the shelf for the third time. She grabbed the six-pack again and dropped it into the miniature cart designed for a shopping excursion exactly like hers. She was only grabbing a few things. A few necessities. *Alka-Selzer, soap, ginger ale, and milk.*

She turned down the aisle full of lotions, creams, and soaps and felt intimidated by all the images of smiling woman with perfectly smooth skin. She decided to keep her head down since she knew exactly where the Dove bar soap would be. When she came to the huge Dove section, which filled the shelf from above her head down to the floor with white boxes of lotions and creams and antiaging serums, she scanned the items and found the four-packs of bar soap. She picked up two. Only a few models to shame her for having a less-than-perfect smile or skin. What a hypocritical company Dove must be to have the same kind of gorgeous models as all the other beauty products. But Dove ran those ads showing how much doctoring was done to those models during the photo shoots and postproduction. What was their tagline? "No wonder our perception of beauty is distorted"? *I guess we must have solved that problem, huh? Because, otherwise, Dove would be just as guilty as any other makeup or skin care brand trying to convince us that using their products made us beautiful?*

Wasn't that ad supposed to teach the impact of skewed beauty perception on young girls? Young girls like Evie. Who wasn't really a young girl anymore. She was probably almost as old as the model in that hypocritical Dove ad. Her Evie, who intentionally wasn't speaking to her that afternoon in retaliation for Valerie putting her foot down on no parties on school nights. Who allowed kids to host parties on school nights anyway? She needed to get to know Evie's friends' parents better so she could nudge them in the right direction.

Valerie laughed out loud at that thought and sheepishly covered her mouth when a fellow customer gave her a confused look. As if she had any right to claim the Parent of the Year Award. *Why do we put up with such abuse?* Thinking evolutionarily, what would have happened to a child who skulked outside the cave, refusing to go in when their parents told them to? They would have been eaten. *Why hasn't obeying been better built into our DNA by now?*

Great! So now I'm advocating for my children to be eaten rather than disobedient. You're just climbing those rungs to better parenting by the minute.

Alka-Seltzer!

By this point, she felt a strong urge to get out of the store as quickly as possible; the narrow aisles were becoming claustrophobic rather than quaint. She pushed her cart forward, perhaps too fast, around the next aisle.

When she found the Alka-Seltzer section of the medicine aisle, she tightly gripped the cart handle to keep from screaming.

"Why don't they just sell the best kind! How am I supposed to know the difference between Alka-Seltzer Plus and regular old Alka-Seltzer? Why does everything need to test my treatment of my kids or husband? Of course David deserves the best, so let's go with the Plus, shall we?" This time, she didn't even look up to see if anybody heard her. She navigated through weeding out the cold medicine Alka-Seltzer and the kind for just indigestion. Only one more decision tree to decipher.

"David really deserves the brand name version," she mused.

He'd been working so hard on his accounting business, especially during tax season. But then again, was there really a difference between the brand name and the generic version? Hadn't the medical companies heard of the paradox of choice? Humans weren't always better off with more choices! She decided on the brand name version because it was only two dollars more and what was two dollars in the grand scheme of things?

Finally, first in line, she gave the grocery store employee-checker a well-meaning albeit pained smile. She was relieved that she'd gotten a teenager checker. Teenage checkers just scanned the groceries and generally preferred silence.

"That'll be $37.16," the checker said in a bored way.

I don't blame him. What a monotonous job. That's why people go to college, kid. Evie will be applying for college this fall. Had she encouraged Evie to go to college enough? It was a wonder that firstborn kids make it to adulthood, honestly. There was still a chance that Thomas would make up for the mistakes she'd made with Evie.

"Sorry?"

"Just tap your card or enter the chip side," the checker said, now impatient, as if he needed to get somewhere or someone else was waiting in line. Valerie tried tapping a couple of times, but she wasn't sure if her card could do that, so she finally just stuck the card in the chip reader.

"Do you want your receipt?" One more question for her to answer. At least this one had a clear and easy answer.

"No. Thanks."

Valerie tried to decide whether she could carry her four items in her hands or if she should ask for a box. *Goodness knows, discarded cardboard boxes are so much better for the environment than plastic bags.* Or, why not just take the cart to her car? Right when she had almost decided on trying to carry the few things in her arms, she heard someone familiar call her name.

"Valerie! What luck. I should have picked up a lottery ticket tonight."

Up to that moment, Valerie would have had to say she wasn't in the mood to visit with any friends, but she changed her mind instantly when she saw who had greeted her.

"Joy! What a pleasant surprise. I guess we shouldn't be surprised to run into each other though, with this town being so small, right?"

"Intimate, dear. Small carries such horrible connotations, don't you think?"

"Definitely. Intimate is much better. You always use just the right words. That's one of the many reasons I want to be you when I grow up," Valerie said, pushing her cart away from the aisle so the checker would stop glaring at her.

"You can't, I'm afraid. You can only grow up to be a better or worse version of yourself. But I think you're on track to experience remarkable things. I'm thrilled to run into you this afternoon because I'm dying to know what arguments you've cooked up for the high school Library Recommendation Committee. Remember, you were telling me about that earlier this week when you were in for your weekly volunteering?"

"I'm so glad you reminded me to prepare for that. My brain has been so distracted lately."

"I thought you had some rather brilliant thoughts this week. About people thinking that not liking a book is the same thing as having grounds to remove it from the shelf. How they can dislike a book but should still hold enough headspace to think that a book might be important to someone else," Joy said, her face lighting up into a cascade of smile lines that enhanced her cropped, gray hair.

"You're right. I was talking to Darla the other day—you know Darla, right? The coffee shop owner?"

"Of course, dear."

"Anyway, I was talking to Darla about the increasing threat of wildfires in the area, and she was completely willing to admit that fire seasons have gotten worse over the decades, but she just couldn't admit that climate change could have anything to do with that."

"You talked about climate change with Darla?" Joy asked with an amused look adjusting her bright-colored scarf.

"Regrettably, yes. People have the same challenge with climate change as with books though. Fire seasons are becoming more severe, and it's not just that the Forest Service hasn't been doing enough timber sales!"

"Preach, sister! Preach!" Joy said, raising her hands as if they were at a Christian revival. "I'd say that's a very compelling argument."

"It really does scare me to see so much interest in banning books," Valerie said, trying to get back on the track that Joy had been on originally.

"For me, it's not so much a fear as a sadness and rage."

There she goes again—using just the right words, Valerie thought.

"I'll let you run, dear. So good to see you, and please keep up the good fight."

"We'll do. Thanks, Joy."

Valerie watched Joy disappear down one of the too-narrow aisles and pushed her cart out the entrance and down the three switchbacks that made up the ramp off to the side of the two sets of stairs that led to the automatic sliding doors, yet another puzzle in Scott's business setup. Didn't most people use carts when grocery shopping? Wouldn't it make sense to make things as convenient as possible for customers to get their wares to their cars?

What a world we're living in. I'll have to see more of it someday, she thought, but a smile crept across her face. She would be seeing more of the world. She'd be rafting down a river in a few short weeks, in fact. That fact had already started to fill some of the gaps in who she used to be. She pulled out of the parking lot with her four items securely tucked away in the back of her cross between an SUV and a sedan. The selling point of the car being that it would provide a lot of the benefits of an SUV in a more manageable size. David had really been sold on it. She didn't like driving, but she made her way toward home anyway, because, as she'd told herself in a self-actualization prayer, she could do hard things.

Just before making the turn into her neighborhood, she decided to grab a copy of the high school library book proposed for removal. She dashed over to the local bookstore fifteen minutes before they closed and bought a copy. As she drove home, she rolled her windows down, enjoying one of the first nights in the mountains warm enough to justify leaving them down. She set her playlist to '90s indie rock and was pleased to hear the familiar sound of a Smashing Pumpkins song. It brought back memories of working on her high school yearbook late into the night, laying things out by hand and developing real-film photos of track meets and pep rallies.

She pulled into the carport, and before she even got out of the car, Evie had raced to the back of it to look for a pair of shoes she'd left there. "Mom, have you seen my clogs? The Merrell ones, not the house-slipper kind you usually wear. Never mind. They're right here. And what's this?"

"What's what, dear?" Valerie asked, grabbing her purse and keys and shutting the car door while awkwardly carrying her four items from the grocery store on her way to the house.

"This book. Nice. Mom's on a teenage vampire kick. I like it," Evie said, squeezing past Valerie into the house. *Guess the silent treatment is over, and all it took was taking an interest in young-adult vampire fiction*, she thought, stumbling into the kitchen.

"Hi, honey. How was the store?" David said from the kitchen where he was cooking something that smelled absolutely delicious.

"It was great, thanks. And Evie is either admiring or making fun of the fact that I'm reading a book for the library board. Why does it often feel like she's doing a bit of both?"

"Because she's a teenager," David said, taking the items out of her hands and giving Valerie a gentle peck on the lips and an understanding smile. "Put your things down and let's eat."

Greenfield Ranch, Frank Church Wilderness of No Return

June 2024

The pine still remembered the days when its first branches grew. They had extended from its spindly trunk as though they were seeking something far away, which, it supposed, was true enough. They were seeking sunlight, and they found it in abundance in those days, after an older pine had fallen, leaving a gash of sunbreak on the exposed ridge for seedlings to fill. But now the pine's trunk was bare of branches far up into its height. Fires had licked up some. Wind knocked off still others. It knew it was a good thing in the end, but every time another branch sluffed off, the pain of loss still registered in deep places inside itself.

TERRY HAD NO CHOICE BUT TO DELAY HIS SPRING BURNING UNTIL the last night before the first day of summer. He didn't pay much mind to the guidance coming from state and county officials that discouraged burning his yard's scrap wood and garbage that late in the year. He'd been burning his scrap for over six decades, and he knew his own land better than any government bureaucrat. So Terry spent a couple of days using his tractor to pile the scrap and then cleared a twenty-foot ring free from vegetation around the pile, just in case. Though, he felt like the new grass that had shot up as soon as the ground was free of ice and snow a month before was still too green to catch fire or, if it did, for the flames to go very far.

And that's what the hundred-gallon jug that he had set up in the bed of his pickup was for. So that next morning, before the sun rose, all was set. He buttoned his work jacket, the kind he could never replace because the work-clothing store he'd gotten it from had closed years ago—back when Salmon, Idaho, had been more of a mining and timber town. He brushed the arms and front of the jacket off and noticed that it was no longer the original chestnut-brown it had once been, but a faded brown that veered toward a light gray in the early morning sunlight, due to the many days he'd spent under every condition—winter or summer.

He put on his rawhide gloves, frozen in the frame he had left them in the last time he'd used them, caked in mud after mucking out his barn. He made a tight fist a couple of times to break up the mud, which fell off in satisfying clumps to the floor of the shed. And last of all, he carried a shovel and his ballcap out of the shed and toward the impressive pile of discarded branches and broken two by fours. He lit the fire in the cool darkness, using a little diesel fuel here and there to encourage it along. Even though it'd been an uncommonly hot and dry May and, so far, June, he could count on some dew and maybe even some frost to have collected on the scrap pile. He'd have to burn through that.

The fire started in earnest just as the sun first became visible over the eastern ridges, though it'd been climbing down the opposite set of mountain ridges for the previous half hour. Terry's border collie came running and stayed at his side most of the morning. His dog sensed there was an important job to do, and border collies never shied away from work. That's why Terry insisted on the breed even though they were ten times more expensive than the dogs he could have found at the shelter in town, and he hadn't run sheep on his land for years.

Terry recognized that he was like a border collie in a lot of respects. He never understood how so many people could sit around home, watching TV or whatever people did on the internet. Having a four-generation homestead just east of the Boise National Forest, meant a couple of things: the work needed to keep the ranch functional was never really finished and was always in good supply, and that work amounted to the ranch getting to a place where it was "good enough" for the time being.

Maintaining the ranch also meant that he was contacted by environmental groups making offers to buy his land several times a year. They tried different tactics—the monetary approach, where they'd try to convince him of how much money the land was worth. *Wouldn't he be better off without needing to work so hard?* Thankfully, they'd learned their lesson on taking that tack. He knew that plenty of the remaining homestead owners had sold their land to such groups, though. The environmental groups would buy the land and then hand it over to the Forest Service to manage in an attempt to protect the wilderness.

He poked around at the edges of the steady fire he had going with a stout branch and then fell back into his camp chair. And with nothing else to focus on, he focused on his wife and kids, which were usually where his default thoughts lay. Terry had named the creek that ran along his property after his wife—Marilyn Creek. After his wife passed three years ago, Terry's kids didn't make as much of an effort to visit him. He certainly didn't blame his kids on that point. His two daughters had families of their own in Meridian, and his son had a thriving dental practice to manage. Plus, there was the headache of getting to the ranch. From Boise, it was quite the trek and included bouncing along Forest Service dirt roads for hours or charting a private plane. The roads were becoming more unruly every year, as the Forest Service focused on its system roads outside of wilderness designations, leaving more of the maintenance to him, though the agency told him he wasn't authorized to do the maintenance himself, sighting something about fish habitat and archeological sites. He didn't know what they were talking about really. Terry never disturbed the obsidian flakes or arrowheads he'd discovered over the decades, and the rivers seemed to still have plenty of fish by his estimation.

A breeze blew down from the canyon that soothed his face after being a bit too close to the flames tending the fire, and he took a step back. He honestly found the remnants of civilizations long past comforting. They reminded him that even though none of his kids had any interest in taking on the ranch when he was gone, he would be leaving a legacy on the land—a remnant marking his presence for generations. And so he didn't have to think about the future too much. At least not farther off than preparing for winter or getting his septic tank ready for the next decade of use.

But in the quiet moments just before sleep, or in first moments after waking up in the mornings when he had to wait for his body to remember how to make blood flow in his veins properly and joints operate in their usual way, he faced the reality that he would likely be the last caretaker of the ranch that had been in his family since the gold rush in the 1890s.

By midmorning, he pulled his camp chair a few yards back, farther away from the ongoing fire, while keeping an eye on the fire's progress. But he didn't just sit there all morning. Burning a scrap pile required real work and constant attention. He adjusted sections of the pile, ensuring there was enough heat to consume the wood and yard debris sufficiently. He didn't want any leftover, charred, half-consumed wood when he was done.

By afternoon, the summer sun was bearing down fully on Terry's ranch, which hugged the mountain foothills from the north end to the south, making a two-mile stretch of tributary, river-valley land. Even during the summer, the high canyon walls surrounding the ranch kept things shaded and cool most of the year, and most of the day. It wasn't until the late afternoon that the heat got a bit oppressive that summer day, especially after tending the fire.

Terry left his chair for a few minutes to go inside for a cool drink from his propane-powered fridge and then returned to sink back into the chair. Thankfully, with a breeze and a cold drink, the heat was tolerable. He took a long draught and let out a sigh. The sounds of the fire blocked out many others, but when he focused, he could hear the gurgling of Marilyn Creek, which had barely enough water flowing across the worn stones and boulders to make its familiar, friendly sound. A cacophony of bird chatter sounded off to the south, an alarm of some predator in the neighborhood. Or perhaps they sounded off for nothing more than to announce their existence to any creature close enough to care or listen. Terry homed in on the birdsong and the river and the crackle of the wood being slowly burned to ash.

The wind gained velocity as Terry drifted to sleep, letting his drink fall gently to the cupholder that was conveniently built into his camp chair. The physics of fire required a lot of energy to ignite a flame, but if the ignition was found under certain conditions, fire could be sustained and grow based on the amount of fuel and oxygen it was fed.

A few stray embers floated majestically in the air—but a bit too far—and landed on a patch of grass that was a little drier than Terry thought it should be that time of year. And normally, those embers would sizzle down to ash to be blown away in the gathering wind. But Terry's several decades of experience did him a disservice that day. Forces had been sneaking past his awareness for years. Marilyn Creek made its last trickling sounds a few days earlier than when he had been a boy. Rain patterns shifted a couple of notches, becoming less frequent in the summertime. Temperatures rose sooner in the summer and degrees warmer. Alone, any one of these factors wouldn't increase fire risk. Combined, they spelled out the perfect condition for those few stray embers to creep along the yellowing grass and transfer their growing energy to branches too small for Terry to worry about gathering into the main burn pile.

The fire caught hold of Terry's outbuildings next and finally latched onto his home. Terry breathed in too much smoke for him to do anything about it, his prepared hundred-gallon water jug useless against the growing fire. Terry never woke from that sleep, but his last living thoughts were of Marilyn and the land that he loved so much.

Krassel Ranger District Office, Idaho

August 2024

The pine wasn't always in a hurry to drop its cones. It waited until conditions were right. Some years, in fact, it didn't even produce cones. That was one of the luxuries of having such a long life—it knew how to wait. Wait for a low-intensity fire to burn open patches of sunlight so seeds could germinate in the new opening. *Wait for a large wind event that might be hard to withstand but would reward it by* helping its cones and seedlings travel to distant soil with less competition. *Wait for a time when the soil's nourishment could sustain the pine's offspring that put down roots far enough away to take in their own sunlight.*

ANDY ENJOYED HELPING OUT AT THE FRONT DESK IN THE DISTRICT office from time to time, when there were lulls in fire activity and his engine crew was waiting for their next assignment. Maybe he would have been a good public affairs officer, if he lived in a world where he could have hacked college. But these opportunities to help provide the public with information were nice breaks from his regular routine. And they were becoming rare, given the severe fire seasons he'd experienced in recent years.

He thought back to his first season as a brand-new wildland firefighter. He'd mainly helped with prescribed-burn fires that the Forest Service intentionally lit and managed to bring necessary restoration to Western landscapes. Now though, his engine was called up whenever they were available. And that was a good thing. His crew needed opportunities to expand their qualifications. They were close to meeting the requirements to become a Type I engine, which was a big deal since they would be the only one on the forest. Most of the crew he managed had seen a major wildfire or two by now. Until Andy saw his first big one, his third year, he didn't fully appreciate why all the training and preparation mattered so much.

This summer was different. It had been oddly quiet so far. It felt strange not going from one assignment to the next from June until late October. In some respects, it felt like the country had finally caught up and staffed enough fire personnel to almost meet the need for the difficult fire seasons it *should* prepare for. And then, of course, they'd experience a mild fire season, more like his first couple of seasons.

There were only so many hoses to check and so many engine-cleanings he could stomach. And his crew tended to get into more trouble if they sat around home. Whether or not the scrutiny was deserved, firefighters in small towns were expected to live up to a higher standard. He knew the PR nightmare that breaking public trust could cause. So he'd sent his crew off to assist with some fires in Canada with the expectation that if there were major flare ups, they'd have to come back early. He'd even been able to delegate the engine boss's duties to Cyrus since he was working on his engine boss task-book training qualifications and needed a few more leadership roles under his belt. That also meant Andy could enjoy some time without having to clean up after the crew in the bunkhouse and enjoy by making nice breakfasts for himself, occasionally without fear of grease fires starting up when he turned on the stove in the communal kitchen.

Honestly though, he understood. He'd been one of those young guys who worked sixteen-hour days as often as he could to make as much as he could during the summer so that he'd be able to live semi-comfortably in the fall and winter when his season ended. After pulling two weeks of long days, the last thing he used to want to do was clean the kitchen. He did encourage his crew to eat some vegetables occasionally and even had a basic-cooking class as a part of the spring orientation.

As much as Andy loved his role as a mentor for the younger crew members, he was grateful for the chance to feel less responsible for the crew. He wished there was an easier way of relaying the instincts he'd picked up over twenty years of fighting fire. That way, he wouldn't need to have conversations like the one he'd had last week with a particularly hot-headed crew member, Warner. Andy had instructed the crew on the proper way of rolling and storing hoses and heard Warner joking with a couple of the guys.

"What was that, Warner?"

"Oh nothing."

"Can you tell us all why rolling and storing hose the right way is so important, Warner?" Andy asked, tossing Warner an easy way to save face and show he wasn't a total goof-off.

"We need water to put out the fire, and hoses that don't work right don't deliver that water." Warner said, striking a pretty cocky pose with hands on hips and his chest out.

"You're not wrong there. Let's focus on what we're working on okay? It could save your life or one of your crew members here."

Warner was making some progress. He'd even opened up a couple of times about some hard things he'd dealt with in high school. Giving him the benefit of the doubt and holding him accountable was key. That's how new firefighters caught the vision of what they could accomplish as a team. It was cooperation that always sealed the deal and kept crew members coming back season after season.

Andy had to admit, though, the chance to sit in the air-conditioned office instead of fighting mosquitoes and yellow jackets in the heat of summer had its perks too. The public affairs officer,

Cheryl Caplan, had asked him to take a look at the forest website for improvement purposes. She was a fun lady who'd been on the forest long enough to get what real work in the forest was like, unlike so many of those recent hotshot graduate-school ladder-climber types.

He was about to finish drawing up a plan for reorganizing the fire safety information on the website when the local district ranger showed up from around the corner.

"How are things going, Andy?"

"So far so good. Thanks, Bill. It's nice to have a week or two inside the office to give my bad knees a rest."

"I hear you there. I think I'm paying for all of those crash landings while skiing as a kid. So getting our website all cleaned up?" Bill asked while arranging some brochures in front of the desk.

"There's no way I'll get it all done, even if you hire me full-time. This website is a beast. But I'm chipping away at it anyway. Cheryl and I have a good plan, I think."

"Cheryl is one of the good ones, for sure. Well, let me know if you need anything. Oh, and Andy, any plans for when you finish up with fire in the next couple of years?"

"Boy, I don't know. I really do enjoy public affairs stuff, but I'd say I have a better view from where I work normally. I'd get stuck in an office so much of the time. No offense."

"None taken. In some ways, I envy how much time you're able to spend in the actual forest. In a role like mine, you'd spend a lot more time in meetings to talk about the forest than actually doing the work to manage it. Not to complain of course. Let me know if I can be a reference for you. Anytime. Seriously."

"Thanks, Bill. I really appreciate that," Andy said, giving Bill an appreciative nod as Bill walked back to his office to answer a phone call.

It wasn't that Andy hadn't thought about that very question, which Bill had asked him many times before. He knew he needed to put together some sort of plan. He only had a few more years to go until his mandatory retirement from fire.

A young couple sporting Patagonia shirts and shorts walked into the visitor center.

"Morning!" Andy said cheerfully.

"Morning. I was thrilled to see your office was open. We're looking to spend a few nights in the Frank Church Wilderness and wanted to make sure we didn't need to register anywhere. I know other wilderness areas we've visited require that, and we weren't quite sure, based on your website."

"Great of you to check. And it's funny you'd bring up our website, because I'm in the process of cleaning it up right now."

"Perfect! That'll be great. Although, I can't help but stop by any time I see your classic yellow-and-brown wooden signs. I guess I'm my father's son after all."

"Your dad work for the Forest Service?"

"No. He was a college professor, but I think he always had an alternate-life fantasy where he'd gone into forestry instead of English. He passed last year."

"Gosh. I'm sorry. But good for you for keeping that alternate life going, through proxy at least, right?"

"I like that thought. Thanks."

Andy waited patiently as the couple shared a few moments of quiet that he guessed were for the man to reflect on his dad. The man, who Andy assumed was the woman's partner, had tanned arms and legs and well-maintained fingernails. Andy didn't make a habit of checking other people's fingernails, but this guy's were unbelievably clean. Andy didn't dare look at the grime he had under his own.

"To answer your question, no registration or permit is required to enter the wilderness. There are several things to keep in mind, though."

Andy spent the next ten minutes going through certain wilderness regulations and best practices with the couple asking engaging follow-up questions at just the right moments. When they left with thank yous and smiles, Andy leaned back in his office chair.

Alternate lives…

Andy rubbed at a scar on his forearm that itched from time to time. It was from a stray ember that made its mark when he'd had his Nomex shirt sleeve rolled up to the elbow. He never did that again.

He didn't regret his career path. He'd made hundreds of friends spread out all over the country. He'd done important work and had helped a lot of people. But seeing that couple drive off in their Land Rover made Andy wonder how many alternate paths he could have chosen.

He turned back to the computer, grateful for a task that would keep his attention focused for the rest of the day. Just when he was getting back into a rhythm, the radio behind the counter, which Andy had set at a low volume, buzzed to life.

"New possible holdover fire reported in Frank Church Wilderness near the Greenfield Ranch burn scar. Do any units copy?"

Andy rushed to the radio.

"Dispatch, this is Miller. I copy."

"Miller, can you go to the Greenfield Ranch with your engine to size up the fire reported there? We have some aerials of the area, but the canyon is too tight to bring aircraft in low enough to do a thorough size-up."

"Copy. My crew is deployed to the Alberta support team, but I can utilize another crew by 1500 today. Over."

"Copy that. Miller will deploy with a neighboring crew by 1500. Thanks, Miller. Over."

Andy set the radio mic down, jotted down the vital bits of information dispatch had outlined and, in his head, rattled off the crews that might be available to check out the fire situation at the ranch. *Schuester's crew is next in line for an assignment. I wonder if they'd let me tag along.*

Andy pulled his phone out of his jacket pocket and called Jared Schuester, a crew lead from a neighboring district.

"Hey, Miller. How's the quiet life without your crew?"

"Peaceful. Nice and peaceful. I miss the guys, though, of course."

"Of course. What's up?"

"You probably heard over the radio, but there's a holdover start flaring up near the Greenfield Ranch burn from earlier this summer. Is your crew willing to check it out?"

"Sure thing. And feel free to roll out with us if you want. I'd hate for you to get too comfortable in those air-conditioned offices."

"Hey, thanks. I'll tag along, if that's okay. It'll probably snuff itself out in a day or two. Those river canyons tend to stay green well into October."

"Don't jinx us. We'll be ready to roll out this afternoon."

"Copy. I'll meet you at your fire cache a little before 1500. See you later."

"Late."

Andy put his phone back in his pocket.

He'd never understood why fire staff tried to cut words and phrases into the fewest syllables possible. It's not like it took any more energy to say, *See you later*. But he was glad to have an excuse to set aside pouring over web pages, for a couple of days anyway, and he really liked Schuester. Andy started an email to Cheryl, letting her know that he would be delayed in getting the fire section of the website plan to her by a couple of days. He didn't try to make it sound urgent. Cheryl could spot bullshit from a mile away and knew that Schuester didn't need supervising.

I had to take a short break from website work to tag along for a size-up at Greenfield Ranch. I'll pick things back up in a couple of days.

He sent the email and walked back to let Bill know he needed to check up on a fire.

"At the Greenfield Ranch? Tragic situation there. It's a good thing there weren't more cabins in the area. But I talked to Terry Greenfield a couple of times. Hard old codger."

"That's right. I remember hearing about that one fatality. Small fires start up so frequently in the Frank Church that I don't keep track of them all."

"I have a hard time most of the time too. But I admired Terry's tenacity, that's for sure. It's a shame he's gone, but I can't imagine him in some old-folks' home or anything either."

"Guys like that make sure they don't end up in senior centers. Are you good to hold down the fort if I head out now? I'm meeting up with Schuester at 1500."

"Go. I've got this. And, Andy?"

Andy had turned to go but spun around.

"Yeah?"

"Be careful, okay? Just a size-up. No active suppression, right?"

"Right. Got it. Thanks, Bill."

Bill nodded as Andy headed out through the back doors of the district office to grab his bag that he always kept ready from the bunkhouse. He switched from the district rig to his fire rig and tossed his pack in the back, then started up the highway that led north to Schuester's district.

He turned the stereo to some generic classic rock station. The only station with a local enough signal to broadcast through the canyon. So much of what fire life really consisted of was driving. Driving to inspect fire reports. Driving to fire lines in the morning, patrolling the burn perimeter when he got there, and driving back to the Incident Command Post in the evening. It was no surprise to him when safety concerns started getting more scrutiny, and reports showed that most firefighter injuries and fatalities weren't experienced at the fire line. They came from driving.

Andy rolled into the back parking lot in front of the district warehouse where a dozen people buzzed around their Type 6 engine, which was basically a green truck with some customizations for fighting fire. Andy hopped out of his rig and headed in the general direction of the action, where he knew he'd find Schuester.

"Glad you could make it. I was about to leave you behind," Schuester yelled from the back seat of the rig.

"Come on! I had ten minutes to spare."

"No way. Remember, fifteen minutes early is on time?" Schuester said, appearing from the back and smiling.

"Ah, yes. I've been repressing those first fire-camp experiences I guess."

Schuester was a few years behind Andy on the way to mandatory retirement, but Andy appreciated the fact that, with Schuester, he didn't have to push off the thought that most of the crews he dealt with were young enough to call him *Dad*. Being buddy-buddy with the crew members wasn't appropriate anyway, given his role as engine boss, but watching Schuester's crew members laugh so freely made him think of the days when his own responsibility was to follow directions.

Firefighting was hard under any circumstances, but there was a simplicity to being a crew member. His whole day, and really his whole six-month season, had been set up for Andy back then. He'd show up for fire refreshers and trainings with mostly returning crew members who he generally liked. He'd do some prescribed fire operations in the spring and fall. Starting in June, most seasons, he'd deploy with his team at least a few times each summer, racking in a lot of overtime that allowed him to save for the months when he'd be laid off.

And even the concept of fighting wildfire was simpler in his early years. Fire was clearly the enemy then. Some science-types were evangelizing that fire was a critical component for forest health in Western landscapes, but the general public hadn't caught up with that idea yet. Not completely anyway, and not in the mountain towns of Idaho. But he didn't have to deal with the groups that advocated for letting fires burn or the groups angry at him for not putting them out faster. Everybody assumed that firefighters were there to put the damn things out, and that's what he did.

Now he was classified as an 18/8 permanent seasonal as opposed to the 13/13 1039 seasonal he'd started out as. He spent his months off at home in Utah, mostly. His parents appreciated the company and the help keeping up the yard that was too much for them. They'd been living there for thirty-five years and the thought of downsizing, though sometimes appealing, was too overwhelming and sad for them.

As a 1039, he'd had to keep his fingers crossed every year that the forest that'd hired him the year before would bring him back on, and if it didn't, that some forest somewhere around the country would hire him onto a crew for the season. Looking back, he realized that it should have worried him more than it had. He never had a backup plan. But he'd always been one of the lucky ones—brought back every season like clockwork, and even to the same forest. He was grateful that as a permanent seasonal employee, he didn't have to worry about being hired back. In fact, now that he was an 18/8, he had a job lined up, guaranteeing at least eighteen pay periods out of the twenty-six in the year, regardless of budget cuts, which could mean reducing the number of 1039s a forest could hire. And the Payette National Forest was even talking about bringing him on the other pay periods, too, if they could find the space to build a new bunkhouse designed to offer apartments rather than just beds and nightstands.

The forest meant it as a reward and a significant benefit, and that's how he tried to react whenever progress to that end was brought up. He was grateful that the forest brought him on and housed him year after year. But the way the forest had talked about divvying up the space in the newly designed modular-housing units had most of the space going to forestry and biological techs. In other words, people with college degrees and huge opportunities for career advancement. Even though none of the foresters or hydro techs he mingled with at fire camps or at the district office ever gave him a reason to, he always felt like he had to prove his worth and justify his actions when he was around them.

All of that mess of memory and thought crashed down on him, but he shrugged it off while loading up his gear into the back of the engine.

"Are you okay, brother?" Schuester asked as he and Andy climbed into the front of the truck.

"I'm fine. Just a bit rusty this year. We haven't been seeing much action so far. This is seriously the first summer I remember where I've had to ship my crew up north to Canada to get some active fire time."

"Weird year, for sure. We've had light fire years before, but not like this."

"Yes! That's it exactly! We have fire, but it's in weird places like Canada and Greece and the Amazon. I mean the Amazon! Are you kidding me! The freaking rainforest is on fire, but not the mountains of Idaho. If I bought into those end-of-days prophecies, I'd sure have some fuel to keep that faith alive."

"Andy Miller, going all religious on me. Now I've seen it all."

"Better watch out, I think it's catching."

"Tell me about it. These days, it feels like people throw their beliefs in your face like it's their purpose in life. Political, religious; hell, even COVID! People are so sure they're right about everything, and if anybody disagrees, they must be stupid and part of the problem."

Andy settled into a nice conversation with Jared that made the three-hour drive to where they'd have to get out and start hiking fly by.

"I hope your boots are nicely broken in because we have quite the hike ahead."

"I held on to last year's, actually. I should be fine."

"Good deal. The fire is burning in the Frank Church, which ordinarily means we don't deal with active fire management, as you know. But the fire is threatening some airstrips, which is getting some wealthy weekend warriors nervous."

"Nervous? Why?"

"Some big hunting outfits rely on those airstrips so their clients can get a taste of the wild without having to work at it."

"Of course. Whoever would've thunk that it would all come down to money and power. When do those things ever come into play?"

"Right. A few prominent citizens with connections reach out to their senators and, somehow, this fire takes on a whole new level of importance."

"Not to say that either of us is bitter or anything." Andy said with a grin, slinging his backpack over both shoulders and adjusting the straps.

"You know me, Mr. Glass Half Full."

"I think I might remember some other nicknames of yours."

"Shhh! There're kids around," Schuester whispered to Andy with a wry smile, then turned to face his crew. "Okay folks! Gather around. Let's chat about what we'll be doing for the next couple of days."

Jared outlined their tasks, which seemed simple enough when he said them out loud, but Andy knew better. Hiking to the ranch in and of itself would be no easy task. After a good day of hard hiking, struggling to follow the trail that eventually led to the single, mainly grown-over dirt road that connected the Middle Fork to the ranch, they'd have to spend a day or two searching for hotspots and smoke columns and drop GPS points. Then, if they were successful at all of that, they *should* be able to relay the fires growth trajectory by radio, once they got to a relay point.

All that arduous effort was exactly what Andy was hoping for when he'd accepted Schuester's offer to tag along. When he had a shovel or a Pulaski in his hands, moving dirt, focused on hitting the ground and moving forward one foot at a time, he could forget about other things like the gnawing question about what he was doing with his life. At least when he was with a crew doing assigned tasks, he knew what was expected and how to be successful. Most everything else in life wasn't nearly that simple.

So Andy jumped in line with the early-twenty-somethings and was proud of the fact that he could stick with them just fine. Although, by the time they found the dirt path that led to the ranch, he'd started to notice his knee more than he would have liked.

He fell into easy conversation with a few of the crew members, and the hours ticked away pleasantly. But then Andy caught the unmistakable smell of smoke, and his nose flared.

Andy fell behind to Schuester, who was taking up the rear.

"Smell that?"

"Catch the smoke?" They said on top of each other.

They both nodded. The old adage *Where there's smoke there is fire*, really missed a lot of nuances that Andy thought through as they got closer to the ranch. It might be true that smoke occurred as a result of a fire having ignited at some point in time, but the reality was that fires often skunked around with little to no flame, still kicking up a lot of acrid smoke.

At other times, billows of smoke blended so well into the clouds that it could be all but impossible to tell where the smoke began, and the clouds ended. In those instances, the best visual came from heat-syncing drone footage, but since Schuester's crew didn't have any certified drone pilots, the next best visual would come from detecting the orange glow at night. When at a safe distance, Andy couldn't help but get philosophical when watching a fire creep through the foothills. The hot debate on whether they should put out any fire they found or use other fire-management techniques with some fires—for natural resource benefits—melted into the background. Watching it weave between trees, scarring trunks and burning off lower branches made Andy certain that fire had as much of a place as any bird or deer in a landscapes like the forest around him.

The canyon that had been carved out by the Salmon River was the second deepest canyon in the country, second only to Hells Canyon, which was fairly close by. It was deeper than the Grand Canyon from the top mountain ridges to the river bottom by quite a large margin. That made for a huge range of climate zones. While conditions might be frigid with windswept high-desert environments at the top of the canyon, things could be warm and humid closer to the river.

They reached the remnants of the Greenfield Ranch just before dark, so they rushed to set up camp while there was still some daylight. Schuester had the crew set up tents on the other side of the mainly dry creek bed that wound around the ranch. The crew ate some dinner as the evening came on, but it didn't get cold enough for jackets.

"It's staying pretty warm. That's not a great sign. No real temperature recovery," Schuester said, sitting on a boulder next to Andy.

"Yeah, there won't be much recovery with these temperatures. Have you seen any active flame?"

"No. I thought I'd walk around a bit tonight to see if I can spot any. Any interest in exploring?"

"I'm game."

Schuester turned on his headlamp, and he and Andy headed cautiously along the rim of the foothills. They hiked in silence, following a game trail that hugged the edge of a ridge, Andy appreciating the fact that they could trust each other not to talk just to break the silence. There was no awkwardness to the silence. It was just open space that would only need to be broken if either of them had something important to say.

They came to a spot where the sporadic trail they were following rose to an overlook before heading below the tree line again. Andy spotted the orange-and-red glow first.

"There. Do you see that?" he whispered, signaling to a point about halfway up the first ridgeline from the creek bed.

"Good eye. Yeah, I see it. Let's see if we can find any others. Fire sometimes creeps through roots and in the layered duff. I've seen that stuff smolder for months."

They scanned left and right of where the orange glow stood out starkly against the darkening trees and hills. Andy caught at least a half dozen other bright spots spread across nearly the entire narrow sub-canyon aside the larger central valley made by the Middle Fork. He fought the urge to rush toward the flame and snuff it out right then. Jared seemed to have the same urge but held back.

"Remember our marching orders. We're just here for reconnaissance."

"You're right, but, man—everything is telling me to knock those spots out while they're still small. I get the newer rules against crews working nights, but—"

"I know. I'm with you there. But we don't know what we'd find. And there's always the concern about us snuffing every fire start even when some might be useful to the landscape. Don't hate me for saying it."

"At least you didn't use the party line of *resource benefit*. To hell with that."

"Careful. Them's fighting words in some specialists' eyes," Schuester said, preparing to head back to camp.

"Specialists who've never faced a fire bearing down on them with fifty-mile-per-hour winds."

Jared and Andy stood silently for a few long moments. Eventually, Jared slapped Andy on the back. "Let's head back. We'll get a better idea of what we're dealing with tomorrow morning."

They made their way back to camp in silence, but once they were just outside earshot from camp, Jared stopped Andy. "What you said earlier about specialists never facing a fire coming down on them with fifty-mile-per-hour winds."

"Yeah. What about it?"

"I've never faced that either. None of us here have. Just you. You can wear that as a badge of honor, for sure. But I'm glad that my crew probably won't ever have to face that situation. So just be careful how you handle that."

"Thanks, Schuester. It just goes against everything inside me to watch fires burn because I've seen the bad consequences that sometimes come."

"I know. Always another fire to fight," Jared said, extending his fist, which Andy knocked with his.

And they both took the last steps into camp.

The pine accepted the fact that large, stationary organisms, like itself, were quite exposed. While mobile organisms ran to shelter or went underground when threatened, there was no running for a tree. The only significant lateral movement trees made once planted was to fall. It was the last thing they ever did. The pine had felt several of its neighbors make the mesmerizing descent when their roots had given out at last. It had felt the sharp pang of losing limbs too close to the ground and the scarring and blackening of its trunk when fire had swept the understory, sending its tendrils of flame into the crevices and folds of the pine's gnarled base. Experiencing fire's effect strengthened the tree. That much was clear. Fire assisted in germinating the pine's seeds. But fire also swept out many younger trees in its wake. The pine once experienced a cutthroat being snatched out of the river by an osprey. Fire's cleansing effect on the forest floor felt similar in some ways. Better for the survival of the species. After the fish was conveyed away, the fish population had a slightly smaller chance of overwhelming the available food supply. But the tree was still desperately sad to consider that striving soul snuffed out. The pine was glad it wasn't a fish. Although sometimes fishes' ready ability to flow where the river took them, to places far away, made the tree long for things it didn't understand or know to want in any clear way.

ANDY SHOWED UP TO THE INCIDENT COMMAND POST FOR YET another fire assignment that summer. He thought there was something magical in the way a fire camp sprouted out from bare ground and became a pop-up town practically overnight. Under the orange sky, Andy watched dozens of neat rows of tents for sleeping go up, followed by dozens more of the larger canvas variety for meals and meetings and public outreach and strategic planning. In more remote areas, fire camps often had more people than the surrounding towns. The logistics of bringing in food services, portable showers, and telecommunication always amazed Andy too. It gave him hope for humanity, honestly—seeing how quickly and expertly his species could put together command operations like the one he was assigned to.

It was 2004. Long enough after the 9/11 terrorist attacks to have the country settled into a new sense of living. Andy had graduated from high school in 2002. Most of the time he didn't want to think about how 9/11 had caused a general loss of optimism, confidence, and prospects for young people like him. Other times, he wanted to grab anybody older than he was by the collar and scream at them for not giving him the same chances that the last couple of generations had been given.

Andy did his best to keep a respectful stance as he stood near the back of over two hundred people dressed in their dirty yellow Nomex, just like he was wearing, except his shirt was several shades brighter than many of the scruffy looking guys, with their thick forearms folded and their faces almost completely submerged in full beards and beat-up ball caps. He looked down at his shirt again. No one would know that he had intentionally left his shirt out in the rain to try to break it in and get some more natural-looking smudges. He was eager to earn some real street cred as he continued his third wildfire assignment during his first real wildfire season.

He didn't really count the last two years. Sure, he'd helped with a couple of prescribed burns, but that called for a lot of standing around, leaning against his shovel and observing the creeping fire to ensure it didn't go anywhere the burn boss didn't want it to go. Last year had been an unusually calm summer for the local crew. A less-severe fire year was technically a good thing. It meant less worry for the towns nestled in the foothills that dealt with punishing heat during the summer. But 2004 was a different fire season with a lot more wildfire hitting the Great Basin region, and he was ready to do what he'd set out to do. Dig line until his arms and legs shook. To be right in the thick of the smoke and action.

At his regular station, he was a part of a local engine crew. His team had been called up to assist with this fire. He stood, mirroring the arms-folded-feet-apart stance that he saw all the fire-operation members take, and listened to the dozen or so different operation leads lay out operational protocols, strategy for the day, safety considerations, and those sorts of things. Despite his relative lack of experience, they were things he had heard dozens of times before during the regular flow of briefings.

Finally, the incident commander finished his diatribe on the importance of not getting complacent so late in the season. And with that, the morning briefing ended, and the crews dispersed. The early morning sunlight was already hot against Andy's back and arms under his long-sleeved fire shirt. He shielded his eyes against the brightness and looked up at the tall red rock canyons that towered above the town of Cedar City right at the mouth of Cedar Breaks National Monument.

He followed his crew toward their unofficial gathering spot near the big tent where they took their meals when they were in camp. The fire's ICP, Incident Command Post, was over an hour away from the fire, so to save the trip, most crews tented nearer the fire in spike camps just off the main highway.

The crew formed a circle around their engine boss, Cecil, a salty, expert firefighter from the old school. Andy always felt small when around him, even though he actually stood head and shoulders above Cecil. He noticed that Cecil's Nomex shirt didn't even look yellow anymore. After too many hopeless attempts at fully cleaning it, it was more of a vague dark-gray and brown. When Cecil spoke, people listened.

"Okay, folks. We're going to be working near Duck Valley, which is a small recreational town near Cedar Breaks and Bryan Head. We've got water drops going, drawing from Navajo Lake nearby, so we're going to be relying on aerial support to keep the fire from advancing while we strengthen lines around the town. Any questions?"

Andy shot his hand up.

"Yeah, Andy. What d'you got?"

"I saw some dozers leave just a while ago. Are they heading up to help dig fire breaks?"

"We pushed hard on that, but the AA—a local ranger—told us that in order to make those dozer lines effective, we'd have to go into the Ashdown Gorge Wilderness, and we're not authorized to bring heavy equipment or aerial support into the wilderness yet—"

"What about bringing aerial support from closer to town? Maybe we could get authorization to fly some air tankers then?" Andy said, interrupting Cecil and regretting that immediately. "Sorry to cut you off."

"It's fine. I get it. It'll make our jobs harder, but these restrictions are there for a reason. We have to live within the perimeters that are set for us. We'll have helicopter support. They can navigate around the wilderness boundaries. No air tankers. Anything else?" Cecil looked around for a couple of seconds. "Okay. Let's head out. Oh, one other quick thing"—Cecil held up his hands to grab the crew's attention back—"this is a major fire operation. From what I hear, we're likely to be upgraded to a Type I command structure next week if things stay on the trajectory that they're on now. There'll be a lot going on when we get to our location, so some reminders: You are already heroes. No need to be stupid trying to prove it. Take care of the guys around you. If you put yourself in danger, you put all of us in danger because we're going to try to get to you. So keep your heads. And I know I say it every day, but what's the best way of surviving a wildfire that's chasing you?"

"Maintain situational awareness and re-evaluate LCES as weather and fire conditions change throughout the day and adjust accordingly," the entire crew said with practiced ease.

"And what does LCES stand for?"

"Lookouts, communications, escape routes, and safety zones," the crew shouted in unison.

"That's right. If we can't ensure those escape routes, we do not move. Got it?" Cecil said panning his arm across the horizon and pointing at each crew member as they nodded. "Okay. Now let's load up!"

The crew jumped into their Forest Service–green engines and rolled out of fire camp. As they headed out of town and started climbing the steep road leading toward Cedar Breaks, the sky got progressively darker. The wedge of sky that could be seen between the towering red rock canyon walls slowly changed to a dark orange-and-red hue while smoke swirled above.

Cecil turned on the high beams of the engine he and Andy and a half dozen others were riding in. Andy didn't know if he'd ever really get used to this awkward time. The time between being briefed and the action kicking into high gear. He glanced left, then right, feigning a neck cramp and stretching out his neck, which gave a satisfying pop as he massaged it.

A blank look had been cast over his fellow crew members. But by the way most of the crew kept glancing out the window at the menacing sky, Andy assumed they were trying to process the same thoughts that were racing through his mind. Trying to remember the day's objectives while not being swallowed whole by the alarming red-hued sky above them. Feeling electrified by the thrill coursing through their veins at the chance to do some of the most important work anybody in the agency ever did while fighting the feeling of smallness in comparison to the growing fire perimeter and the scope of the operation.

Cecil turned off Highway 14 and pulled onto a shoulder just past Navajo Lake but before Duck Valley. The crew jumped out of their engines and slung on backpacks and shouldered their shovels or Pulaskis. The side of the road was already packed with fire rigs. Andy scanned the delicate golden waist-high grass in the wide field in front of him, which ran through the valley until it hit the timberline. From there on up the mountainside, there were ponderosa and lodgepole pine growing thick on all sides of the valley. Duck Valley was centered in the bottom of the bowl with cabins tucked within the forested area along with hundreds of other structures within the grassy central-valley area—structures, he noticed, with cedar shank roofs and lacquered log walls.

Andy sighed as he joined the crew in a single line, moving to an area where he could see a couple dozen other firefighters heading in their direction with smoke-blackened faces. He knew how easy it was to forget fire danger when someone's home was nestled under the shade of a lovely forest canopy. He certainly didn't blame anybody for wanting a cabin like the ones he saw tucked in the trees around him. If he didn't normally think about what a tinderbox a place like Duck Valley could be under the wrong conditions, how could he blame any member of the public for not considering it? No one seemed to notice until fire was at their front door.

Andy's crew nodded to the crew they were replacing. The outgoing crew was unusually quiet. That made Andy more nervous than the bright orange he saw flaring just over the next ridge. The other crew must have had a hard fight to be so subdued right when they were being relieved. He swallowed the saliva pooling in his open mouth and adjusted the knob on the back of his hard hat, tightening it a couple of turns.

It might be true that *that which doesn't kill you makes you stronger,* but that struggle sure felt like hell sometimes. Andy was grateful for the calluses that had gradually formed over the season of digging line. After repeating the same motion a thousand times, it didn't matter how good his gloves were. Andy knew the busted knuckles and blisters on the pads of his hands and feet intimately. They were just the price of doing the work he did.

Every year, firefighters got labeled as heroes during the late summer. Andy remembered the signs hung on fences around town from his last assignment. Encouraging phrases like *Thank you heroes!* Those sentiments were certainly well meant, and they did mean a great deal to him. He wondered, though, if that would wear off after he had several seasons under his belt. A time when, push came to shove, he woke up in his tent on the hard ground, smelling like smoke and groggy after several nights of sleeping in far-from-ideal circumstances. A time when his first thought wouldn't be about how excited he was to be a hero that day.

As he scanned over his crew members, he didn't think the excitement of working alongside them would ever wear off. They'd quickly grown to be as close of friends as friends could be. That was the feeling and fervor that moved him forward.

But this fire felt different.

The whole crew was quiet while driving their tools in the reddish dirt and shifting aside for the next man so that, by the sixteenth driving thrust of the shovel, a deep enough furrow was established that it might slow down the progression of the oncoming flames. The real goal being to dig a wide enough barrier that was free from fuel so that the fire would have nowhere to go and stop in its tracks, forced to fall back on the blackened ground it had already traveled.

While they worked on getting line in place, the crew would conduct back burns, burning out fuel before the oncoming wildfire reached it. All these actions were based on simple and solid scientific principles.

Andy thought back on his fire-behavior classes. Fire needed three things to burn: fuel, heat, and oxygen. Take away any of those three things and an existing fire might continue to burn for a time, but the fire's growth potential would be snuffed. Some theorists argued that an active wildfire met the current qualifications of a living organism. Wildfires responded to changes in their environment. He'd already seen fire adapt quickly during his first active season. It climbed up tree trunks and from there hopped from one needle-rich crown to another, sending its embers forward, ever searching for new consumable material. And fires could grow—that was a given. But that growth came in mysterious ways at times.

Andy had witnessed firsthand instances earlier that summer when he had prepared the defenses of one of the small communities tucked in the foothills and tried to decide when he should retreat to a safety zone. As inexperienced as he was, even he knew it hadn't been a question of if but when. He'd watched the fire rush uphill, driven by near-tornado-speed winds. And then, as if by divine intervention, the gusts shifted and the embers blew past some homes, sparing them entirely, while dozens of whole neighborhoods were rendered to ash.

Andy wasn't a religious man in the least. He knew, intellectually, that natural forces had scientifically backed causes. But when he flew over the blackened hillsides after wildfires had burned through, it was hard not to wonder what good deed one family might have done so their home was spared when so many others had been completely lost.

As the day progressed, hope rose like the hot air blowing smoke and ash. More crews arrived by the hour. More aerial support was diverted from other incidents of lower priority. Andy's crew as well as dozens of others were making some headway on establishing solid line. Not containment. Those percentages that the news media always homed in on wouldn't start climbing for several days. He drove his shovel in with extra energy, thinking that he'd have to keep his head any time he was in town for groceries or other supplies. Without fail, several folks would walk up to him and ask if there was any progress on the fire. He needed to talk to some public-affairs folks to figure out the right answer to that question. All of his immediate answers included far too much condescending sarcasm.

He normally took a folksy gosh-darn approach so he could just say that everybody was working really hard to protect their homes and community. That satisfied most people. Andy couldn't honestly say that about the homes around Duck Valley, though, not with the fire he was looking at during his brief water break.

"Man, it feels like a lost cause kind of, doesn't?" he heard someone next to him ask.

Andy lowered his shovel to the dry dirt and did his best to smile, looking up to see a green firefighter named Daniel Rodrigues. Even though Andy only had two more seasons than Rodrigues did, he felt an obligation to cheer him up. "Hey, we get paid whether or not it burns, right?" Andy wiped his sweaty forehead with the bandanna tied around his neck, pleased to see Rodrigues's smile.

"That's true enough, I guess. But still…"

"I know, not the best. But we do the best we can, right, man?" Andy reached out his gloved fist for Rodrigues to bump with his own.

"Let's give it hell before it gives it back," Andy said, taking in as much of a deep breath as he could against the smoke. He picked up his shovel again and jumped back in line with his fellow crew members.

By the end of that first shift, some of his initial fear was replaced by simple fatigue. But Andy certainly noticed that the nervous agitation he'd felt all day had taken its toll. When the two engines rolled back into the spike camp that night, he didn't feel up to any friendly banter with the other crews. He picked up his food, which he ate alone in silence, and then crashed in his tent, totally spent.

Against all odds, all the maps shared during morning briefings the next day showed that they were actually making progress. The crews had established good line around the north and west flanks of Duck Valley. Constant water-drops on as much of the fire as could be reached forced the fire to lose most of its forward momentum. Now if the wind just cooperated for a few more days, they could establish some real firm lines around the perimeter.

After a couple of days on the line, Andy volunteered to help local families get their properties better prepared for potential wildfire. Andy found he enjoyed public outreach once he learned strategies to better handle community members' questions when they were asked in ways that ordinarily pushed his buttons. If he didn't love the physical hands-on appeal of being a crew member so much, he would've even been tempted to move over to the public information world. *Maybe that would make for a good retirement next-career.* He shook that thought from his head right away as he considered the long thirty-some-odd seasons he'd have to rack in before he could move on any such plan.

Andy wasn't surprised to see that the residents of Duck Valley appeared to take a nonchalant stance with Level 1 "Get Ready" orders. But as the Level 2 "Set," or *prepare for evacuation,* orders came later that week, there seemed to be a much stronger sense of urgency. He'd returned to digging line and back-burning with his crew a few days after his first stint helping clear fuel on Forest Service-managed lands near homes of potential fuel, but when the next assignment to help community members came, he jumped at the chance.

Unlike last time, though, the prospect of the wildfire reaching their homes was not just a theoretical idea that sparked some fascination for community members. Thankfully, though, the fire still didn't have much forward thrust in the area near the town. The greatest threat was on the southeast quadrant and the fire there was mostly creeping through low-lying fuel like brush and downed trees. That kind of fire behavior was beneficial. Andy knew that. Although, it was sometimes hard for him to admit that fire wasn't always the enemy. After decades of suppressing all wildfire, in some sectors, the Forest Service was finally gaining some ground in establishing that fire was an important part of the Western ecosystems and that suppressing it completely only led to fires supercharged by excess fuel that normally would have been cleared out by naturally occurring low-to-moderate-severity fires.

"Why don't you guys just put the thing out?"

Andy looked up and broke from his methodical chainsaw work and his own thoughts to see a teenage girl who looked about thirteen or fourteen, maybe, in jeans with holes in both knees that he suspected were put there by design, a ball cap with an emblazoned Hello Kitty design and a ponytail sticking out the back, and Converse high tops.

"Jenny, leave the firefighter alone so he can do his work," a smiling older woman called out to the girl from the porch of the log home whose property Andy had been working near. Andy waved in the woman's direction.

"It's okay. It's a good question. It must seem really weird that we haven't just put it out. But let me ask you a question," Andy said, putting down his chainsaw.

Jenny folded her arms but nodded.

"Look past your property out there," Andy waved his arms in the general direction of the thicker forest. "What do you see?"

"A lot of trees," Jenny said defiantly.

"Good! I see those too. How healthy do a lot of those trees look?"

Jenny looked again, and Andy stifled a chuckle as the realization hit her.

"They don't look healthy at all. A lot of them look awful. But won't the fire just kill them?"

"Some of them, probably. But that's actually a good thing. It'll give the healthier ones a better chance of growing strong. And see all of those little skinny trees growing like crazy all around the bigger trees?"

Jenny nodded enthusiastically.

"Those are tricky. They're what we call ladder fuels. If a fire has a lot of fuel like that, it can creep up those smaller trees and jump up into the upper story of the larger trees and into the crowns, and then the fire can jump from crown to crown, and that is exactly what we don't want. So if we can have a bit of fire creeping around, taking out some of those smaller trees and brush and stuff like that, it'll keep the fire from climbing up the trees we want to keep. Makes sense?"

"Yeah, I guess," Jenny said, standing with one foot tucked behind the other and tapping at the ground nervously for a few moments, but then she ran to be with whom Andy assumed was her grandma.

"Thanks for the lesson on fire ecology for my granddaughter. She's a smart cookie, isn't she? I'm Carol, by the way?"

Andy smiled and caught the embarrassed look spreading over Jenny's face as her grandma gave her a side hug.

"Absolutely. Great to meet you, Carol. It's important that we ask hard questions. None of us has all the answers, but we're better off if we watch out for each other." Andy's words certainly received a more grateful reception from the grandma than from Jenny, but they surprised even him. He didn't even know he had those words in his head.

I guess some things have sunk in from all those fire trainings, he thought as he attempted to start his chainsaw again. After a couple of attempts, he checked the fuel gauge and realized it was running low, and he'd have to get back to his rig to fill up. But something drew his attention.

It was a subtle shift in the air. There'd been little to no wind for the last few days, and so the breeze had fallen into the back of his mind, like habituating to a ticking clock after being in a room for a while. He hadn't given it much consideration because it had been so consistent, instead giving his attention to things that seemed more important. But now the wind was blowing hot across his face from the west—in the direction of the Ashdown Gorge Wilderness.

Fire prevention folks talked a lot about defensible space. Not that the goal should ever be a fireproof property, but that when and where fire did occur, the homes and communities with a defensible space could be better defended because firefighters would have anchor points to push back against oncoming flames. That's why Andy spent the time helping alongside local families to prepare. Encouraging them to limb up trees, cut back brush, set sprinklers, clear rain gutters. He'd even had the new experience of wrapping a historic guard station in what looked like aluminum foil. It was supposed to help protect it from the radiant heat of the fire.

As much as wildfire had a reputation of being the enemy, Andy knew, in an intellectual sense at least, it couldn't really be blamed for destroying homes full of memories and, in some tragic situations, the people trying to protect those memories. It just followed natural laws like everything else. But as his anxiety paralleled the rising wind, Andy thought about how fire's effect could feel a lot more personal than other natural disasters. Earthquakes rolled entire landscapes and whole cities. Tornadoes' funnel clouds were sometimes so wide that they took huge swipes at communities. Rising sea levels during storm surges could rise only as high as the water level. None of them could send out arms of personalized destruction. If a home was on the flood's path, it would be impacted. If it was above the threshold, it might get pelted from above by torrential rains, as with hurricanes, but with floods, homeowners didn't have to worry about deviant waves seeking out their individual homes.

Fire was different. A single floating ember miles away from the main front could ignite a rooftop or the last year's dry duff that lined a rain gutter or the kindling section of a well-ordered wood pile. Modern homes were literal tinderboxes with highly flammable furniture and carpets and combustible electronics. That single ember could spell a home's demise, so it was easy to understand how people who lost homes to fire felt more victimized—as if some punishing divine direction drove the embers.

That flood of thoughts and fears crowded Andy's mind that moment in that afternoon as he saw Jenny and her grandma go back into their home. There was a slight uptick in wind. And after he'd finished his work near their property and left, a wind rose steadily over the afternoon, changing the direction of the wildfire's focus to bear down on Duck Valley.

Andy passed the only real grocery store in Duck Valley, which was barely more than a glorified convenience store. He picked out the two public information people wearing Forest Service uniforms and standing in front of a card table and a large piece of plywood that displayed maps of the fire. Ordinarily, Andy would roll by to check in and joke around with them, partly because they were usually fun people, but also because they had good information with updates he appreciated.

This time, though, as he drove past the store, he felt an uncanny urge to yell for everybody, anybody, to drive down the canyon as fast as they could. His eyes darted around the exterior of the store, looking for anybody he could warn. He couldn't trust his instincts. Not yet. He hadn't paid the price of a dozen fire seasons that added up to scores of fires fought. So, he rolled his shoulders back a couple of times in a mostly vain attempt to flush out the adrenaline that was starting to cause a nasty taste in his mouth.

He paused at the four-way stop and noticed his heavy breathing, even though he'd only been driving his rig and was prepared to turn left up the hill to where most of the hand crews were stationed, trying to strengthen the line. There was a reason why fire command didn't rush to declare increases in the percentage of containment. They only called that higher percentage when they were certain the fires had very little chance of jumping the established lines. When the news people threw out their reports about the progress of fires, they liked to play up the drama by declaring the small containment percentages or layering on video footage of flames and firefighters walking in single file and toting chainsaws or establishing shots of the hundreds of fire operators standing in solidarity and paying close attention to an evening briefing under the fire-stricken sky.

But Andy knew how many thousands of strikes at the dry ground it took to build those small percentages. Those gains were made by shovels held by real people with names and favorite places and jokes to tell and lives to live. He pulled a glove off one of his hands and massaged the callused pads of his palm. *Those calluses were blisters first.* The anger and frustration building inside of him mixed with the growing fear.

He woke from his thoughts, realizing he'd been sitting at the intersection for quite some time. He blew out the air from his lungs and took in a deep breath. But then he glanced to the north, out of his left window, and he couldn't process what he saw. A line of fire had just crested the nearest ridge, leaping forward from crown to crown, incinerating clusters of hundred-year-old trees in its wake. He ran a rough calculation of how long it would take for him to get back to his spike camp. He pulled out his radio.

"Dispatch, this is Miller in Duck Valley," Andy said, tightly gripping the radio in his sweaty hand.

"Miller, this is dispatch. Go ahead."

"Dispatch, I'm returning from some prep work in Duck Valley. Can you give me a status check on the hand crews on the northwest flank of the fire perimeter?"

"Copy that, Miller. The hand crews on the northwest flank of the perimeter are being emergency evacuated at this time. We advise you return to your safety zone and await further instructions from your engine boss." *Damn. That's not happening. There are no more safety zones.*

"Copy. Miller out." Andy slowly put the radio back in its holster. He didn't pay attention as dispatch gave its obligatory last statement over the radio, documenting the time of the conversation for their recordkeeping, as was protocol. Protocol dictated that he return to the ICP. There were no safety zones anymore. Not with a fire rushing toward him with more force than a hundred freight trains and enough heat to melt trees. Fire that could make its own atmosphere.

Andy made a U-turn at the four-way stop and headed back the way he had come. The public information people must have received word on their radios, the same message he'd just received from dispatch, because their rig was gone and their displays stood alone. He turned onto Highway 14, headed back to Cedar City. He flipped on the headlights as the ashfall darkened the sky and drifted past his windshield like fleecy snowflakes.

But when he saw the road sign leading down the dead-end road, he swerved off the highway and took the gravel drive down to where Jenny and her grandma, Carol, were still biding their time, hoping not to receive the Level 3 evacuation order to get out as fast as possible—clinging to that Level 2 notice to merely prepare for what might happen next.

Andy came to a jarring stop, spitting gravel in front of the cabin near where he had spent most of the day. He rushed to the front door, jumping the two steps and pounded on the door frame. He heard the startled rustling as someone walked to the entrance. Andy saw Carol's alarmed face through the screen.

"Andy. How nice to see you again. Is everything okay—"

"We need to get you and Jenny out now!" Andy yelled, fighting the urge to sling both Carol and Jenny over his shoulders and carry them out to his rig.

"Oh, okay," the grandma said as reality sank in. "Oh! Jenny!"

Carol turned back inside and hurried up a few steps toward the loft. Jenny came out to the railing with a puzzled look on her face.

"Dear, we need to go. Grab your emergency bag right now!"

"Okay, but I need—"

"No, dear, there's no time. We need to get out right now!"

Andy could read the fear in Jenny's stance even from where he stood on the porch. He reached behind to swat at something that fell on his neck. Ash. He turned around. The sky had turned a sinister red, and below that and the awesome gyre of smoke-blown clouds, he saw the fire roaring toward him. Every second counted now.

"Hey, we really need to go. If the fire crosses the highway, we won't have any escape routes!" Andy yelled into the house.

Jenny stumbled downstairs, carrying a backpack on one shoulder and a carry-on suitcase in her opposite arm.

"To hell with protocol."

Andy swung the screen door wide and dashed to grab the carry-on bag from Jenny while frantically looking around the room for her grandma. She finally appeared from the kitchen, carrying a large carboard box.

"Jenny, get to my truck now, okay?" Andy said, looking straight at her eyes to ensure she was paying attention.

She nodded nervously and took the carry-on bag that Andy had left at the foot of the porch steps. He raced back to take the box from Carol.

"Got to go now. Come on!" Andy said, hefting the box against his hip and pulling Carol toward the door.

"Wait, do I have everything—"

"There's seriously zero time for that now. We just need to get out while we still can—"

Andy stopped cold on the porch, looking north to where ash was falling much heavier now. The fire had jumped the highway. He had minutes to prepare to defend the area the best he could before the wildfire burned over the home.

Krassel Ranger District, Idaho
August 2024

Fire normally burned in a patchwork pattern of low-intensity flame that simply licked up the grasses, shrubs, and trees too young to have developed sufficient bark. The pine didn't get sentimental about that anymore. It was nature's way, and it was for a wise purpose, though it recognized it might be self-serving for it to believe things should be the way they were simply because the system had directly set it up to reach its full potential. Not all trees were so fortunate.

It appeared to it that nature did more than self-correct by making allowances for landslides and burn scars. Nature was better than that. Nature self-enhanced. From broken things, it found a way to strengthen the system itself. Through those landslides new habitat could come. Fire recirculated nutrients and ensured those most likely to propagate could grow more easily. And nothing was ever wasted.

AFTER SPENDING ONE MORE NIGHT AT THE GREENFIELD RANCH with Schuester's crew and then a day of traveling back to the district office, Andy said his goodbyes. It was late by the time he got in at his office, and the janitor was vacuuming the conference room.

He didn't keep anything in his cubicle really. He used the warehouse where the engine was parked as his base of command. They had a small gym there, too, where the crew did group workouts. He plopped down on the desk chair that he'd never bothered adjusting to fit him, and called his boss, the fire management officer for the district.

"Hello, this is Mike."

"Hey, Mike. This is Andy. Just wanted to let you know I'm back."

"Thanks. How did things go?"

"Fine. We scoped out the fire. It's just skunking in the duff and leaf litter mostly."

"Okay. Glad you made it back safe. When will your crew be back again?"

"They still have eight days, officially."

"Good deal. Glad you set up that experience. Hate to see them sitting around with nothing to do."

"Agreed. Thanks. Have a good night, Mike. Oh, and Mike?"

"Yeah?"

"What do you think about me doing a PIO stint one of these days?"

"Public information officer, huh? Definitely something worth talking about. Let's chat tomorrow when I'm in the office. Good night, Andy."

Andy hung up and leaned back in his chair. Even though the chair could use some adjusting, he was amazed at how comfortable its design was. For a few moments, he contemplated closing his eyes and falling asleep right then and there, but then, with a sigh, thought better of it. He stood and nodded to the janitor as he passed her on his way to his rig. He'd crash at the bunkhouse for the night.

The next morning, he was working the front desk again when Mike found him.

"Hey, Andy. Thanks for checking in last night. Hope you caught up on some sleep."

Andy turned to face Mike, who was wearing a slightly crumpled button-down shirt untucked, trying to hide the paunch that he'd collected after the last few years of being stuck behind a desk most of the time. Andy had actually worried a bit after seeing Mike's heavy breathing and sweat streaming down his face after trying and barely making it through the annual arduous-level pack test that was required to get on the fire line as a firefighter.

"I think that'll be a task for the next few days, but yeah, it felt good to sleep in my own bed," Andy said, though saying it made him contemplate homeownership, and that distracted him enough that he missed Mike's first sentence. He could tell by the expectant look on Mike's face that he couldn't get away with a sly smile and nod. "Sorry, Mike. Come again?"

"You really do need to catch up on some sleep. I just asked if you knew of any fires in the region where you could take up a public information officer trainee assignment," Mike said, running his fingers through his thinning brown hair streaked with gray.

"I haven't been keeping tabs on that, but I could check with dispatch. I'm sure there's something going on."

"Okay. Why don't you look at some options and send them my way. I was thinking it might be a great launching point for you when you 'graduate,'" Mike said with air quotes and a grin.

Andy chuckled, but somehow it didn't seem quite as funny for his boss, who was easily five years younger than he was, to joke about his mandatory retirement.

"Will do. Thanks for considering it. I think it could be a great fit."

"Righto, and good luck with the website. Sounds like Cheryl has you really dialed in on that?"

"She and I have a good plan at least. It'll be a work-in-progress for a very long time though. Thousands of pages to deal with. But I'm making some headway, I think."

"Good man. Carry on, then. And let me know when you have a couple of PIO assignments for me to look at."

"Thanks, Mike." Mike walked back upstairs, his heavy footsteps falling on the stairs above Andy's head.

Andy looked up Cheryl Caplan's cell number. She was like him—an old-school person who preferred talking to people for real rather than sending them a chat message or text.

"Hey, Andy! What's up?" Cheryl said in her characteristically chipper voice, picking up after the second ring. It almost sounded like she was serenading anybody who called.

"Hey, Cheryl. You'll never guess what Mike just told me to do this morning…"

By the end of the conversation with Cheryl, Andy had a couple of good leads on teams that might be looking to bring on some public information officer trainees, and Andy spent most of the morning trying to nail down lead PIOs to find a team that would be called up next. Eventually, he connected with a guy named Glen Sacchet who still led a team, although he'd formally retired from the Forest Service a couple of years before.

"Hey, Glen! This is Andy from the Krassel District on the Payette. How's it going?"

It took longer than Andy was anticipating to home in on the real purpose of his call because Glen insisted on connecting all of their mutual acquaintances in the fire world, not to mention their shared fire experiences and all of the possible times the two of them might have worked the same fire at the same time without knowing it. Andy wasn't in any hurry, and it was an early Tuesday afternoon, which was notoriously slow in the visitor center anyway. But after wading through all of the side roads the conversation took him on, he confirmed that Glen's team was open for PIO trainees and were next in line to be dispatched.

"Granted, we might not get called up this year, with the fire season turning out to be so mild compared to the last several," Glen said.

"Very true. I had to send my crew off to Canada to find action."

That opened up a whole new line of conversation, which Andy was surprised to discover he actually enjoyed. Fifteen minutes later,

Andy hung up and wheeled his chair around to his desk and computer, committed to knocking out a few web pages.

Now it was time to play the waiting game, see if any fires rose to the level of needing a Type 2 PIO team. Over the next couple of days, he fell back into his old routine. He exercised alone at the gym in the warehouse. He went for long daily runs on the trail that ran past the bunkhouse and up to an old lookout that showed signs of disrepair from decades of neglect. Andy had proposed to the district that his crew replace planks in the wood flooring, reinforce the stairs, and even do some significant landscaping, but he'd been told the area was eligible for consideration on the historical register, so they'd need someone from heritage to run a survey first.

That was unlikely to ever become a high priority. The heritage folks always had more than they could handle. The lookout would probably just continue to fade until the district decided it was past saving, then, for most intents and purposes, forget it was there. It would lose whatever historical value it might have had before being set aside because it once had *historical significance*. It just made no sense.

Andy was running past the lookout two days before his crew was due to return from their Canada assignment and stopped, as he generally did, when he got to the site. Somehow, by his estimation, between the Forest Service's founding and now, the agency had been knocked off its moorings a little. Like the lookout. It still functioned and could still be useful, but its proud legacy had shifted. Every fall, Andy nailed gray boards over the windows of the lookout to keep the glass intact and at least pretend it had enough value to keep it from falling into total disrepair. Maybe he'd been knocked from his moorings a little too.

The Forest Service prided itself with having a can-do attitude about things. And from Andy's twenty-year experience working for them, he could see how that played out. It wasn't that the fish biologists he'd tagged along with when they needed an extra hand—or the timber-sale administrators he and his crew had helped burn slash piles—or the recreation specialists he'd helped cut trails with sat around or complained about their jobs in the breakroom. It was that the agency had allowed itself to become less proactive.

In Andy's career, he'd rubbed shoulders with specialists from all kinds of programs, and he saw the same problem. Instead of sending a trail crew to log out trees that had fallen atop trails, the rec managers focused on building relationships with volunteer groups who did some of the work some of the time. Instead saying flat out *no* to mining projects that would undoubtedly damage the forest landscape in irreparable ways, the agency spent thousands of hours working for the mining companies, essentially for free, describing how the mining project should be conducted to minimize impacts to the landscape. Talk about putting lipstick on a pig. Sure, we can't stop you from cutting a road through one of the last remaining stretches of non-wilderness wolverine habitats, but hey, we can make sure that you tell us any time you transport petroleum to and from your facility.

And it wasn't really the Forest Service's fault either. He'd never met a group so dedicated to protecting public lands or willing to put in extra hours to protect their resource, whether that be fish or watersheds. The agency had just lost its spine and confidence. Andy was sure that the Forest Service of fifty years ago would have had a crew on that lookout long before major repairs became necessary. Granted, there probably would have been a lookout operator living in the lookout too.

So many operational components of the agency—the truly cool and romantic pieces—could be performed faster and cheaper by technology now. He was honestly glad that he was retiring when he was. He couldn't handle the thought of sitting around a compound, watching a screen while a drone did all the fire spotting or hotspot checks or even started prescribed fires, using what the agency affectionately called PSDs, or plastic sphere dispensers. A drone would essentially shoot out a bunch of ping pong balls that exploded to start prescribed fires.

And it wasn't just in fire either. Timber markers that used to spend their summers painting tree trunks to lay out timber sales would likely be replaced by Geographic Information System layers. Forest disease and insect technicians would lose their usefulness to LiDAR-enabled drones. Fish biologists would be replaced by sophisticated camera systems. No more need for snorkeling in the shallow river waters to count juvenile salmon or to wade in the stream with fish-shocking backpacks to count and measure fish.

Andy glanced at the shed near the lookout where he'd stored all the tools he and his crew would need to get the lookout back into shape, on the off chance they'd get the privilege of doing that labor. And before his worries of what the forest leadership would think or how the heritage people would get after him, he unlocked the padlock on the shed door, pulled out a saw and some fresh pieces of plywood and set to work, repairing what he could on his own.

He wasn't due at the district office for a few hours, so he cut the boards needed to replace the warped and rotten stairs. There was something satisfying in ripping out the rusted nails and prying up the old boards and driving home new galvanized steel studs into the boards. The progress that he could see so clearly was intoxicating. By the time he stopped, he'd replaced all the stairs and half the interior floorboards and had painted and sealed the exterior walls.

If he could do all that in a morning, what could the Forest Service, with tens of thousands of dedicated employees, do? If they could only be set free. Not only to worry about fixing outdated information on the website, but to have a reason to update it. Fill it with new and exciting adventures for people to explore in the forest and, by connecting to that newfound purpose, gain tons more prospective Forest Service employees.

But, for now, Andy sat down at his desk in the visitor center at the district office, which was quiet even for a Monday. He buckled down to listing suggested changes that the forest could make to its dysfunctional website. He did it because that's what he'd been asked to do and because that was what the current Forest Service felt was the best use of his time. He couldn't resent the agency for being timid any more than he could yell at the shy kid on his crew to have more confidence. He knew there were reasons for the way the agency functioned, a lot of which he probably didn't understand. But he also knew he was going to finish laying the new floor in the lookout and that the next day, he'd stain the new boards and go about the landscaping. That much, he could handle on his own.

The phone rang.

"Payette National Forest, this is Andy."

"Hello, Andy. This is Glen. Still up for an assignment as a PIO?"

"Yes, definitely. What fire are we working on?"

"The Greenfield Ranch Fire. It really blew up last night. Freak wind event with fifty-mile-per-hour gusts. Pretty incredible."

"Sounds like it. I scoped that area out when the fire was first called in by dispatch. Where should I meet up with your team?"

"Could you make it to Salmon tonight?"

"Definitely. It'll give my engine boss trainee a bit more experience anyway. I'll grab my things and head right out."

"Great, see you there."

Andy hung up and sprang from his chair, more excited about an assignment than he remembered being in years. Just as he made his way around back behind the visitor center, it dawned on him—he still needed to get the green light from Mike. He gave him a quick call, and after Mike had gotten over the fact that Andy had basically committed to the assignment without running it past him first, he gave the go-ahead.

The lookout repairs would have to wait a couple of weeks. That work would be waiting for him when he got back, for better or worse.

The pine had interacted with rafting groups that cut wood to burn during the dark nights along the river. It remembered further back, even, when the early homesteaders cut live trees that were about its current age back then to make cabins and fence cattle. It watched how the trees had grown from a flurry of grasses and then new saplings. It supposed in some respects, having some trees gone helped others grow, but the bond it felt to its neighboring trees and the chemical connection that built its underground community made it doubt the efficacy of intentionally felling of those experienced trees for the sake of lifeless structures, especially to keep penned animals inside.

MAGGIE DRAGGED HERSELF INTO WORK AT THE RIVER-RAFTING shop in town, one business among a number of storefronts dotting a strip mall. The one she worked out of was in the northern part of town in a community called Eagle, although the entire region had exploded in population in recent years, so Eagle was pushed right up against Meridian, which butted up against Caldwell, which was meshed in with Nampa. Heading west, there was just a brief division between the urban sprawl of Boise and Oregon's eastern border now.

To the north, though, there was a very clear dividing line to indicate where the urban zone ended and the more rural parts began—mountains. Maggie loved the fact that there were still some areas in the Southwest Idaho Region where it was difficult or expensive enough to build new subdivisions that builders couldn't access the canyons leading up to Cascade and McCall. Of course, that meant that housing was at a premium in those small mountain towns, so she couldn't even dream of living there. Still, she took comfort in knowing there were wild places close to town.

The river-rafting shop where she worked was about as wild as a domesticated labradoodle though. She entered the shop from the front entrance. The storefront had large flatscreen TVs on all four walls, flashing scenes from river-rafting adventures. And polished light-colored wood floors and countertops that Maggie always thought would be more appropriate for a cellular phone or computer shop than an outdoor-adventure company. But retail was certainly not her thing. She brushed her hand across one of the plush couches in one of the cozy-corner seating areas where customers could be shown—in glossy trifolds—all the grand adventures they'd have in exchange for a single-ticket price worth more than her car. She gave a wave to the customer-service rep standing behind a counter, sporting a crisp light-blue polo and khakis and spotless high-top sneakers. Another reason she was glad she ran rafts instead of working the retail end—she wore what she wanted. She looked down at the leggings and t-shirt she wore appreciatively.

Maggie was just about to say something to the customer service guy, but then froze for a second. Is his name Jackson? Why are there so many Gen-Zers with names that start with J? Jaime, Justin, Jacob, Josh. And when did it become acceptable to wear sneakers as business casual? With a deep sip from her gas station cup of coffee instead, she decided that the wave she gave was sufficient and easily pushed the thoughts out of her mind as she drifted back to the workshop section behind the retail portion of the building. And as she got closer to the familiar smell of rubber rafts and oiled machinery, her breathing got easier and her shoulders loosened. Even though she hadn't worked for the company long, the workshop felt like home.

"Hi, Jay, is it a Monday again? It sure feels like one."

"Hey, Maggie. No, it's actually Thursday. For most of us normal nine-to-five, Monday-through-Friday, modern-service workers, Thursdays are so close to Fridays that they're almost exciting. Almost," Jay said, adjusting his glasses that were the only real indication that Jay belonged to Gen X not Gen Z, despite his name starting with yet another J. He fiddled with knobs and tightened some screws on a camp stove without looking up. After surveying the stove for a few moments more, he turned the igniter knob and after a couple of faint clicking noises, the stove burst into flame.

"Look at that! It lives!" He shouted, clapping his hands and bringing them together as he crouched down close to the camp stove to inspect it further. Jay looked at all the angles around the small stove and shut off the flame with a satisfied nod.

"Okay. Now let me greet you properly." Jay stepped away from the workbench he was standing behind and gave Maggie a bear hug with his arms entirely enveloping her skinny frame. Jay's hugs were always the best, not only because he had the mechanics of a proper hug down perfectly, but also because when he gave hugs, which he gave to everybody Maggie had ever seen enter his workshop, it felt like a momentous occasion. As if Maggie hadn't seen him in years and they were reuniting for the first time.

"Thanks, Jay. Best part of the day and working for this company is definitely your hugs. And I swear that if you weren't so happily married to your fabulous Leanna, and if you weren't twenty years too old for me, I'd force you to go out with me."

"Ouch! Twenty years? Really? It's just as well. Leanna and I have basically adopted you by now, so it wouldn't do at all to venture into the dating thing," Jay said, pushing his red aviator glasses back up on the ridge of his nose and pulling his long dark hair that was streaked with gray that Jay never seemed ashamed of behind his ears. Then grabbing a broom, he began exuberantly sweeping the shop floor.

Maggie dropped her bag on a coatrack standing against the far wall of the workshop next to a long pegboard where dozens of tools and gears hung. "One of these days, you've got to show me how to use these tools. I can't be tied to a raft forever. Got to develop some other marketable skills, right?"

"I'm not sure I'm the right person to talk to about marketable skills. I've been running the operations for this rafting thing for over a decade now. Not a lot of upward mobility in my line of work either."

Maggie plopped down on a worn, overstuffed corduroy armchair. "That's something I've been wondering about for a long time. You practically run this whole operation. Have you ever thought about asking for a corporate job?"

Jay stopped sweeping and let out an infectious laugh that made Maggie giggle. "Can you imagine me in a suit and tie?"

Maggie looked at Jay's huge muscular forearms and defined chest. "Yeah. I can. I think you'd kill it with a well-tailored suit. You'd draw every eye in that boardroom." Maggie chomped down on an apple that she'd grabbed from a bowl of fresh fruit near the coatrack.

"Well, corporate life is definitely not for me. Way too many pointless meetings and working weekends when I'd rather be taking my camper out in the woods. Speaking of which, looks like we have a couple of tours for you to look at." Jay pointed to a printed sheet on a clipboard hanging on the wall opposite the workbench Jay was working at. Maggie got out of her chair with a sigh and strolled over to the clipboard, pulling it off its hook and scanning the sheet.

There was an updated calendar of rafting groups needing guides. The company offered all kinds of outdoor adventures, from weekend horseback trips to weeklong rafting tours like Maggie normally led. There were also guided trips in Europe, backpacking to many exotic-sounding places Maggie had never even dreamed of visiting, and many others. But she focused on the light-blue color code for rafting. Jay was right. There were several rafting groups scheduled to run the Middle Fork the next week.

The way the scheduling worked, she wasn't automatically assigned to specific tours or groups. To be assigned, she would have to log into her employee portal and indicate she was available and willing to take a tour. Then she would show up at the launching location and get more specific assignments from trip leads to decide who did what and when throughout the trip. It would be easier to just have people initial on the clipboard sheet next to a tour group on the calendar, but there were databases involved and tracking software that Maggie was glad she didn't have to understand.

She leaned her elbows up on the tall counter and squinted at the screen of the low-tech clunker computer next to the clipboards that was intended for employees to use to sign up for tours. *I really need to get my eyes checked*, she thought. Another issue she couldn't afford to worry about right then.

"Your mission, if you choose to accept it," Maggie said, clicking past the home screen and logging into her portal page while trying to sip the last drops of her coffee.

"I knew you were a spy in disguise!" Jay joked, disappearing into the small warehouse in the next room where the rafts and other outdoor gear were stored.

Maggie found the right week range and tour and checked the box next to "Assign tour." She got the confirmation on her screen and logged out of her portal, then wandered back to the armchair to pull up details from the automated email on her phone. There, she started reading details about the clients in her assigned group.

One seemed to be a batch of three old college buddies. At least that's what she gathered from the fact that the group had inside jokes and jabs and references to each other in their profiles. That was somewhat interesting. She looked at the photos that had been included with each groups booking. Most were of folks enjoying various outdoor activities and grinning quite contentedly. A few families, a son and father duo, and a few couples.

Her eyes focused on a small family. A husband named, David; a wife, Valerie; and a teenage daughter named Evelyn. At first glance, the family seemed so normal. David was an accountant. Valerie stayed home with one younger child who was too young to join the rafting trip. Valerie was also a freelance technical writer. That sounded kind of interesting. Although, Maggie had to admit she didn't know what technical writers did.

"Hey, Jay. What do technical writers do," Maggie shouted in the direction of the warehouse.

Jay popped his head into the workshop and pulled out his ear-buds. "What was that?"

"What do technical writers do?"

"I thought maybe an intruder was taking over the shop or something because I was sure you wouldn't ask me to stop everything for anything less important," Jay said, grumbling to himself.

But Maggie saw a sideways smile creep up his face. That made her certain he didn't mind being useful, even in silly opportunities like these. She reflected on how many invitations to dinner with Jay and his wife she'd accepted over the past year alone. Jay was important, or at least important to her.

"But since this is vital information, I'm sure, I think technical writers write things like manuals and text for websites and stuff like that. Or there's this magical thing called the internet that can answer all your deepest questions. At least, that's what I've heard." Jay disappeared again.

"Thanks Jay," Maggie called after him as he disappeared in the warehouse again, then pulled up a couple of descriptions of what technical writers did on her phone. Reading through some details, she was certain she'd be able to strike up a few conversations about Valerie's work. Technical writing had some creative components to it, and she was sure she and Valerie could talk about books.

And then Evelyn. Sixteen years old. Starting her junior year of high school that fall. There were several sentences gushing about how she was on the honor roll last year and was involved in a play and had aspirations for college and an interest in trees. All that added up to one thing—Evelyn's mom had written the description, and she was trying to convince Maggie that Evelyn was not going to be a problem, which meant that Evelyn would definitely be a problem.

She remembered Nate's promise after the last tour with the family with the jerk son and clueless mom—the dad tried. She supposed the kids had spent too much time connecting to screens and not enough real face-time with parents. Their complaints about having no cell coverage and being bored in the middle of a vast wilderness made for a very long and challenging week on the river. The son had been especially challenging. Maggie almost felt sorry for the kid when he fell out of the raft and had to be rescued on their last day. Almost. But, either way, it meant she had first choice from the groups to take particular care of this time.

Maggie thought about wandering over to the warehouse to help Jay, but she knew she'd really just be in the way and slow him down. And she knew Jay well enough to know he'd be listening to an audiobook that he would stop listening to if she helped. He was too polite to ignore her while she worked alongside him. So she just poked her head around the corner to say goodbye.

"Check you later, Jay!" she shouted over the din of a power washer. Jay shutdown the washer.

"Leaving so soon?" Jay popped around a stack of rafts.

"Yeah, got some errands to run before I head up to Stanley for my next tour.

"With your technical-writing buddies?" He smirked.

"No. I'll make Nate take special care of that group. I'll probably end up spending most of the week with a bunch of old college buddies."

"That's a shame. Family dynamics are good learning experiences, but the college frat boys will probably be easier to manage."

"That's what I figure. But I think I've earned an easy one this time."

"Fair enough. Well, be careful. You never run the same river twice, right?"

"Right," Maggie smiled at the very familiar adage. Jay always offered that bit of advice before she left for every tour she'd ever signed up to guide. "I think it's sweet that you're such a fan of that Disney movie. Wasn't it *Pocahontas*?"

"What are you talking about?" Jay said while marking some rafts with tags.

"The movie. Remember? 'The thing I like about rivers is you can't step in the same river twice…' and then she jumps in her canoe."

"Oh! I think Disney was taking that quote from Heraclitus. The ancient Greek philosopher?" Jay said, appearing from behind a raft near Maggie.

"Oh. Easy to confuse the two, right?" Maggie smiled sheepishly and gave Jay a wave.

Jay waved back.

"Thanks, Jay."

She exited the way she'd come and dropped into her car's front seat. The reality was, though, she didn't have any errands to run. Sure, there were plenty she would run if she had the means to afford them. She'd get her eyes and teeth checked. She'd drop off her car at the mechanics. She'd load up on groceries so she'd have plenty of good food waiting for her when she returned from the rafting trip. She'd splurge—buying three bestsellers from her favorite independent bookstore downtown.

Someday, maybe, she thought as she turned the key in the ignition. At that point in her life, she was just grateful her car started and she could rev it up well enough to get it out of the parking lot. Having nowhere else to go, she headed toward downtown Boise's greenbelt. As she got close to the river and the path that ran alongside it, she stopped for a traffic light. Boise State University was just outside her driver's side window. It was the tail end of the summer term, which meant the university was a bit less bustling than during the spring and fall semesters, but there were still plenty of students milling around grassy fields in front of the large college buildings.

The light turned green, and the car behind her gave a polite honk to let her know. She stepped on the gas and waved behind her shoulder, though there was no way the car behind her could see the apology. She pulled in at a small parking area where a couple of picnic tables stood empty.

She pulled her phone out of her back pocket—force of habit—and checked her social feeds. After the first few reels, seeing her friends' trips to Thailand or family photos in front of their lovely homes was a bit much for her as she realized she could barely handle keeping gas in her beat-up car and lights on in her apartment. There was no home full of kids.

She wasn't sure she really wanted that kind of life, but it felt like the social media friends her age had leveled up a couple of times, while she still struggled to make headway.

She closed the social apps and sat with her back against the picnic table, facing out toward the river. She did her best to enjoy the sun warming her face and the soft gurgle of the river as it flowed past worn stones. That was good. That was real. And nobody got more or less of such experiences, whether they lived in New York in a fabulous apartment like one high school friend had managed or a studio with threadbare carpeting and run-down appliances. And the sun was the same in Thailand. *Isn't it?* The hum of a river might be slightly different, but it was the principle she was driving home.

A runner in leggings and a sports bra that looked like they had never been worn before and probably cost a great deal more than

Maggie's monthly grocery budget passed her. The runner was maybe a few years older than she was. It was hard for her to decipher ages anymore. So many people tried to look older when on the younger spectrum or younger when on the older spectrum.

How did you get to where you are? She sent the silent thought in the direction of the runner who wound around a bend in the foot path. She fought against the cliché trophy wife idea, although it was a bit hard for her to dream up many other scenarios for why someone in her mid-twenties would be free on a Thursday at 10:00 a.m. Maybe she took the day off. Or maybe it was her birthday. Or maybe she had a flexible work schedule. Lots of companies were offering those now. So long as employees got their work done, the companies didn't care when it got done. What would that be like?

Then she looked past the river and could just make out the tops of the university buildings. That explained a lot of the success stories she saw on her feeds and probably explained that unusually well-kept runner's success too. They'd all graduated from college with degrees that were actually useful. English Literature majors were fine, but they required more planning. You get that degree with the larger goal of law school. Or you double-majored in engineering and English to make yourself more attractive to employers who wanted engineers that could hypothetically write and communicate decently.

Or you planned to pursue a PhD to teach and write. The thought of standing in front of a bunch of students like she had been held zero appeal to her. The writing part might be good, but she also bought into the theory that it takes genius to write much of anything worth reading, and she had taken enough creative writing courses to know she didn't harbor any hidden talent that just needed to be tapped and nurtured.

It did gnaw at her that she hadn't at least finished her degree. There were certain pieces of her identity that she used to pride herself in and that she'd once thought about using as themes in college-scholarship application essays. She wasn't a quitter. But as she considered the major turning points in her life over the last few years—graduating from high school, going to an out-of-state college, dropping out, finding any work that would allow her to stay where she was—her chest tightened and her breath came in shallow anxious bursts.

By any estimation, she was exactly that. A quitter. But she didn't have to stay that way. She pulled up a browser on her phone and flipped to the Boise State home page. She tried to log into her student portal, hoping they didn't clear out inactive accounts at regular intervals, but she couldn't remember her password. She almost abandoned the effort entirely, then she thought about how ridiculous it was, allowing herself to be defeated by a forgotten password when she could request a new one through her phone. Right there in a lovely park by the river.

She got a recovery password, and a couple of moments later, she was staring at her Boise State student dashboard. She pulled up her unofficial transcript. She had twenty-four English credits. One more full semester and she could graduate. She already had her general courses knocked out. And she realized for the first time that she had enough credits to consider a communications minor. She just had to apply to the communications program.

Communications. Technical writing would fall under that category, right?

She clicked on a link labeled "How do I re-enroll?" After five minutes of wading through unhelpful frequently-asked-question lists, she found the link to enroll again. She filled out the online application right then. No thought of getting back to it later. She amazed even herself. She had no idea how she would pay for the last semester or two that she needed to knock out her degree. But a surge of possibility run through her at that moment. She'd figure it out. She could get loans, and *Who knows?* Maybe she would shift her major to communications. If Valerie the raft client found a job as a technical writer, maybe she could too.

By the time she stood up from the picnic table, her muscles and joints stiff from inactivity, she had re-enrolled in college. And though the river and sun and overly attractive runners were the same, she viewed them differently, in a weird way that she didn't really understand. She tried various analogies to describe the difference as she drove home to get some things together for her river-guide stint that weekend. Maybe it was like eating a time-tried-but-personally-avoided, new-to-her dish only to realize it was her new favorite. Not quite right.

She jiggled the key in the door to her apartment, pushed the door open and flipped on the light. No, it was like a river. A river she had gone down several times before but was experiencing in totally new ways.

Because you never run the same river twice. Jay's saying took on an alternate meaning. It used to be about nothing more than safety and unpredictability. But now she realized it was also about perspective and becoming an adult. In that moment, Maggie felt like an adult. She wasn't sure if she ever really had before. So many things had been out of reach or not worth the effort to grasp.

She dropped her keys on her kitchen counter, and for the first time in months, she noticed an empty pot with a packet of sunflower seeds tucked inside. Adults could plant seeds and actually see them grow. She walked back outside, the pot in hand, to a dirt patch on her apartment complex's property where some scraggly bushes were barely holding on. She dug into the dry dirt and added a few handfuls to the terra cotta pot, making a mental note to get some kind of fertilizer or mulch to add to it. Those bushes were really sad.

Back inside, she added some warm water to the soil, which turned black and kicked up an earthy aroma that made Maggie wish she had more than a single pot with a single packet of seeds. She carefully tore open a corner of the seed packet and poured a dozen oblong black-and-white-lined seeds into her hand, then did her best to evenly distribute them around the surface of the soil in the pot. She gently gathered the pushed-aside soil and covered the seeds with a thin layer of moist dirt and brought the pot to the one sunny windowsill on the far side of the room, opposite her main entry.

She surveyed her work. It was just a small pot, but there was something significant in starting something that had the potential to grow now that the right conditions were in place.

Just like my life. She knew what a cliché that was, but at that moment, she didn't even care. She reviewed the back of the seed packet a couple of times to verify watering instructions, and the little sun that reached her apartment worried her, but her new addition would do for now.

The seed packet still had several dozen seeds left inside, so she tucked it in a kitchen drawer for future planting, and as she did so, she remembered when her mom had given her the pot and seeds as a house-warming gift. Her mom would be thrilled to know that she had finally planted some of the seeds. But Maggie felt the surge of adult-like confidence waning.

This will do for now.

 he tree never complained about the shoddy soil that its seed had been planted in. Partly, perhaps, because it had never known any other soil, but also because with that poor soil came certain advantages. From its ridge, it could experience the constant battle for sunlight that the trees planted closer to the rivers' edge—where water was plentiful—fought. A seedling planted there would never make it under the shade of the existing trees.

No upstart trees with aspirations of being the tallest in the forest ever came to encroach on the pine's access to sunlight or water, and that made it easy to distribute its cones. If it hoped to pass on its genetic code, which it supposed was its only real reason for existing, it had to make sure that the cones fell well beyond its own shadow and then hope the seedlings had the fortitude to grow strong amidst the nutrient-poor landscape.

"WE HUMANS HAVE A FASCINATION WITH FIRE. IT'S NO MYSTERY why that might be. Fire is the reason why our species was able to abandon our fearful caves and start the quick, in geological terms, ascent to domination of the entire planet. We hide the fact that, despite all of the grand advancements in technology, with circuits and airplanes, we still rely on fire to fuel most everything."

Andy turned off the podcast in frustration.

"Have you ever been on a fire line, Dr. Snodgrass? I dare you to think that fire is so darn fascinating when a lightning strike–caused fire is burning near your home," Andy said out loud in his rig as he parked in an expansive field in Salmon, Idaho. One thing from the podcast kept circulating through his thoughts—when wildfire threatens homes or people's livelihoods, like ranches and farms, it's always seen as the enemy. And a burned-up forest doesn't attract many tourists to towns that need those tourists to visit, eat in their mom-and-pop restaurants, and stay in their struggling motels. Andy shook the thought from his head, opened his door, and climbed out of his rig. It was late, but because of the late-evening sunlight of summer, it was still a good hour before dusk.

Andy still found the setup of a fire camp thrilling. So many firefighters missed the true magic of having the framework for a group of people, often larger than any of the surrounding towns, pop up overnight. There were so many logistical considerations at play. Generating power, providing food and showering facilities, water systems, lighting, traffic control, security, internet, telecommunications, and more. He knew that by tomorrow morning, in time for the 0600 morning briefing, large canvas tents would be set up for all the different functions of the Incident Command Post, each with a neatly laminated placard on its entrance: Logistics; Planning; Operations; Incident Command, or IC; and Public Information Officer. He hoped he could avoid assignments where he'd be stuck in the tent. He'd much prefer setting up trap lines at local grocery stores, handing out information, and giving updates to residents.

He checked in with Glen and set up his own tent, and after walking around the Incident Command Post once so he could get his bearings, he decided to head in for the evening, in preparation of an early start the next day. There were some things firefighters just had to learn about living in a fire camp for a two-week assignment. Massive floodlights were on all night long, so Andy carried a sleep mask to block out the light. Even if tents were set up far away from generators, there were other disturbing sounds, like boots on dry grass, walking right past tents, or the sound of food or gasoline supply trucks making deliveries any time—day or night. That's why he carried noise-canceling earbuds. He didn't sleep very well in sleeping bags on the ground, so he'd brought his own foldout cot, sheets, and comforter. Young firefighters take rough nights as a mark of being tough, but the men and women who lasted as long as Andy had, knew that sleep was one of the most important things he needed to function during the day. He defended that sleep.

The next day, Andy woke an hour before the morning-briefing call. He put on his running shoes and jogged around the perimeter of the camp twice, which was nearly a mile each loop. He shoveled down some scrambled eggs and bacon and grabbed a couple of apples to stuff in his pack for snacks throughout the day. He had to remind himself not to overdo his eating this assignment. Normally, on a fire assignment with his engine, he was working fourteen-hour days of hard labor, burning thousands and thousands of calories every day, so it was hard for him to take in enough calories to counter the amount he was burning, but PIO work was a lot more standing by tables or updating social media feeds. Not exactly the most cardio-intense work.

He showered and put on his Nomex pants with their gasoline smell that carried with it so many memories. He decided on a simple T-shirt with a print from a fire a couple of years previous. As he put the shirt over his head, he thought of how many camp T-shirts he'd bought over the years. If someone figured out a good way to distribute them online for all the fire operations throughout the year, they could make a killing by printing and selling camp shirts. With the hundreds of crew members all eager to mark the experience, most jumped at the chance to buy a shirt. Something to supplement the retirement, maybe, he mused.

Andy wandered toward the group congregating in front of a large wooden board where several maps were hung. Other meetings would use digital screens, but morning briefings were only for firefighter operations, so rather than messing with shared screens and email invites, low-tech means were preferred.

"Morning, Andy. How was your night?"

Andy smiled at Glen's pleasant face. Somehow, Glen's graying hair was always perfectly slicked to the side, and he almost always had a genuine smile on his face. He nursed a mug of coffee, taking long sips.

"Morning, Glen. Slept really well. You?"

"Fine. Just fine. I'd imagine sleep isn't normally hard to come by on your regular gig, after pulling those insane hours of hard work, but I'm thrilled you're trying out PIO work here too. I've found it to be very rewarding."

"How long have you been doing the PIO thing, Glen?"

"Oh boy, let's see, I guess this would be around my forty-second season maybe?"

Andy let out an impressed whistle. "That's more of an endorsement for PIO work than anything, I'd say. Either you must enjoy it or else you're a masochist. I don't know you that well yet, but I don't think the second option quite fits."

"Gosh, thanks."

"Mic check," someone said from the front by the maps.

"Yo!" several people shouted back from within the crowd, which had grown a lot since Andy had joined it just moments before.

"Thanks. Good morning. I'm Andre Williams, Planning Chief for Great Basin Team 6. Thanks so much for being willing to help with this incident. We had our in-briefing last night at 1800, and our team assumed command of the Greenfield Ranch Fire at 0600 this morning. We're going to run through group lead updates, and our intent is to have you out of this meeting by 0630. So first up, operations, and then we'll just run through the order from the daily sheet here." Andre held out a half-sheet of paper and waved it around, then the ops. chief took the microphone from him.

"Morning. Tim Lundell, Ops. Chief. The fire grew overnight under moderate northeast winds to roughly forty-one thousand acres, burning in heavy timbers in the Frank Church Wilderness. No structures are currently threatened, though the Greenfield Ranch was lost. Potentially, some weeks ago. The cause of the fire is under investigation but is believed to be an escaped campfire or burn pile near the ranch. Looking at the maps here…"

Tim walked the group through the day's strategy, which was to start building line on the southwest side of the fire to protect Stanley, and the northeast side to protect Salmon and keep the fire burning in the wilderness. After Tim, Logistics talked about camp setup and protocols. Finance focused on timesheets. The assigned agency administrator welcomed and thanked the crew for their help, and then the incident commander stepped up in front of the map board.

"Morning everybody. David Buck, IC for Great Basin Team 6. I'm so grateful that you have all accepted this assignment. I know the work you do isn't easy, but it's so important that we protect local communities and natural resources like this beautiful landscape." David started taking a slow half-circle, walking past the crowd of people mainly dressed in dark-green pants like Andy's and yellow Nomex shirts and well-worn heavy leather boots.

"I hope you don't mind if I wax a bit philosophical here for just a second. I'm an old man, after all."

Several crew members chuckled in response, and David smiled under his bushy mustache and well-shaved chin.

"I've seen a few dozen fire seasons. Some have worked out better than others. The ones that stick in my memory are usually the ones that go really well or really bad. These days, I don't measure a fire season by how quickly we put out the fire or how many accolades we get from the local community. Believe it or not, I don't count the number of *We love you firefighters!* signs anymore."

The crowd continued to warm up to David's dry humor, and this received appreciative laughs from most of the crowd.

"No, I measure success based on the objectives set each day and on seeing that all of you get back to camp safe and sound each night. Will you help me do that?"

The whole crowd nodded and several shouted, "A-firm!"

"Thanks. I know we have our safety officer here, and we really appreciate what safety does, but it's really everybody's job to watch out for those around us. Now to the philosophical bit. I promise I'll only go there this first morning." David cleared his throat and took a moment, no longer pacing.

Andy felt the urge to lean forward in anticipation of what the IC would share.

"I didn't know Terry Greenfield all that well, but we knew each other, and I respected him. Over the years, I've served a few assignments in the Frank and a couple have been close enough to Terry's ranch that he and I have spoken on a number of occasions, mainly because Terry insisted on being told straight from the IC what we were going to do to protect his land. Terry never showed up to public meetings, but he wasn't the sort of person to be uninformed about things that could impact his land. He knew what was within his rights, and he got what he needed."

David took off his ball cap and scratched the fringe of scanty white hair that rimmed his bald head. "Terry lost his life because of this fire. We don't know if he was burning piles or if a back-packer left a campfire unattended or something else. But every life matters. Terry's life mattered. And this land mattered a lot to him, and it matters a lot to a whole bunch of other people still with us. So let's work hard and smart and see what we can do to get this wildfire under control, shall we?"

The crowd let out a roaring cheer, which Andy had never seen before. Most of the time, these morning briefings were stoic affairs. But he hadn't worked with this particular crew or IC before. He liked what he'd seen so far.

"So last reminders," Andre said when he got the microphone back from David. "Your Incident Action Plans are on the logistics table right over there." Andre pointed with his mic to where two women in polos and cargo pants stood behind a card table with stacks of printed IAP booklets. "And last. Don't be reckless heroes out there. Let's be smart so we'll all get home safe tonight. That's it. Have a good day everybody."

The crowd quickly dispersed with most people heading toward the commissary tent. Andy walked in that direction with Glen.

"That was different," Andy said, taking his time to get to the tent as he saw the line forming up already.

"Different in what way?" Glen asked, taking another sip of his coffee.

Andy picked up whisps of escaping steam as Glen tipped his thermos. Each tendril joined the foggy morning air that was finally warming up as the sun progressed down the surrounding hillsides.

"I don't know. The IC's message was just different than I'm used to. More human, I guess."

Glen chuckled at that and held the door flap open to let Andy enter the dining area ahead of him.

"David is a great IC. He really cares a lot about the crew, about the communities, about the landscape. He's just a caring guy all around. I'll see you at the PIO tent at 0700."

"You're not eating anything?"

"I have some things in my rig. Don't worry about me."

"Fair enough. See you at 0700."

Glen left Andy feeling a bit foolish for having entered the commissary now that Glen wouldn't be eating. He reminded himself that he'd already eaten, probably more than he would need for the day, given the work he'd be doing. So he grabbed a Greek yogurt and, as he sat down, nodded to several people. People he recognized from past fires but hadn't worked with closely enough to remember a name or attempt to catch up with over breakfast.

"Hey, you're, Andy, right?"

Andy looked up and greeted the woman who slid into the bench opposite him. She had a tight ponytail pulling her dark-brown hair back so her chiseled chin stood out prominently.

"That's right. Andy. And you are?"

"Katie. I'm one of the lead PIOs who works with Glen. He told me you'd be joining us. You don't mind if I sit with you, do you?"

"Not at all. I welcome the company."

"Good. There aren't a lot of true introverts in the PIO world."

"I'm sure you're right. I bet they get weeded out pretty fast as trainees. We'll see if I can hack it."

"I was wondering about your experience. So you're a trainee?"

Andy nodded. "I'm a lot younger than I look. You see, I have this disease that makes me age quicker," Andy said with a straight face.

"Really?"

"No. Totally joking. I've been working on hand crews and engines for over twenty years. I'm just trying out a new way of helping."

"Experience *and* a sense of humor. You and I will get along just fine, I think." Both Katie and Andy ate quickly and in silence, realizing that 0700 was getting close.

"I'll leave you to it. See you in the PIO tent at 0700," Katie said, grabbing her tray and sliding out from the bench.

"Great to meet you, Katie. Thanks for saying hi. See you in a couple minutes." Andy watched Katie step out into the gray light that was just starting to warm up the surrounding mountain peaks. He had worked closely enough with PIOs over the years to know that there were definitely different norms and expectations in that world than he was familiar with on the fire line. It'd been years since Andy had taken the Myers-Briggs test, but he'd been pretty firmly in the middle on extroversion. And he knew he had shifted more toward the introvert side in recent years. But he knew how to play the game. He was a very well-adapted introvert, and he knew how to meet expectations.

Five minutes later, Andy tossed his yogurt cup in the trash and headed straight to the PIO tent a few minutes early. As he ducked his head into the tent, he found a few people intently looking at laptop screens and a few others chatting in the corner. For a fire of this complexity, there would be several more PIOs. And there was one cultural norm he'd have to get used to. Meetings really started at the appointed time. Not five minutes early like the ones he'd grown to expect.

As it turned out, the meeting started at 0705 with Glen welcoming the group and asking them to do some get-to-know-you games because, Glen explained, there were a few new folks and the old folks could use all the help they could get in remembering names. Andy did his best to hide his annoyance, but his jaw tightened, and he found it hard not to fold his arms in disapproval. Another PIO difference.

Throughout that first day, though, Andy realized that those get-to-know-you games served a broader purpose. On the fire line, he worked closely with people. In some ways, a lot more closely than he had with the PIO team that day. But on the line, he didn't have to come up with creative ways to solve problems as a team, not the way he discovered he had to as a PIO. All day long.

He'd worked on a social media post, run it past a lead PIO, and had an in-depth conversation about the drawbacks of using the word "catastrophic." And the amazing thing was that the leads were right to questions single words like that. How many times had he been at a grocery store or gas station and heard members of the public use those kinds of words. He knew they'd picked them up from the news. And the news took their verbiage from PIOs' messaging. The word "catastrophic" meant something different to a mom of two kids than the word "developing" did. It wasn't spin, exactly, he decided. It was more like PIOs trying to teach the public where to place their attention. He could definitely get behind that.

Andy learned quickly that a fourteen-hour shift setting up various social media accounts and drafting messages via computer went by much slower than one on the fire line. He had been somewhat prepared for that, but by the end of the first day on the assignment, he was pretty stir crazy. Glen reassured him on that front though. "The first day is always spent setting up shop. Tomorrow, we'll have you out in the community, talking to folks."

"That would be great. Today was a bit longer than I remember fire days being," Andy said, closing his laptop and drinking the last sips of his soda and tossing the can toward the recycling bin on the other side of the tent.

The can landed neatly in the bin.

"Nice shot. Have a good night, and I'll see you in the morning." Glen left the tent and Andy followed him out moments later.

Andy felt tired, but not how he normally felt tired on fire assignments. This was mental fatigue, which was a thing he'd never really believed in before. He always assumed that when people talked about that they were really talking about boredom, but he knew what they meant now.

He didn't feel up to reading a single word the rest of the evening. His brain felt depleted, even though he knew he'd learned more that day than he had in years. His well-adapted introversion had been on overdrive all day too. He was in one, decision-making, small-group huddle after another. People always seemed to be *just stopping by to check in*. It was a small miracle that anybody got anything done. But they all did. They got a lot done actually.

When he left the tent, he didn't have any destination in mind. The 0600 morning briefing would come awfully early, he knew, but he also knew he couldn't go to sleep until he could shut his brain down. So he debated between going for a run and getting food. Remembering Glen's warning about pacing himself, he decided he'd better just take a walk. So he made a loop around the perimeter of the camp, which was fully operational, given the additional twenty-four hours of setup.

As he was making his third turn around the large rectangular grid, he caught a glint of blue light in his peripheral vision. His eyes followed it and picked up its source. A TV monitor had just been powered up in the GIS mapping tent. That was something else he hadn't fully gotten used to—the dramatic transition to digital tools within fire management. He felt comfortable using most of it, but there was something less satisfying in pointing at an image on a screen than marking up a large paper map that everybody could gather around.

As he got closer to it, the TV monitor suddenly shifted to a map showing the fire boundaries for the current fire. It must have been based on a recent aerial-surveillance mapping flight because the map showed areas that had burned that he wasn't aware of yet, even though he'd been monitoring the fire's progress all day to update communications. The fire was fanning out in multiple directions, but it was plain to see that its primary force was driving west—in the direction of the Middle Fork of the Salmon River. The next morning, he'd have to ask Glen about evacuation orders and communication to rafters and people staying at the historic lodges and private homesteads along the river.

he pine didn't know the meaning of friendship. Not in the human way at least. Those emotional bonds were as foreign to it as the feeling of flying. But it did know connection. Deep abiding connection. The way its roots intertwined with its neighbors' made it hard for it to separate itself as an entirely individual and disconnected thing. It liked the thought of links. Links between seed and soil. Links between needles and sunlight. Links between fungal networks that reached much farther than its roots could ever hope to explore. In some important ways, it was more connected to those things than human families could ever hope to be connected to each other.

THE NEXT MORNING, MAGGIE SWUNG BY THE RAFT SHOP AND entered through the back. She'd gotten an uncharacteristically early start and arrived well before the retail operations opened. She flipped on lights as she passed the warehouse with the rafts and then into Jay's workshop, where she grabbed a set of keys for the company rig she'd be driving up to Stanley. A little perk of the job. She got to feel a bit like a big shot, at least some of the time, when driving the company vehicles.

She checked one more time to ensure that the tour was still on at the start of that weekend. Now that it was Friday, if she drove up, the company would pay her for the full week regardless. They'd already charged the tour groups the full amount, with no refunds. Then she did something she'd never done before.

She went into the warehouse and looked over the rafts. There were easily over fifty of them in a variety of sizes and designs, each intended for use in different types of white-water conditions. There was even some simple fishing rafts made of less sturdy rubber. She found the section where the smallest four-person rafts were stacked and looked over each raft in turn, trying to imagine that family group—Valerie's family—using that raft. For all she knew, the family might be perfectly happy sticking with a more stable oar boat. In that case, selecting the right paddleboat wouldn't matter at all. But she wanted to find the right one in case they turned out to be a bit more adventurous.

After scrutinizing each raft carefully, she started to imbue her ability to select just the right craft with completely unrealistic importance, as if her choice would make or break the family's experience and, based on the clear signs she'd read in the description and her past experience with family groups, maybe make or break the family too.

She found a raft that was a cheery yellow color made out of solid materials. If she were Evelyn's age and in her situation, that would be the raft she'd want to float in. She brought out a sticky note that she'd grabbed from the workshop and wrote a note to Jay.

Maybe load up this raft, for sure, this weekend. Trust your judgment totally though. See you next week. Maggie.

She threw a heart down in the corner of the note for good measure and stuck it squarely on the raft where Jay was certain to see it. She really did trust Jay completely, so if the raft she had identified wasn't right, she wasn't going to lose sleep over it. She'd picked up a few things about the classes of white-water rafts and other kinds of equipment, mainly by hearing banter between Jay and the part-time workers the company brought in for particularly busy seasons like the one they had just gone through. This was one of the last full-week rafting excursions the company offered. The river's flow was sufficient on the main stem to float down year-round, but weather started to get cold, even dicey, by early October, and of course, normal people didn't dream about rafting trips during the fall. It was a summer thing. Most people had other aspirations and commitments in the fall. Like starting school.

Maggie got a small jolt of pride, realizing her re-enrollment application was nestled in the registrar's database, awaiting determination. She had wracked her brain to recall any reason her re-enrollment shouldn't be accepted. She'd left with a good academic standing. She didn't have any incompletes or withdrawals. She'd even been on the provost's honor roll a couple of semesters.

College had been hard, but she'd met the challenge. She'd heard that some of the rising stars from her high school, a couple of people she might have even called friends back then, had totally flamed out when they saw how much more demanding college was than high school. There was no easy on-ramp from the sheltered, supportive environment of high school, where students were cheered on as they acquired scholarships or did better than average on standardized tests, to college, where professors didn't care what kind of high school hot shots were in their classrooms. Papers were expected on time with no exceptions. No retakes on tests or extra-credit points were given to buffer bombed midterms.

Maggie had figured all that out and, in some ways, even excelled at the college game. She'd shown up for class, asked good questions, wrote the kinds of research papers and creative writing pieces she thought her professors would give good marks on, and most of the time, she'd been right on target. She hadn't flamed out, but as she started eyeing her graduation in the not-too-distant future, her next steps became murkier with each passed exam and paper written. The prospect of three or four or even seven or eight more years of school to get her master's or PhD made her heart race and her chest tighten.

At first, she'd only taken a year's deferment so she could re-evaluate what she wanted to do after graduation, rather than rushing toward a path she would later regret. That year had come and gone. She connected with the rafting job the summer of the second year she was away from college, and somehow, it had become more important to make it through the week and keep gas in the tank rather than look any farther. She couldn't look farther, at least not until yesterday.

She checked to make sure she hadn't left anything in the workshop, and she was about to leave when Jay unlocked the back door and walked in with a backpack slung over one shoulder and a big thermos of coffee in his free hand.

"Well, good morning, Maggie. I didn't except you for hours. Good on you for getting a jump on the day."

Maggie smiled and waited for Jay to drop his things so he could give her one of his bear hugs. "I thought I'd get an earlier start so I can get to Stanley at a decent hour and avoid driving the canyon after dark."

"Smart move there," Jay said, putting on his leather apron and turning on various pieces of machinery."

"And let's be honest, I wanted to snag that new F-150 too. It's the only one with Bluetooth, and you know how I like to get on with my tunes." Maggie showed her sad dance moves by snapping her fingers out of time and swaying awkwardly.

"Good luck with that. Nate will be disappointed about the new rig being gone, but you earned it this time. The early bird and all that."

Maggie was about to leave, but having Jay mention Nate reminded her of something.

"I'd almost forgotten Nate signed up for this week too. I need to have a talk with that boy."

"Yeah. Is everything okay?" Jay looked up from inspecting and wiping down a shelf full of patching supplies with a bit of concern written on his face.

"Of course. Nate's great. He just owes me a favor because I took a rough tour last go-around. He said it would be my choice who I wanted on my raft this time. And I'm thinking I'll go against my better judgment."

"Oh right. The family or college buddies. And you're deciding what?"

"If I want to take on a mentoring role as well as be a raft guide."

"Take on the mentoring role every time. No question. There's no better role."

Maggie walked up to Jay and squeezed his tattooed forearm.

"That's because you're so darn good at it."

"Years of practice. Seriously though, the extra effort is almost always worth it, and even if it ends up not being worth it, there's no better way to learn important things about ourselves. Total win-win." Jay beamed a warm smile in Maggie's direction, clearing his throat awkwardly. "But I'll stop blathering on. You've got to get on the road. Have a safe trip and good luck with that family. You're going to change some lives."

"One way or another, I guess. They won't forget the trip down the river. No one ever does. For better or for worse."

"You'll make it great for them. And either way, come by next weekend for dinner. We'll look forward to hearing all about your adventures. Okay?"

"Sounds great. Thanks, Jay."

Jay gave Maggie another hug, careful not to get grease from his apron on her jacket.

Maggie walked out the back door that Jay had propped open. But she turned around, remembering something.

"I left a sticky note for you on a raft. Let me know what you think."

Jay nodded and waved, and Maggie unlocked and started the new truck with its remote, having to use the grab handle to pull herself up, given the truck's incredibly high clearance. She connected her phone to Bluetooth and started her road-trip mix, beginning with Third Eye Blind's "Semi-Charmed Life." She drove toward the street but stopped before pulling into the morning traffic. She took a deep breath and adjusted her grip on the supple leather steering wheel, which felt luxurious in her hands. She was ready for another tour.

About an hour from Boise, she lost her data connection, and thus Bluetooth, as she got deeper into the mountains. She fumbled with her phone and got it plugged into the USB port, glad to have left early enough to avoid a lot of traffic as she weaved around the road a bit. She decided on a couple of downloaded podcasts instead of music, trying to keep her focus on the road. The drive was beautiful. No doubt about that. But like all things, she reached a point where there was just too much landscape. And she was ready to arrive at her destination. She pulled in at the lodge where she would spend the night in preparation for the rafting participants to arrive the next day.

She backed her rig in so she could drive straight out of the parking stall—per company policy—and walked inside the rustic, wooden entry to the lodge. There was nothing rustic about the inside. Well, the large wrought iron mantle above the stone fireplace that ran up a couple of stories had a nice effect; Maggie had to admit that. But the light-sage carpet that added an extra bounce to her step, the subtle fragrance with notes of pine and vanilla that was piped all around the lodge, the soft piano riffs that were always present but never obtrusive reminded her that there was no chance she would be able to afford a room under normal circumstances. Doing so now was another perk of the job.

She approached the front desk and the person behind it looked at her skeptically until recognition hit him.

"Maggie! You're back to stay with us again. Excellent! You have a room with a king bed and kitchenette, with a lovely balcony view of the river. Will you be staying with us for two nights like usual?"

Maggie put her arms on the tall counter.

"Sounds great, Frank. You know me so well," she said with a slight edge that she hoped was obvious enough for Frank to realize she'd noticed he was about to dismiss her.

"Glad to have you back with us, Ms. Bushman."

Maggie nodded and gave Frank an appreciative smile as she took the pocket-sized folio containing her two keys. It was strange to hear her last name. She heard it so rarely that it almost startled her when Frank had used it. As she wandered down the long corridor that she hoped led to her room, it struck her that maybe her name had started her off on the path to her current job.

"I mean *Bushman*. How can a kid not get hints that nature is good with a name like that?" Maggie said, speaking her thoughts out loud.

She found her room, dropped her backpack by the desk in the corner, which was beside a leather recliner, and was immediately drawn to the balcony Frank had talked about. She pulled open the sliding glass door, stepped onto a small balcony, and sank into a clean beige wicker chair, one of two sitting at a comfortable angle where she could imagine having long meaningful conversations—if there were anybody in her life to have those meaningful conversation with in a single-king-bed room. It was never lost on her that her chosen style of room was geared toward couples. Two terrycloth bathrobes in the closet. Two nightstands on either side of the bed. Even two soft cookies on the dresser that, by some magic of culinary goodness, were always slightly warm when she gratefully ate both.

The rooms on her side of the lodge all had balcony views of the river, and though there were dividers between balconies, she could see about half of the space on the neighboring balconies and even more on the ones farther out because of the way the lodge curved to follow the bend of the river. If she were to ever come back with someone, she'd definitely never do anything spontaneous on the balcony or, at least, not until it was completely dark.

She chuckled at that thought—dozens of guests at the lodge having intimate moments without realizing they were on display for dozens of others. But then her nose flared at a distinctive and familiar smell. The acrid smell of wildfire smoke. Instantly, she lost interest in the balcony and walked back inside, shutting and locking the door, as if locking the glass door would do more to keep the smell and anxious feeling that was creeping into her chest at bay.

She had dealt with some smoke during past tours of the river. The steep canyons of the Middle Fork funneled any errant nearby smoke right through it, so smelling it along the hundred-mile stretch of river was pretty much unavoidable. She'd even heard the spiel on how fire was a naturally occurring part of Western landscapes, which included a gentle prod at federal land managers who had suppressed fires too much over the last century. Apparently, that had led to fuel buildup, which now contributed to larger-than-usual wildfires.

But she didn't remember ever picking up the smell so quickly or strongly in Stanley. The air felt unstable, almost like it was full of static electricity that would make her hair stand on end if she stepped outside. If the wildfire was burning in the wrong place, it might make for a pretty nasty breathing experience for her clients. Maybe for the whole week. She pulled out her laptop and logged into the lodge's Wi-Fi to see what she could learn about the nearby wildfires. She pulled up the National Interagency Fire Center's current fires page. She clicked around to find her bearings and saw that the entire state of Idaho was covered in red, orange, and yellow fire graphics. She didn't remember seeing that much fire activity during the few seasons she'd lived in Idaho. And all that fire activity had to have sprung up in the last couple of weeks, because she remembered Jay commenting back a month or so ago on how little wildfire activity there was. She had been grateful that she didn't have to deal with constant smoke on her last couple of runs down the river. But she also knew how quickly the fire situation could change. Rapidly. Large swaths of Idaho sometimes got hit by dry-lightning storms, and the landscape was ripe for fire with the extremely dry summer. At this point, no measurable rain had fallen since early May.

As she zoomed her screen in to where her rafting tour would launch and then scrolled down river, she saw that their route would take them within a dozen miles of the western side of a fire perimeter. And if the fire was headed in their direction with any kind of wind driving it, it could easily burn to the Middle Fork within a matter of days, if not hours.

She knew that federal land managers rarely closed access to the river when fires burned in the Frank Church Wilderness, partly because some portion seemed to burn every summer. If they closed areas every time a fire burned, the public would cry foul, for sure. But Maggie also knew the main reason. There was way too much money at stake with the grandfathered-in homesteads and landing strips where private hunting trips took off along the river that was accessible only by boat or plane. Homesteads with landing strips that relied totally on summer tourists to make their annual income.

And there was a ton of money made by the rafting industry. Goodness knew that her company was no non-profit. On a good year, even after all of the gas, raft-upkeep, supplies, and staff salaries, she was sure the company pulled in a healthy profit. Last year, she had even been given a small bonus with a thank-you barbeque, and a complimentary carabiner emblazoned with the company logo. And the state of Idaho prided itself with that rugged individualism too. She imagined having a federal agency tell Idahoans that they couldn't go hunting or fishing would be dangerous for any political leader's future.

So, the show would go on, no matter what the fire forecast looked like Monday morning when the rafts launched. It would just mean another thing for her to feel anxious about. She did her best to push thoughts about the fire out and to focus on that sage-vanilla fragrance wafting into her room. She was determined to fully enjoy her night's stay in the lodge, in part because she realized that, with her acceptance back into college pending, it could be her last rafting tour. Best to enjoy where she was right then and take full advantage of every scrap of goodness she could latch on to.

McCall, Idaho
August 2024

he pine couldn't be conscious of its own compulsions—its longing for sunlight or rain or milder wind. Though those pulls toward such wishes filled full days for the pine as it quivered in hope and anticipation, its cells buzzing in preparation to embrace the water molecules, and its fine-threaded needles poised to take in the sunlight—no words were possible. It just was. Hungry for sunlight when it was. Thirsty for water to soak up its xylem and circulate to every branch and leaf when it was. Lonely in a way that no hiker who passed by could ever possibly understand. Standing on a ledge for a hundred years, watching younger trees be swept off by wind and water-driven earthflows—the tree was just what it was and hoped that was enough.

VALERIE HAD NEVER CONSIDERED HERSELF OBSESSIVE OR EVEN very particular when it came to preferences. She had strict standards for her professional work, of course, but she never thought packing a car in just the right fashion mattered so much to her.

What do they call this type of SUV again? A hybrid? No that's about electric cars and gas mileage, right? She nicely wedged three sleeping bags in the back corner of the rear storage area—*Cross something or other. Cross breed? No, not that either*—pulled the sleeping bags back out and re-evaluated the placement. The sleeping bags were put back in place. The same place as before, but in a different order. *Crossover! That's what it is! What am I doing?* She pulled the sleeping bags back out one more time and put them in the same spot, this time sure that it was the right spot. She moved on to placing a cooler next.

So things went for another hour. She had the time to get it right. She needed to get it right. Her family needed her to get things right this time. It might be her last big gesture to show that she cared—that Evelyn mattered to her. She couldn't shortchange things like getting the back of the car packed.

If I cut corners on packing, then it'll show all the other things I've shortchanged, like that Halloween costume five years ago. Evie had wanted to go as an evil nurse. But how was Valerie supposed to explain to an eleven-year-old that costumes like that were more for adults or rebellious teenagers and not her sweet fifth grader?

This time she wouldn't mess anything up.

By the time she had things tucked away for the fourth time, David was pulling into the driveway behind her. He got out and inspected her packing job.

"Wow, Val, you've outdone yourself this time."

"Really. You think things look okay? I know where everything is, so we won't have to dig around either," she said, leaning into David's chest.

He draped an arm around her shoulders. "Really. It looks tight and orderly. I think we're ready."

"I just so want things to be as close to perfect as possible. This might be our last shot."

"Last shot for what?"

"For having Evie."

"What about Evie?"

"You know!" Valerie pulled out of David's arms and leaned against the car, suddenly feeling very tired and frustrated and alone. "The last shot at having Evie in our lives. Last shot before seeing her off to college and never really having her back ever again. The last shot for her to like us again."

Valerie started breathing heavily. She planted both of her fists on the side of the car and laid her head down on the smooth metal frame.

"Oh, Val." David pulled Valerie back toward him, and she fell toward him and buried her face against his shoulder with her arms tightly wrapped around his neck. "We are both brilliant people. You especially. But I don't think anybody has any idea how to ensure the well-being of a teenager. We just have to keep doing our best. That's all."

"That's part of the problem though. How do I know if I'm doing my best when it feels like I'm failing more than succeeding, and no matter what I do, she still pulls farther and farther away?"

"That's why being a mom is the hardest job in the universe." David gently pulled Valerie's head up and kissed her forehead, letting his lips rest on her skin for a long moment. "Come on, let's just make it through today together, okay?"

Valerie nodded and allowed David to lead her inside the house.

As soon as they stepped into the kitchen, Thomas starting singing loudly and milling around them.

"Late last night when I was home in bed, Mrs. O'Leary took the lantern to the shed and when the cow kicked it over, she winked her eye and said, 'It'll be a hot one in the old town tonight!' Fire! Fire! Fire!"

"Nice singing, dear. Maybe take the volume down three notches though, okay?" Valerie said, running her hand through Thomas's bushy sandy-colored hair and then grabbing some things to start making lunch.

"You probably don't even know what that song is about," Evelyn said, perched on the couch in the living room without looking away from her phone. "It's about the Chicago Fire. One of the worst disasters in America's history, just in case you wanted to know."

Thomas rushed out the kitchen to the living room. "Really?"

"Yeah. That's why Chicago started building skyscrapers. Because they needed to build in smaller spaces since so much had burned."

Thomas stood there with a curious expression on his face for a moment and then broke out in a rueful smile. "Late last night when I was home in bed…" Thomas started singing again, even more loudly than before. And now with a purposeful grin.

"God! What an idiot!" Evelyn rolled her eyes and let out a disgusted sound, then headed toward her room.

"Hey, honey, don't call your brother an idiot. And, Thomas, remember, three notches quieter."

Thomas started whispering the song, which somehow carried just as well as his full-voiced version had. Valerie debated asking Thomas to find a quieter game, but decided it wasn't worth it.

"He's just trying to make sure we're going to miss him while we're gone next week, aren't you pal?" David said to Thomas. "Come on. Help me decide what boots I should pack for the rafting trip, Tommy."

Valerie mouthed the word *Thank you* as David led Thomas toward the back of the house. Now alone, she looked at the items she had taken out of the fridge. A block of cheddar cheese, a head of lettuce, a package of sliced turkey, mustard, and a bag of tomatoes. She was surprised she had all the makings for decent turkey sandwiches, despite the fact that she didn't remember making that choice consciously. Her thoughts being hundreds of miles away in the mountains on a river. She had second thoughts to deal with now too. All the possible what-if scenarios started running through her head.

What if Evelyn has a horrible experience? Then we'll be down $10,000 and no closer as a family? What if David has a heart attack on the river? There's no way they'd be able to take him to a hospital in time. What about ticks and bears and cougars? She remembered watching a documentary about cougars and how they knew people were around a lot sooner than people knew they were. The documentary had called them *the ghosts of the forest* or something. Climate change was impacting wildlife, including cougars. She'd seen those horrifying videos of cougars following hikers for miles.

How could she possibly take her child and husband to a place where a deranged animal could kill them in their sleep. Wasn't that the whole point of evolution and our species' dominance of the natural world? *What's the point of that if we're going to willingly go where animals can eat us anyway?*

She stood up, smoothing her clothes as she realized she had been leaning against the granite countertop for several minutes. She glanced around to ensure neither of her kids had seen her like that. She pulled a steak knife from the wooden knife block and sliced up some cheese and tomatoes and tore apart the head of lettuce, putting the fluffy wet shards in a bowl. She pulled down plates and glasses and milk and put it all on the table.

"Lunch is ready!" she yelled toward the back of the house, trying to sound more confident and cheery than she actually felt.

Bread! How are they going to make their sandwiches without bread!

She rushed to the bread box, praying they had some and racing through her to-do list to recall if picking up bread was one of the things she had left undone for the day. She gratefully pulled out the fourth of a loaf from the box and put the slices of nine-grain bread on a plate, then carried it to the kitchen table just in time for Valerie to hear Evelyn open her door and David and Thomas's voices grow louder as they walked toward the kitchen.

The family sat down in their seats—where they always sat, even though the seats had never been assigned. Evelyn started sitting on the left-hand side of tables because she was left-handed and got angry when bumping elbows with right-handed people. Valerie had learned it was better to put Thomas on the opposite side and as far away from Evelyn as she could so she usually sat next to him. That left David sitting the farthest away from her, too, which she had secretively always resented.

"Do we have everything?"

"I'm a vegetarian, if you recall. So I'll make do with what we have," Evelyn declared to the room.

Valerie looked at David questioningly. He shrugged. Evelyn must have decided that recently because the last weeks' worth of meals had all had some component of meat, and Evelyn had eaten all of them. Hadn't she? Now Valerie wasn't quite sure. Had Evie told her before? And Valerie continued making meat dishes as usual? She was all but certain she would've remembered. Then again, why did everything have to revolve around Evelyn? As she sat down at the table, grabbing a bowl of apples as a last-minute addition to the meal, she realized for the first time that even their regular seating chart was based on keeping the peace with Evelyn.

Everyone else was already making sandwiches when she sat down. A thought flashed into her mind that they should have a blessing on the food first. Having grown up in a Christian home but deciding with David well before Evelyn was born to not actively participate in their local congregation, some rituals still stuck in her mind, and surprisingly, in some ways, she missed them. Honestly, blessing the food had had a nice way of pulling everybody around the table and had stopped disagreements in their tracks in her parents' home. Too late now though. She knew what hell Evelyn would raise if she even suggested that the family consider organized religion.

By the time the rest of the family had the things they needed to make their sandwiches, there was only a small heel of the loaf left for Valerie, but that was fine. She added extra meat and cheese and lettuce to the flimsy flap of bread she had to work with. She really should talk to David about his thoughts on church stuff again. They hadn't talked about it since Thomas was born, when they discussed whether it would be good to bring him up in a religion.

She was so lost in her thoughts that she hadn't taken a bite of her sandwich yet. Although she had held it up to her mouth for over a minute, ready for that first bite. Valerie caught the concerned look David sent from his corner of the table. She smiled and mouthed *I'm fine*. She took a bite, realizing too late that she had put on far too much mustard. With so little bread, that extra mustard oozed out of her mouth. She struggled to keep it from spilling onto the table, and she covered her mouth, her hand getting slathered in mustard too.

Valerie put her open-faced sandwich down on her plate and took a look at her shirt, which was now spotted with dark-yellow splotches. She had forgotten to put any napkins on the table, so she did what she had always taught her kids not to do. She used her shirt tail to wipe her face and hands. Then, after glancing at her reflection in the mirror hanging on a nearby wall—to make sure she didn't have any stray spots of mustard on her face—she smiled back at herself.

It was the sort of thing she had done with her kids. She'd done it a bunch of times—held her young children up to mirrors, pointed at their shared image and asked, "Who's that? Is that Evie? Yes, it is!" All with that sing-song tone of voice mother's somehow instinctively knew to use. She supposed it might help kids develop a healthy image of themselves—that by coaching her kids to not be afraid or ashamed at what they saw in the mirror, they might accept who they were and who they wanted to become as they got older.

But in that moment, the mirror's image only shone back at her. And for the first time in her life, she pointed at her reflected image in the mirror and said softly to herself, at first, but gaining in confidence with each word of the well-used phrase, "Who's that? Huh? Is that Valerie? Yes, it is!"

She broke down into exhausted, uncontrollable laughter mingled with punctuated sobs. It had been too much. Too much worry. Too much caring. Too much restraint. Too much sending out love only to get disgust in return. Too much loneliness. Too much convincing herself that everything would work out. Too much sleep deprivation. Too much planning. Too much hoping.

She knew her family was confused by her behavior. She'd caught Evie's disgusted look at seeing the mustard stains all over her shirt. But that look of disgust changed to confusion and maybe even a bit of fear once Valerie had started crying.

Good. You should be afraid of some things. Valerie thought about all the things she had grown to be afraid of. Things she never planned to fear but that came with married life and especially with motherhood. All the fears about her kids that haunted her. *What if they get hurt? What if I hurt them?* What if they do drugs or go to prison or fail at school or don't go to college or don't care about Van Gogh or don't like *Casablanca. Or get pregnant before being ready, which means ever.* Or what if they got hurt or died before she did or they didn't have good relationships with their grandparents. A million other messy fears ebbed and flowed through her, according to a completely unpredictable schedule that struck her hard enough sometimes for her to need to sit down, to feel the ground beneath her, to connect to something real and solid. To assure herself that if she focused on changing the laundry or getting the mail, she wouldn't curb her chance at raising happy, healthy children.

"Excuse me," Valerie left the table and dropped her plate in the sink on her rush to get to her room where she could be alone with the thoughts that felt too big and too complex to understand. But she had to find a way of containing them anyway. Like that old saying, *How do you eat an elephant? One bite at a time.*

Except no one actually ever ate an elephant. They were amazing, strong and useful creatures. The emotional consumption of mothers, on the other hand, required elephantine immensities every day. And with no thanks.

She heard David say, "Keep track of your brother for a bit, okay?" Which meant David would be coming to check up on her.

That was the right thing for a husband to do. She knew that. So why did she feel frustrated by the fact that he felt obligated to check up on her? For so much of her last sixteen years, she had felt like she was rowing a boat with a partner but she was the only one with the ability to steer it. David's help had built momentum and helped move things forward, but she felt—not unkindly or with resentment, at least not until today—like if she didn't add her subtle tweaks to the rudder, he would have driven the ship aground dozens of times. Yet, he was okay, and she most certainly was not.

"Honey, can I come in?"

"If you dare," Valerie replied, lying flat on her back on the bed with a pillow over her face.

The door opened, and David slipped inside and shut it quietly behind him. He left the light off, even though the room was nearly dark. Valerie appreciated that.

"Come on. You're not that scary."

Valerie lifted the pillow off her face. "No. Not scary. Crazy. Do you remember that week I volunteered at the psych unit at the jail? I think I'd be among the best of them. I don't know what got into me earlier."

"You've been dealing with a lot," David said, gingerly taking a seat at the edge of the bed.

"Mothers who stand in front of tanks in African nations during civil wars deal with a lot. I should be able to keep things together in 21st-century America. We're upper-middle class, for God's sake. We're among the lucky ones."

"It's really not fair to compare that way. Our reality is our reality."

"True enough," Valerie said, putting the pillow back over her face.

"No, really. No comparison, you're right. Those horribly tragic people take the cake in misfortune. No question. But different stresses call for different kinds of strengths. I doubt many mothers in sub-Saharan Africa have to remember that their daughters are playing vegetarian for the day."

David gave her a hopeful smile, and Valerie removed the pillow.

"That's a horrible comparison. Make sure you never use that analogy at dinner parties with any smart people."

But David's statement had the desired effect. She couldn't explain it, but the level of her anxiety dropped several degrees. Then David seemed encouraged to run with the analogy a bit farther.

"They don't have to do the delicate dance of encouraging their daughters to start on their SAT-prep while also making it seem like standardized tests don't matter, all the while conveying that they are loved no matter what route they take, even though Mom knows that a lot of those routes are just not good. Oh! And not overemphasizing that fact, either, because then they'll make themselves miserable by making horrible decisions just to spite their moms. That's one of my favorites."

"No denying it. Teenage girls are categorical monsters." Valerie said, sitting up and putting her hand over David's mouth.

Both sat still for a moment.

Valerie listened for any sign that Evelyn or Thomas was listening behind the door. "Not so loud. You can't say those sorts of things within earshot of the kids."

"Oh, Evelyn knows it too. She just calls it independence and feminism." David smirked and playfully caught one of the fingers that was covering his mouth in his teeth.

"Grown men have become more and more monster-like too, I've heard," David said in an ostensibly sinister voice.

"Yeah. It's been known for a long time that all you men are brutes who are only after satisfaction for your lust of flesh and power."

"Don't sell us short. We also lust for a few other things." David pulled Valerie's hand off his mouth and brought his mouth to her lips while massaging her back with firm, methodical strokes.

"We can't do this now. We have things to do, and I need to convince our kids that I'm not completely insane," Valerie said regrettably.

"That lust for the flesh can be very strong sometimes," David said in Valerie's ear, nibbling on her lobe.

"I mean it. Save it for when we're in the wilderness. Then you can let your true primal instincts run wild." Valerie grabbed both of David's hands and brought them to her mouth for a kiss.

"All right. I'll do my best to fight my brute tendencies. And by the way..."

Valerie had gotten off the bed and was looking at herself in the tall mirror hanging in their walk-in closet and adjusting the new shirt and sweater she'd put on to replace the mustard-stained top. She looked toward David while running a brush through her hair. *"By the way... What?"*

"You're certainly not completely insane."

"Just mostly then."

"I'd go as far as partially. But who isn't these days?" David wound his arms around Valerie from behind, completely encircling her frame, and kissed her cheek while both looked at their image in the mirror. Daivid's stubble tickled the nape of her neck. And David pointed at their reflection. "Hey! Who's that? Huh?"

"It's me," Valerie rolled her eyes but secretively relished the childish attention.

"Is that Valerie? Yes, it is!" David gave Valerie one last squeeze and spun her around to face him.

Valerie was taken off guard by that. She didn't know her husband had dance moves like those.

"Are you going to be okay? Because we can bail on this rafting trip if you feel like it's not a good idea," he asked with piercing seriousness.

Valerie gave the question a moment of serious reflection, closing her eyes tight and holding her breath. At last, she burst out the breath, relaxed her shoulders, and reopened her eyes. "No, let's go for it. It'll be good for us. For our family. For you and me. And just for me, maybe even."

"Great. Now that that's settled and we both know that the car is packed with a professional's care, let's have a fun evening together. This will be the longest time Tommy has gone without family around."

David took Valerie's hand as if to lead her back to the kitchen. Valerie squeezed David's hand. "I'll be right there. Just give me one more minute."

David nodded. "I love you, you know that right?"

"Of course I know it. Thanks for loving me despite my craziness."

"I love the full package, so that includes the craziness, not despite it." David gave Valerie a warm smile and returned a squeeze to her hand, then opened the door after clearing his throat. "Who's up for pizza and a movie tonight," he announced in the direction of the kitchen.

David had closed the door behind him, which meant Valerie had one extra moment to be alone. She went back to the closet and looked at herself in the mirror one more time.

That's definitely Valerie. For better or for worse. She pulled down the tail of her teal wool sweater and pulled up the sleeves of her three-quarters shirt to above the elbows. "Here we go. You've got this." Valerie gave a fist bump to her refection, opened the bedroom door, and shifted gears the best she could.

Stanley, Idaho
August, 2024

 *The pine had no sense of the passage of time, but it did mark the days and nights. Its cells retained chemical reactions that responded to days filled with extra rainfall, and its roots communed with fungal networks that passed on the story of their interactions.*

"SO WE DON'T NEED SLEEPING BAGS OR OUR OWN TENT OR FOOD or any of that?"

Valerie gave David a puzzled look from the passenger seat of their car as they continued the drive to Stanley, Idaho, to meet up with their rafting group for their trip orientation meeting. Cell phone coverage had been spotty along the drive, so she had missed a call from their rafting-guide company as well as an email. But as they drove through one of the small communities nestled in the mountain valleys that offered a bit of cell service, she called the company back.

"And electronics are allowed?" She stopped and listened for a while.

Evelyn perked up at that question, looking up from her phone. "They can't force me to leave my phone behind. But I guess it doesn't really matter since we won't have reception the whole trip, right?"

David nodded toward Evie's reflection in the rearview mirror. "That's right. Six whole days with no phones to bug us. Won't it be heaven?" David whispered.

"Something like that." Evie sat back and touched her earbud, which indicated the conversation was over.

"Okay. So we can leave the car there at the lodge and pay for it to be shuttled up to Salmon, and we can leave everything except for clothes and any personal items we need? Got it. Thanks, Jay. I'm sorry for not reading the trip-planning guide more carefully beforehand. We jumped at some extra slots that freed up a few weeks ago, and this is our first time doing anything like this. And I realize I'm rambling now. You don't need to hear my whole life's story. One more question though. Lodging tonight. Is there a block of rooms set aside for the tour group or—"

Valerie stopped again and listened, nodding every few seconds. Eventually, she pulled her phone away from her ear and whispered to David. "It looks like we'll be camping tonight. I guess this gear will serve some purpose after all."

"What? We're camping tonight too? I thought we were staying in a lodge?" Evie sat forward and gripped David's seat with both hands, leaning her head between the driver and passenger seats.

"Sit back, Evie. Do you have your seat belt on?" David asked, waving Evie back with his free arm while keeping his eyes on the winding road.

"Yeah, of course. I'm not stupid."

"Glad to know that. It's such a relief to know my daughter isn't stupid. Leaning forward like that and distracting me while driving these canyon roads isn't the smartest things to do in the world though. I'm sure your mom will reveal all once she gets off the phone." David reached a free fist behind his seat while still keeping his eyes on the road.

Evie bumped his fist with hers, adding an annoyed sigh.

"Thanks again, Jay. You've been very helpful. I'm sure it'll be a great experience. You too. Bye-bye." Valerie put down her phone and gave David a concerned look.

"So, here's the deal. Since we were so lucky to snatch up a few seats with this tour so late in the game, the guy I was just talking to from the rafting company told me there is almost no chance of any of the lodges having rooms available. But—"

"No rooms. I already checked at all of the hotels in Stanley. Yay us," Evie said with a withering look that Valerie pretended she hadn't seen.

"But we're lucky because there are lots of great camping areas near Stanley that almost always have one or two sites available."

David craned his neck to glance back at Evie. "Hey, since you were so good at looking up hotels, do you mind finding us a camp-site for tonight, and unless you want to camp when we reach our final—what do they even call it? where we get off the river?"

"Disembark site, maybe?" Valerie offered.

"Maybe. I'm sure we'll learn all the rafting lingo during our orientation tonight. Anyway, could you also look up hotels in Salmon for Saturday night?"

"Count on a Gen Z to do everything with technology. Typical."

"Oh. I'm very comfortable with my millennial technical aptitude. It's just a lot more fun putting you to work."

Evie gave her dad a dirty look but started scrolling on her phone anyway.

"So we'll have time to set up camp tonight before orientation at the lodge—"

"The lodge where we should be staying," Evie said to herself interrupting her dad but loudly enough to make sure her parents heard.

"At the lodge which won't be nearly as much of an adventure as camping will be. And then we'll launch tomorrow morning!" Valerie said with some genuine excitement.

David held up his free hand. Valerie put up hers against it.

"Come on, Evie. You're always trying to be environmentally conscious. How can you say you care about nature if you never go there?"

Evie sighed dramatically again, but put her hand against her parents'.

"*Team* on three. One, two, three."

"*Team!*" All three said it slightly off tempo so it was more of a rapid-fire declaration, but Valerie appreciated her husband's effort.

"We'll have to work on that before we get to the rapids so we don't embarrass ourselves in front of all those cool rafting guides. Remind me, honey, don't we have some information about our river guides?"

"Yes!" Valerie pulled out her phone again and opened the informational email about the river tour. "There's Nate and Ryan, it looks like. Maggie will be another one of our boat captains, or whatever they call the leaders of the rafts. She looks like a nice girl."

"Nice woman," Evie interjected.

"Right. She seems like a nice woman. She is twenty-four from the East Coast but lives in Boise. She's working on her college degree in communications. I bet you two will get along just great, Evie."

Evie didn't say anything, but Valerie took the fact that Evie wasn't quick to dismiss the possibility as a good sign. With that, the road tucked within high canyon walls, and they lost cell coverage until they approached Stanley, Idaho. They used their car's satellite GPS to stay on track, following Highway 21 past tree-covered ridges and valleys that burst into view around corners where small farms nestled within the foothills of imposing mountains.

David had been so certain that the time given by their GPS was wrong that he'd insisted they get on the road by late-morning, at the latest, to be on time for their orientation.

"I'm sure glad we left things in such a hurry this morning because—*gosh!* if it isn't 2:30 p.m. There's no way we could have been ready for the orientation with less than four hours to prepare," Evie said, laying the sarcasm on thick.

"Yeah, yeah. And my greatest strength is my punctuality. I get it. But this could be a good thing. We'll have time to set up camp and explore a bit before orientation. And hey, we're here."

They pulled off the highway and down a short gravel path with a thick canopy of pine boughs overhead that left a thin strip of blue sky running between the two sides of the road. David slowed the car to a crawl, tires making a gritty sound as they rolled slowly over the gravel. They found their campsite. Number 012. Valerie was glad to see that their site was close to a small stream and not next to the outhouses. They pulled into their site, and Valerie felt like all three of the occupants in the car were waiting for one of the other two to make the first move.

"Right. So first thing to do is to set up the tent, I'd imagine. I intentionally packed that last so it would be easily accessible." Valerie opened her car door and the other two jumped into action too. She pulled out the long nylon bag holding the tent from the back of the car.

"Great. Mom will direct the unloading since she has a great system for that. Evie and I will start getting that tent up, and Val, you set aside the things we need for tonight. Evie, grab the other handle on this tent to give me a hand."

"Perfect. Sounds like a plan." Valerie gave her husband an appreciative smile as he walked toward a flat, circular patch of ground off to the side of the fire ring that she assumed was the spot for tents. She surveyed the plethora of other things in the back of the car, which was packed to the gills with things they wouldn't need. The food would mostly go bad, but if they kept the cooler shut and sealed, the person shuttling the car from Stanley to Salmon wouldn't notice too much stink. Hopefully. Plus, the mountains cooled down at night and in the early morning. She tried to convince herself of that and almost believed it, doing her best not to assume the worst-case scenario: having no shuttle company willing to take their car to Salmon because of the offensive smell.

All they really needed were the camp chairs and maybe roasting sticks, if they decided to roast marshmallows after the orientation. They could easily get a bite to eat in town, so probably best not to dig around for the coolers. And the one thing the tour company guy, Jay, had said they would want to bring were clothes and personal items. Those bags were conveniently tucked at the very back.

"So much for well-laid-out packing plans," she thought out loud, having to laugh at the absurd amount of time she'd spent fussing and worrying about the proper way to pack their car.

"I see nothing funny in the world right now. This tent has twenty poles of varying sizes and purposes, and I'm not even going to allow you to look at the instructions because it will shame your technical-writing profession." David walked up to the back of the car and wrapped his arms around Valerie from behind.

"Thanks for protecting me from the bad technical-writing people. They can be pretty evil," Valerie said playfully, reaching behind her to pat David's cheek.

"I think the tent stakes might be in a separate bag. Or they're hidden really well in the tent one," David said, starting to rummage around the back of the car.

"Stop that. Remember, I'm in charge of orchestrating the unload. Did you check the side pockets?"

"Side pockets?"

"I thought so. They should be there in one of the side pockets. The zippers are kind of hard to find because there's a waterproof flap that goes over them. But I promise they're there."

"Excellent. Secret compartments. Very useful to have those in tent bags."

"Okay, Mr. Sarcastic. Let's try to keep things positive. This is, after all, our very last and best chance at saving our daughter from sure and utter destruction."

"When you put it that way." David gave Valerie a wry smile. "Evie! Did we check the side pockets?"

"What side pockets? Oh got 'em!" Evie said, pulling out a small pouch of stakes.

"Like father, like daughter, I suppose. Doing okay, Val?"

"Yeah, I think I am. I'm great actually. I think this wilderness thing will be very good for me. It might even motivate me to jump-start that landscape-photography side hustle I've been talking about for years."

"Well, look at you! Way to be. I knew there was a reason I married you."

"Only one?" Valerie asked with a seductive voice.

"You do have many other great qualities." David turned back and tucked his arms through Valerie's and pulled her close.

"Dad, can you help me with these stakes? This ground is full of rocks. Hope you thought to bring ground pads or something," Evelyn yelled from where she struggled to drive the stakes into the hard ground with a rock, mostly missing the mark.

"Be right there, Evie," David shouted in their daughter's direction. And then craned his neck toward Valerie. "You really are something, you know that, right?"

Valerie tucked her cheek against David's chest, smiling, enjoying the warmth of the afternoon sun that radiated off David as well as the filtered sunlight through the pines.

"You're doing a good job as a mom too. There isn't a definitive how-to manual for parenting teenage girls. This trip is a very good thing."

"There should be, you know." Valerie pulled her head up to face David directly.

"Should be what?"

"A definitive manual on how to parent teenage girls. Maybe I should write it. I mean, manuals are kind of my jam."

"True. But seriously, this will be a very good thing for our family. And I'm so proud of you for pushing for this." He pulled Valerie closer so he could whisper, "for not giving up on Evie. Goodness knows, I certainly have thought about it once or twice."

"Or every day, with that infuriating eye roll move of hers." Valerie tried to mimic it. "See! I can't even do it properly. She's mastered it."

They laughed, and with that laughter it was as if layers of caked-on worry and anxiety and fear mixed with a bit of anger and betrayal were dislodged so they could drift away. For Valerie, it felt as if that pent-up knot of hurt feelings she'd been carrying alone for so long could be better dealt with somehow. Regardless, she'd find a way to navigate it.

"Dad! Come on! I can't do this by myself."

David and Valerie looked at each other and grinned. David rolled his eyes.

"That's it! You do it so much better than me," Valerie said, giving David a playful shove.

"That's because you're a better person than me," David said, turning to help Evie with the tent stakes. "You seem to be doing just fine without me, but let's see if we can find a bigger rock to pound those in…"

David's voice faded into the hot afternoon air, mingling with the occasional cry of a hawk somewhere in the trees and the distant crackle of a fire at one of the nearby campgrounds. For some reason, Valerie focused on the sound of the fire. *Wasn't there a burn ban in place?* She ran through her packing plans. That's why she'd brought food that could be eaten without a campfire. But then again, she'd brought roasting sticks and marshmallows too. She'd have to check with the camp host.

After digging around for the sleeping bags and ground pads, which they laid in their freshly set-up tent with its stakes secured, Valerie closed the back of the car and sank into a camp chair. She closed her eyes and let the sunlight heat her face, feeling a sense of renewal wash over her like a new coat of paint. She'd gone through the painful experience of scraping the old coat off her walls. The primer was set. Now she'd get to enjoy rolling a bright new color onto the thirsty wooden walls. At least she hoped. And in that moment, hope was enough.

That night, they explored the few shops in the cute town of Stanley and grabbed dinner at a fun diner full of other folks taking advantage of the great recreational potential in the area. They made it to the Mountain Village Lodge for their orientation just in time, which was a good thing. If they had been earlier, they would have had even more reason to regret booking their trip too late to stay at the lodge instead of roughing it at the campsite.

They found their way to a small conference room with polished stripped-log walls and a massive stone fireplace, which wasn't lit, thankfully. Valerie was almost certain that the lodge hadn't been updated to include modern conveniences like air conditioning and a pool since it was first built, and the AC system clearly couldn't maintain a comfortable temperature when it was ninety-five degrees outside. David must have been thinking along the same vein because he wiped his forehead, which was beading sweat, as the three of them moved toward some vacant seats near the back rows of chairs. "These great old buildings must have been built without climate change in mind, eh?"

Valerie gave a polite chuckle, and Evie ignored it completely. It was a fact though. Similar grand lodges were spread throughout the country. Valerie remembered a trip she and David had taken to Yellowstone about a decade before. She'd been impressed by the Old Faithful Lodge and the other lodges at the other nearby National Parks, but they all showed that people then used to value different things when traveling. She had stayed at the Timberline Lodge for a work retreat once and was amazed at how small and simple the rooms were. There was a full-sized bed and a very small bathroom. The small lead-based window that looked to the south had had an amazing view. But that was it. No stylish desk. No walk-in closet. No mini fridge. Hotels were for sleeping back then. The joy of traveling came not from hanging out in a hotel room, but from getting outside. That and from the sense of community that gathered in the space. Hence the cavernous main lobby and other communal spaces at the Mountain Village Lodge, and what she assumed were modest-sized guest rooms.

"Welcome folks! My name is Nate. I'm one of the river guides who will be going on this tour with you-all. I'm thrilled to have you here tonight and even more thrilled that we're going on an amazing adventure together. Please take a seat, and we'll get started in just a few minutes."

Valerie looked at Nate and then at Evie, who seemed to be paying attention now, her eyes still scanning Nate. Valerie fought the urge to say anything. If she commented about him in any way, Evie would instantly lose interest in Nate and anything he represented. So she covered her mouth to hide the spontaneous grin on her face and turned away from the front of the room.

With her eyes diverted from her daughter, she scanned the few people in the back of the room near the entrance, memorizing their descriptions in preparation for learning their names. When Nate called the group together and had each member introduce themselves, Valerie did her best to keep the names and brief descriptions straight. There was a teacher who had taught for thirty-four years and had retired the day before and was celebrating by taking the rafting trip.

There was a retired veterinarian with his son. Valerie created a story in her mind, one that perhaps was completely wrong, but it seemed to her that the son was trying too hard. And as she learned about the vet's other son, who had died due to opioid addiction, some of the son's mannerisms clicked into place for her.

There was a couple, Darold and Sheila she thought their names were, from Washington, who joked about how much easier it was to get around in the wilderness when they weren't trying to keep their elk from a pack of thirty-seven wolves.

Speaking of packs, Valerie learned a bit about three old college buddies, who were now marketing executives or engineers living in Minnesota or Wisconsin. They seemed completely at ease with their geekiness, and she liked them instantly.

There were others, but Valerie lost track of names and stories. Though, she made a mental note to have conversations with all of the other participants. Her curiosity was piqued just from their introductions.

There was a short interlude while Nate worked with some of the other guides to locate bags that the participants would use on the river. Valerie looked around at the few people who hadn't introduced themselves yet. She noticed a young woman wearing the same khaki button-down shirt and the same shorts as Nate—with the rafting company's logo on her shirt pocket. Valerie had missed her when she'd entered. They had come in through the other set of double doors. *She must be Maggie.*

"Come on, Evie, let's meet one of our river guides, Maggie," Valerie said, putting a hand on Evie's shoulder to encourage her to follow.

"No, Mom. We'll meet her in a second when things get started again."

"We have a few minutes. Come on. It'll be fine. She's just standing there. We'll start to get to know each other a bit earlier. Never hurts anything."

"Mom, no, seriously. We'll meet her later—"

"Hi, you must be Maggie!" Valerie called after the young woman. She waved and dragged Evelyn with her as she approached.

"Hi. Are you Valerie?"

"Sure am. Thrilled to meet you." Valerie said, extending her hand, which Maggie shook warmly.

"Likewise. It's not like we have a ton to go by, based on descriptions clients give us, but I have been honestly looking forward to meeting you."

"Did you hear that, Evelyn? A young, surely brilliant and talented person is excited to meet me. That's a novel idea, isn't it?"

Evelyn looked like she was trying to disappear into the wall, but Maggie turned her focus to her and smiled.

"Hi, I'm Maggie. You must be Evelyn?" Maggie put out her hand for Evie to shake, which she did with some visible trepidation.

"It's all right. Meeting new people, especially people your parents really want you to like can be totally awkward. We can warm up over the next couple of days. Love your earrings by the way." Maggie pointed to the silver dolphin earrings that Evie reached up and touched as if just realizing she was wearing them.

"Thanks." Evie anxiously swayed from side to side, but the start of an uncontrolled smile was creeping across her face.

"Dolphins are my favorite animal. Maybe one of these days I'll be a guide at one of the Florida Keys so I can swim with them, and in water that doesn't freeze your hair solid."

"Okay, folks. If we could all take our seats again, please." Nate stood up at the front again.

Valerie saw Maggie lean toward Evie a moment before they had to find their seats.

"Nate is such a guy. Always loves being in charge and the center of attention," Maggie smirked, and Evie smiled more confidently this time.

Valerie felt a flood of relief wash over her. *This is going to work.* It had to do some good things to see a strong woman like Maggie in her element. And it didn't hurt that Maggie seemed to already like her and was warming up to Evie. So far, so good, though Valerie had to admit that being a twentysomething's fan was weird. But Valerie decided it had to be better than starting at a disadvantage. She would take anything she could get to give Evie the best possible shot of having a good experience.

"Okay, looks like we're all back. Sorry about the short interlude. We needed to check up on a few things. Thanks for your patience. Welcome everybody! I'm Nate, again. Don't worry, we're going to get to know each other really well over the next couple of days, so if you forget my name, I guarantee it'll be burned into your memory by the end of the week, for better or worse. And yes, I'm being mostly funny, so feel free to laugh if you feel so inclined."

The group gave Nate a courteous chuckle. Maggie leaned forward between Valerie and Evie and whispered, "That's his go-to punchline. Watch out for the torrent of dad jokes he'll throw in during the week."

Valerie and Evie grinned and stifled their laughter when they noticed Nate looking in their direction.

"And I'd imagine that my co-host and partner-in-crime, Maggie, has already set all of you against me, so I might as well have her introduce herself too. Come on down, Maggie. Give her a hand, folks!"

Maggie shuffled her way forward with her hands in her shorts' pockets. Valerie was thrown off by Maggie's display of shyness, but she bet it was an act.

"Aw, shucks, folks, I'm not all that. It's really all about the little people who helped me get to where I am. Little people, like Nate for example."

This got genuine laughter and a little bit of scattered applause. Valerie scanned the audience. They were all fully engaged. She was impressed by how quickly Nate and Maggie set everybody at ease and made themselves instantly likable. She wished she had that kind of charisma.

Nate mostly took over, as Maggie predicted, and outlined the itinerary for the week, dispelled some common concerns, and opened things up for questions. The whole orientation would have been done in fifteen minutes and all the legally required pieces would have been knocked out fine. But Nate had the group stand up.

"Okay, we're going to have some fun now," he said and then put on a wry smile. "Even if it kills us. You see where you-all are sitting? Look at the row opposite you and find your mirror image, then count two people over to the left. If you're at the end of the row then jump to the other end of the row and count two over that way. Got it? Okay. Break!"

The group awkwardly separated and focused on counting the right number of seats. Valerie got confused and was certain she settled on the wrong person, but decided it really didn't matter for the purposes of the icebreaker. She found herself standing in front of a polished looking woman wearing a nice cashmere pullover sweater with a beautiful silk scarf around her neck and new hiking shoes on her feet. It was really hard for Valerie to decide how old the woman was because her skin was perfectly smooth despite her ankles, which revealed loose skin, and the age spots on her calves, which were partially visible at the hems of her knit travel pants.

"Hi, I'm Sylvia Newman, pleasure to meet you." Sylvia smiled, and only then did Valerie detect a few light smile lines around her eyes.

"Hi, I'm Valerie. I absolutely love your scarf. It's beautiful!"

"Oh, thank you! I found it when I was hopelessly lost in Marrakesh last summer. I feel so incredibly fortunate to have seen that beautiful city before the tragic earthquake."

"Absolutely. So fortunate." Valerie nodded with a solemn expression, trying her best to look the way one should when expressing remorse for the loss of a place she couldn't quite place on a map. *Marrakesh, that's in Morocco, right? Near Casablanca? Maybe?* One thing was clear—this woman was way out of Valerie's league. Like not even in the same ballpark-like league. She could almost imagine herself with smooth and perfectly toned skin, and it made her question practically every decision she had ever made. She could have had the life that Sylvia lived now, maybe. If she had abandoned marriage and children and invested her efforts in her career. By now, she would have had twenty years under her belt, and if she had hit the right notes, she could have been a marketing VP for a mid-sized corporation. She almost justified her own choices by glancing over at Evie and David, who were acting very appropriately and engaging properly. Then Sylvia introduced Valerie to her husband, who fit Sylvia perfectly.

He had a crop of flawlessly tousled curly hair that gave him a youthful and adventurous look. Although, his silver hair clearly meant he was older. He had that same even, natural tan and exquisitely smooth skin, even around the eyes, which amazed Valerie. She'd enjoyed smile lines as early as her twenties.

"Let me introduce you, Valerie, to my husband. This is Eric Amsel. Eric, this is Valerie. She's absolutely lovely and complimented me on my scarf."

Valerie shook Eric's hand. *Just the right pressure. Perfect again. I want to be you two when I grow up. And what is it about all professional women keeping their own last names?*

"If you spotted the scarf, you must have impeccable taste. I think it's one of Sylvia's finest pieces. Although, between you and me, I think she wears it as a conversation starter," Eric said at a conspiratory whisper.

"Hey, it worked for me. Mark that in the win column, for sure," Valerie said, making a checkmark in the air with a swish of her hand.

"I love that phrase. Mind if I steal it?" Sylvia asked while giving Valerie's arm a warm squeeze.

"Go right ahead. Wonderful to meet you and thrilled to get to know you both better on the trip."

"You too, dear. Talk again soon."

Sylvia and Eric both flashed their shockingly white teeth in generous smiles.

"Okay, folks! You'll have plenty of time to get to know all about your fellow rafters over the coming days. Ready for round two?"

The group let out a communal groan.

"Wow. Rough crowd. Just kidding. I'll let you go because we'll have an early start tomorrow. We'll meet up in this same room at 0700 tomorrow morning. Don't forget to grab your wetsuits and bags. Don't worry, you really can pack a lot in those bags, but in case you're still on the fence about using them, this is the only big bag we almost guarantee will keep your stuff dry. Almost. Rest up and get ready for the time of your life."

On cue, Green Day's "Time of Your Life" started blasting through the conference room speakers.

Nate brushed his unruly curly blond bangs back from his eyes with a fluid whoosh that caught Valerie's eye. He gave Valerie a warm, intense smile. *Evie is going to lose her mind when she gets to spend five minutes around that guy.* Thankfully, Valerie figured just about every straight woman who shared a raft with Nate felt the same way, so an awkward sixteen-year-old probably wouldn't be the target of his true affections. Maybe some flirting would even be good for Evie. It might force her to give up the whole "the world is screwed, and I'm, therefore, completely justified in acting completely miserable" routine that Valerie found so boring and tiring. When Valerie was growing up, it was 9/11 or Princess Dianna. Choose your tragedy. Now it was school shootings or climate change. Kids always had someone else to blame for why their lives weren't shaping up exactly how they'd envisioned them. Thankfully, later in life, some people figured out that most of the good in life was built by themselves, rather than handed to them.

"Hi, Valerie, right? Are you okay?" Nate asked with a worried look.

"Oh! Yes! I'm sorry. Yes, I'm fine. Long day of travel, I guess."

"Totally get that. Travel knocks us all down a peg or two."

"Great orientation. You and Maggie make a great duo."

"Maggs and I play off each other pretty well. Yeah, I guess you get to know someone pretty well after going on half a dozen river tours together."

"I can only imagine, but I bet you would, for sure. Say, we weren't able to get reservations at the lodge, so we had to scramble a bit to find a place. We're camping about ten minutes from here. Anyway, long story short, do you know where we should leave our car and keys?"

"Yeah. You can leave your car in the gravel parking lot on the other side of the road. And… I'm not quite certain about the keys. I think the lodge has a lockbox or something. Hey, Maggs!"

Maggie looked up and raised her pointer finger without saying anything because she was tied up in a conversation with Sylvia Newman, of all people.

"Did you know that Sylvia's fabulous scarf came from Marrakesh. That's in Morrocco." Valerie was very pleased with herself to have remembered those details from her earlier conversation with Sylvia and her polished husband, Eric. Two people she knew she would never grow up to be, even if she became a bit more world-wise as she aged.

Nate didn't bother filling the silence with chatter. He gave Valerie a dashing smile and was off with another whoosh of his hands through his hair and a hand on her shoulder that was even warmer than the sunburn she already felt developing up her forearm. Maggie cut out of the conversation with Sylvia and sprinted across the room.

"Hi, Valerie. Sorry about that."

"Not at all. Those two are very engaging, aren't they?"

"Yes! Scary engaging actually. I can't help but get sucked into their vortex and before I know what I'm saying or doing, I'm agreeing that the Mongolian highlands are the next big adventure destination. As if I know anything about Mongolia or its tourism industry. Anyway, how can I help?"

Valerie felt a rush of maternal well-being for Maggie. It wasn't what she said, but how she said it that made Valerie instantly want to invest in Maggie's future. The right combination of unassuming humility mixed with obvious intelligence and a good dose of natural poise.

"I was asking Nate where we should leave our car and keys. He said something about a lockbox?"

"Yep. You can drop the keys in the lockbox just outside the main lodge entrance. You're getting your car shuttled to Salmon, right?"

"Yeah. And then we just tell them where to hide the keys, right?"

"That's right. A bit old-school, but it works since we won't have any way of reaching out to the shuttling companies until we get into town in Salmon at the end of the week."

The end of the week. *I can't believe I'm doing this*, Valerie thought while keeping a pasted smile on her face. "Great! Thanks so much. I'll see you at 7:00 for the start of our ride."

"Have a good night, Valerie."

Valerie waved on her way back to connect with her family. She relayed the good news, and the three walked out of the comfortable lodge on their way to their tent. At least the ice cream shop stayed open late during the summer. Valerie soon forgot the lodge's deep, supple leather couches in front of the enormous stone hearth thanks to the sugary goodness of Fudge Ripple and Pralines and Cream.

It was dark when they made it back to their campsite, especially with the thick canopy of trees overhead. Valerie was glad they had set up camp beforehand. All she needed to do before heading into the tent was make sure their three bags were ready for loading onto the bus the next day and find her toothbrush and toothpaste. With her neatly packed back-of-the-car totally askew, both tasks took more effort than they should have.

After finding the nearest campground spigot, her teeth felt clean and her body felt very ready for sleep. So ready, she decided it wasn't worth changing into pajamas. She climbed into bed, wearing her shorts and the shirt she had worn all day, promising herself to go for a refreshing swim in the cold water of the river first thing the next morning—once she got there.

 *The pine lacked the ability to worry, but it prepared for contingencies. It dropped low-hanging branches as it matured, removing ladder fuels that could provide fires a path to its canopy. It slowly drained its water content in the fall so there would be less chance of freezing in the bitter winter. And it kept its growth proportionate to the resources available at the time—not allowing its ambitions to overcome current realities of water, soil nutrients, or sunlight.*

VALERIE WAS UP WELL BEFORE DAWN AND HAD EVERYTHING EXCEPT what David and Evelyn had in the tent packed an hour before either of them were up. At first, the urge to get going was built on the desire to be on time, unlike every other step of the way throughout the trip so far. She wanted to catch them up so they wouldn't be a burden for the guides. So she wouldn't be a burden for Maggie.

But after everything was packed except a bag of protein bars, crackers, and a jar of peanut butter—in case David or Evelyn didn't feel like grabbing breakfast on the way to the lodge—Valerie realized she had jumped up and tiptoed out of the tent so early for a deeper reason. She was genuinely excited for the adventure. There were so many impactful sides to becoming a wife and a mother, ones she hadn't predicted. Her time was no longer her own. Before meeting David in college and even when they'd started seriously dating, she'd relished her independence. She was always fastidious about building healthy routines, sure, but back then, she'd made plenty of room for spontaneous adventures too.

She'd gone on weekend road trips to The Wizarding World of Harry Potter in Florida, backpacking trips in Yellowstone, and houseboat trips to Lake Powell. And she did a lot more than just tag along. She was a big value-add to those trips. How was it possible that she hadn't kept in contact with any of those college friends? It'd been almost twenty years. But twenty years wasn't that long ago, and she felt some of her old self waking up gently as the sun progressed down the hillsides toward her expectant face that morning.

If anybody ever asked her if she regretted the path she'd taken since college, she would have given a resounding no. She had chosen the path, one of many successful possibilities, and it was a good one. But in the unsettling quiet moments, rare as they were, when the paths not taken became more palpable to her, she experienced a low rumbling sense of loss. And that loss felt as if a path had been taken from her before she even knew to value things like independence, personal discovery, and adventure—independence from her marriage and kids. It was as if she had always known the taste of ice cream, been able to enjoy the sweet, creamy dessert whenever she wanted, only to wake up one morning to the sad realization that she would never taste ice cream again. It was the cost she paid to take her next step. People her age often got married before that window of opportunity closed. Having kids had been her next step, and in her naïve worldview back then, she was certain that raising children would bring powerful new experiences and help her grow into a stronger woman.

She hated the fact that it was Donald Rumsfeld who always got quoted when people talked about *unknown unknowns*. But he wasn't wrong. The unfair thing about life was that so many of the biggest choices hovered around unknown unknowns. How could she have ever ensured that her husband was the right fit? Or been able to run any kind of accurate cost-benefit analysis before having kids? She had no way of knowing how giving up her place as star employee would impact her self-worth. These days, it was tied to how well-behaved her kids were. How well she kept house.

She shivered, realizing she was quite cold. And her arms and legs were stiffening because she was sitting on the bench of the picnic table rather than a camp chair, which she had already packed. She heard rustling noises from the tent and made the mental shift. The mental shift she made dozens of times a day—to show up, kindly and encouragingly, for her family.

Having time to reflect that morning, though, was like writing a set of instructions in a manual that clearly led to a finished bookshelf. Instructions she was more conscious of than ever before. The brightening of her eyes, the straightening of her back. Her energy level poised one rung above an even keel, which required some form of caffeine pick-me-up by the late afternoon. Those instructions came automatically. But now that she saw herself so clearly, she couldn't navigate her way back to where she'd spent the last twenty years. She didn't want to.

The tent door unzipped. Evelyn climbed out, prepared to resent the day, and David, who was not a morning person, followed her out in what Valerie could only describe as a fog he had to fight his way through. She loved them both. She was more certain of that than anything. But why did family relationships have to be so damn complicated?

"Hey guys. Good morning. I have protein bars ready. Let's get a move on so they don't shove off without us." Valerie held out the bag of protein bars and gestured to the crackers and peanut butter. "And look, Evie. It's even all vegetarian. Am I good to you, or what?"

They finally got ready and ate some food and stuffed things they would leave behind and checked the bags they'd take on the rafts one more time.

"Make sure you're only bringing things you really need. These bags are pretty compact," Valerie said, fighting the urge to sort through Evie's bag and ensure she had the necessities, quite certain that she would forget something and complain later.

At last, they loaded into the car. Valerie didn't even suggest that they stop at a local café for a more substantial meal, so they actually made it to the Mountain Village Lodge with half an hour to spare. She reviewed the instructions. Since they were going to have their car transported down to Salmon, Idaho, where the trip ended, they checked in at the lodge and left their key in a labeled envelope in the box outside the registration office, then met up with the tour bus.

On the bus ride to their launch point, Valerie had that weird feeling she got in dreams where she knew she needed to run, but for some frustrating reason, her legs stood frozen in place while whatever she was chasing after got farther and farther away or what was chasing her crept ever closer. She shook it off the best she could, and stared out the window.

As soon as the bus pulled off the main highway and entered the narrow dirt road, the view opened up to broad fields washed over by clusters of purple lupine that twirled below the burn scars from past fires. Tall gray snags crowded the edges with a flurry of young lodgepole pines.

When they reached the launch site, Valerie wasn't prepared for the immensity of humanity on display while surrounded by millions of acres of wilderness. Maggie had said something about it being a mad house, and she was right. Four school buses were pulled to the side, and those groups circled around river guides who gave safety briefings and got gear sorted. Fifty or so rafts were pulled to the side of the parking lot. People swarmed in various stages of dressing and undressing. Putting on wetsuits. Taking off layers to more comfortably accommodate wetsuits and splash jackets.

When they finally parked, Valerie was the first to burst off the bus. "Whoa, Val. Hold up. Wait for us!" She heard David call after her.

She fought the urge to rush into the river, realizing there was a quarter-mile hike down to it. She paused and turned around. Maggie was next off the bus, and she almost managed to hide an uncontrollable grin at seeing Valerie itching to go. Maggie nodded in her direction. "Almost there. Give me twenty minutes, and we'll be on the river, okay, Valerie? I promise."

Valerie smiled back sheepishly, but realized she didn't really care that Maggie had seen her desires. She got the sense that Maggie thought her eagerness was cool. It seemed to her, as she waited for everybody else to make their way off the bus, that everyone was moving in slow motion. She felt a giddiness she hadn't felt since she was a kid.

The group formed up around the guides, who ran through safety protocols and basic paddling techniques. But the whole time, Valerie wished she could be that obnoxious cool kid who said something snarky but also captured what everybody else was feeling. *We all know how to paddle! We get that if we get stuck under water too long, we drown! Let's get on the river!*

The supercharged energy faded a bit when Valerie saw David and Evie standing a few yards away. Was it possible that she had forgotten that she was a mom responsible for a daughter and a wife with a husband? How did she do that? She felt a mixture of shame and excitement and curiosity that was exhausting but also thrilling. Her whole body lit up.

Nate clapped his hands twice. "Okay. Enough talking. Let's shove off. Ready, Maggie?"

"You know I am. David, Evie, and Valerie, you're with me today. I'll be leading one of the oar boats, which won't get you quite as wet, but might be a nice way to meet the river and ease into the idea of rapids. And whoever is going with Nate, make sure you give him a hard time for me, okay?"

"Don't listen to her. She's just jealous she can't ride in one of the cool paddle rafts today, am I right?" Nate led his group to their raft, and Valerie stuck right with Maggie as she led the way to theirs.

David fell into step with Valerie. "Hi, I'm David. You haven't by chance seen my wife anywhere, have you?" David put his arm across Valerie's shoulders and gave them a few massaging rubs.

His touch tickled, and Valerie shivered, rolling her shoulders around and laughing. "I'm sorry. I don't know what's gotten into me—"

David stopped walking and ignored Evie's annoyed gestures as she stuck with Maggie on their way to the raft. When Valerie lowered her head, he pulled at a few strands of her dark hair that had fallen in her face. "You are amazing. After nearly twenty years of marriage, you keep surprising me." David cradled Valerie's face in both hands and kissed her deeply.

At first, she worried about what Evie would think, but when David didn't break the kiss right away, like he usually did, she stepped into the moment. She felt the slight tug as David's upper lip searched across hers. She noticed the slight twitch of his cheek as one of the hundreds of small muscle fibers in his face misfired. By the time David did end the kiss, Valerie's cheeks were flushed and her eyes glistened. Maybe she had developed some tears, but she didn't feel the ache that usually accompanied tears. She felt relief. As if a big spool of string wound messily within her chest had finally given way. And as she stepped into the frigid water for the first time, hand in hand with David, that reflexive, startled intake of breath felt so unhindered and free.

"Are we going to ride this river, or would you two rather stay here and get a room?" Evie said with dramatic eye rolls.

"Well, we've come this far. I suppose we might as well go for a ride?" Valerie said. Though, deep down, she did feel cheated out of time alone with her husband. That feeling of regret left quickly.

Instead, she remembered the feel of her feet in the refreshingly cool river as she climbed onboard the raft and awkwardly made her way to the front to help Evie and David get onboard.

Maggie pushed their raft off the bank and into the current with remarkable grace, then dropped down to a long blue vinyl cushion draped over coolers and other supply boxes in the middle of the boat, just behind the bench Valerie was sitting on. "David and Evie, come sit up front with Valerie. I think you and I have a lot to talk about," Maggie said, nodding to Valerie and testing out her two long oars as she adjusted to the current.

Valerie was thankful that Maggie could do all the navigating that first day. She was ready to enjoy the river and let the spool of responsibility and worry that had wound across her chest unravel into the rushing water.

Valerie quickly got caught up in the nuanced bumps and swirls and waves of the river. For the first twenty-five miles of their trip, the raft floated past massive landslides that Maggie told them had completely changed the character of the water's flow. And Valerie understood how that could be—a three-hundred-yard field of colossal boulders ran across the river at an angle. It was amazing that the rock hadn't blocked the river completely. What would it have been like to witness that monumental earthflow, she thought. Her reverie was interrupted by the first rapids.

"Hold on!" Maggie shouted excitedly. Maggie faced the raft's broadside, putting Valerie on the side closer to the rapids.

The raft dipped down and climbed again, cresting the wave made by some submerged boulder, but it sank again, this time smacking the next wave, driving a wall of water over the raft, thoroughly drenching Valerie.

Valerie had been anticipating that first splash for days, but the chill and power of the water still took her breath away. She understood then why the guides had insisted that participants wear wetsuits for the first day of the trip. She was instantly cold, but the bright sun soon warmed her, and she was pleased to see that Maggie adjusted the raft so the next splash thoroughly hit Evie's side.

It amazed Valerie to see how expertly Maggie controlled the raft. "It must be incredible knowing how to read the water and control a raft like this," Valerie shouted toward Maggie over the roar of the rapids.

"Yeah, after going down the river a few times, you kind of learn how to read it. Like, *I need to avoid that hole. I need to get the raft to this side of the river so we can avoid a strainer.* It kind of forces me to stay completely in the moment, you know?"

"Yeah, I bet it's a great feeling," Valerie said, facing forward again.

"Want to take over for a while?"

Maggie dropped her oars, which were thankfully anchored to the raft, and leaned over with a serious look. Valerie panicked as she saw the raft start to turn toward a significant dip in the river—toward rapids that she had no idea how to navigate. But then a broad grin spread over Maggie's face. "Just kidding! Maybe one of these days."

After they made their way past that first set of rapids, they pleasantly floated in calmer water. At first, Valerie wanted to keep small talk going, but she sensed that David and Evie were trying to take in the scene, and Maggie seemed happy to take in the warmth from the sun while methodically moving the oars in slow circular motions. So Valerie put her feet up on the front of the raft and leaned back against one of the bright-yellow waterproof bags clipped to it. She found the rugged rock formations that seemed to grow out of the steep hillside fascinating—they looked almost like they'd been planted there by some giant, ancient gardener.

She was surprised to see so many homesteads as they drifted past airstrips and good-sized homes with attached airplane hangars. "Wouldn't it be amazing to own one of these ranches?" Valerie asked David with a tap on his shoulder after they had drifted past one particularly posh-looking wooden structure she couldn't bring herself to call a cabin.

"Sure, maybe for a week, until we ran out of food."

"We could fly in supplies. They have airstrips."

"Oh, so we'll have a plane as well as a ranch in the wilderness? That opens up a whole host of possibilities then." David gave Valerie a wry smile, and she gave him a playful shove.

"Most of these ranches have been owned by the same families for generations. They don't go up for sale often. I think I heard one did a while back, and it sold for something like twenty million or something crazy like that," Maggie explained.

"I believe it. Such an amazing place. And what a weird thing that people can fly into the middle of the wilderness," Valerie said.

"It really is. I don't know the entire backstory to how the Frank Church Wilderness was established, but I know that keeping these private ranches and airstrips was super important. I think they chalked it up as being important for wildfire protection. That doesn't seem to be much of a worry for the Forest Service anymore. Though they still maintain the airstrips they manage."

Valerie made a mental note to research the history of the Frank Church Wilderness. Political jockeying was a reality, but after seeing her fifth plane fly overhead that morning, she decided there was something strange and sad in allowing the river be so readily accessed. The irony of benefiting from that easy access to the wilderness wasn't lost on her either.

The hours slipped by as easily as the river lapped against its bank, and Valerie experienced a level of contentment unlike any she'd ever felt. It was a different kind of contentment, grown from her realization that she could do hard things and still find beauty and excitement, even while facing those challenges. It made her wonder what else she might be capable of, given the right kind of motivation.

It was midafternoon by the time all the rafts arrived at the group's camping spot for the night. Most of the paddleboats were already tied up at the base of a small rocky hill above which a large flat grassy area extended hundreds of yards in either direction underneath stately ponderosa pines.

"We're here!" Maggie shouted as she maneuvered the oar boat alongside the other rafts.

Nate was there to tie off the raft to a sturdy boulder jutting out from the riverbank. Valerie waited for Evie and David to get off first, and then she did the same, self-conscious of how clumsy she must look. It felt good to feel her feet on solid ground again, and though she hadn't done any paddling, she was exhausted just the same.

When she reached the long plateau, she was amazed to see a large circle of camp chairs already set up near a kitchen area within view of the river and several side canyons beyond it. She took off her wetsuit and splash guard and eased into one of the camp chairs, letting the sun warm and dry her soaked shorts and shirt. She was more tired than she had any reason to be, and so grateful for the camp chair that she debated with herself over leaving it to walk the few paces to the cooler for a soda.

One day down, she thought as she hoisted herself out of the camp chair, liking the idea of the cool drink more now that her clothes were drying and she was gradually warming up. She grabbed a ginger ale and smiled as she reflected back just a few weeks before when she'd purchased that same brand of soda in the grocery store. She felt a thousand miles away from who she was back then.

Valerie was eager to head to bed early that night. She brushed her teeth and decided she'd wait until morning to experience what the raft guides called the *groover*. She assumed it was some kind of makeshift latrine. *Something to look forward to tomorrow.*

She was the first up the next morning and tried to make herself useful to the raft guides as they prepared breakfast, but after a couple of vain attempts at offering, she decided to take a brief walk around camp to prepare her legs for sitting on an oar boat most of the day.

Valerie's second day on the river was much like the first. This time, lots of good conversation with Nate as their oar boat captain. She noticed Evie seemed more interested in the conversation than she'd been the day before. She figured Nate's natural laughter and substantial forearms had something to do with that.

Time on the raft had a strange quality. In some respects, Valerie felt like time stood still, especially after a particularly large splash. Yet, before she noticed how late it was, Nate was navigating their boat to their camping spot for the night.

That night, pleasant aromas drifted to her nose from the make-shift kitchen, and she turned to see a few crew members already hard at work setting up a table with a cheese board and assorted other snacks.

"Hey, folks! We have some snacks here to tide you over until dinner."

Valerie hated to leave those pleasant smells, but she remembered that she'd left her go bag on the oar boat, and she'd want that for the evening. So she pulled herself up and out of her chair, her knees protesting. *I'll have to find a better position to sit on that boat tomorrow*, she thought as she headed back down the rocky bank to the boat.

On her way back up to the camp, she was startled to see, yet again, for the second day, dozens of tents set up, tucked away on a modest-sized bluff. This raft company really meant it when they said they would take care of everything.

That night slipped by in a blur. Though Valerie had several hours to spend before bed, by the time she'd found her larger bag on the raft that had gone ahead of the group earlier that morning, set up her cot and sleeping bag, ate some dinner, and took a bit of time to explore the roughly defined Middle Fork Trail with David and

Evie, the sun had already dipped below the high canyon walls and it was getting chilly.

She spent a half hour or so chatting with some of the other participants and saw Sylvia and Eric, who she'd met at the orientation and who were engrossed in a conversation about yak milk and mint tea. She hardly believed that people could be so passionate about those things. Though, she might have misheard. She lost focus on their topic of conversation when she caught sight of Sylvia's expertly pedicured feet. *How have they stayed so clean after a day on a paddleboat?* Her toenails practically stood out in the dark. *How do I grow up to be Sylvia*, she thought yet again.

"Doing okay?" David said, putting his hands on Valerie's shoulders.

Valerie looked up from Sylvia's feet and gave her husband a tired smile.

"I'm okay. Thanks. Tired for some reason. It's not like we did anything except sit all day, but I'm beat."

"Yeah, I'm feeling it too. All that sun and core work, trying to stay in the boat, I guess."

"I think I'll head up to our tent. Need anything?"

"No, I'm just fine. I'll be up in a while." David kissed the top of Valerie's head and gave her shoulders a gentle squeeze.

Valerie wandered past the rows of tents to a clever hand-washing station with one bucket sitting atop another with a faucet attached to the top one and a tube running into the lower one and with a foot pump on the ground. She ran the water over her hands, pleased to discover that it was even warm water.

That night, Valerie was ripped from sleep by a rustling in the tent.

"Mom, I'm getting wet."

It took Valerie a long moment to remember where she was and why, but eventually she turned to Evie. She was right. A gentle rain was falling through the roof of their tent, which they'd left open to the night air, forgoing the rainfly. Valerie ran through her options. None of them seemed promising. She was so tired after the day on the river and the disruptive sleep in the new environment, and the surprising silence—other than the river's quiet churn—that the last thing she wanted to do was to get out of her warm sleeping bag to put on the rainfly. On the other hand, if she didn't do something, all their things would be drenched without enough time to dry come morning. A mildewed wetsuit was not something she wanted to experience.

Right when she decided she'd have to do something and tried to steel herself up for that reality, two red pools of light came from nearby headlamps, appearing translucent through their tent. Two of the rafting crew put up the rainfly in less than a minute. She felt a wave of gratitude toward whomever was assigned the task. And the fact that they were clearly practiced at doing it made her realize just how institutionalized the guiding trips had become. Which wasn't a terrible thing. But it chipped away at the rustic appeal of the wilderness environment. She didn't even have to put up her own rainfly when a sudden cloud burst emptied on her tent. Imagine that.

In the morning, their third morning on the river, all of her things were still dry. She never discovered who had come by her tent in the middle of the night to ensure she and her family had a pleasant sleep. So she sent out a silent well-wish to the whole rafting crew and started breaking down her tent and cot for the lead raft to take to their next camping spot farther down the river. She was ready for another day.

Salmon, Idaho
August 2024

he human-rafting groups that floated below the pine's branches, who chatted excitedly about rapids and dinner late at night had their way of communicating, but the pine's lack of vocal organs didn't mean it had no way to send out important messages. It had its way of communicating too. Its roots sent messages to nearby trees through their microbial-symbiotic relationships and the aboveground portion sent pheromones throughout the air to worn and remind and protect itself and its neighbors.

BY THE END OF HIS FIRST FOURTEEN-DAY ASSIGNMENT BEFORE HIS mandatory three days R and R, Andy was getting the hang of things on the PIO team. And though the work was clearly less physically demanding, he loved the interactions with community members. There were plenty of blanket gratitude and praises for the firefighters, which he was used to. But he was thrilled to discover that his favorite kinds of interactions were the hard ones that most PIOs skirted around or tried to defuse.

Andy would throw himself fully into the discussion. He didn't debate, exactly. He gave facts when he had them and admitted it when there weren't enough facts to make a fair assessment of things. And his decades of experience on the fire line and running crews meant he was very willing to correct people when they were mistaken, which they often were, about the professionalism and skill of those making decisions about fire-behavior modeling and tactics.

At first, Glen seemed nervous about Andy's methods, but after Andy demonstrated how quickly members of the public warmed up to him, he gave Andy free rein to engage as he saw fit. After one particularly heated conversation with a burly man wearing a leather vest and a tight gray ponytail at Salmon's one real grocery store, Glen strolled up to Andy. "I thought the sparks were flying mostly in the canyon. But now I'm not so certain," he said with an encouraging smile.

"Yeah, that one did get a bit spicy, didn't it? Seemed to end up okay though."

"True. Most PIOs are eager to please and to leave the public happy and satisfied. That inevitably leads to downplaying bad situations and focusing only on the good."

"Ah, you mean they spin it."

"No. It's not like that. They're not intentionally misleading at least. Public affairs' jobs are hard because they have the task of telling the truth about the Forest Service's actions, some of which aren't neat and tidy. And as much as we like to say our decisions are based on the best available science, sometimes politics gets thrown into the decision space too. That's why PIOs love those side stories about firefighters waking up a family just in the nick of time to escape the fire or fire crews spending time to fix the water feature at a local community center. Anyway, you just tell it straight."

"Sorry. I don't have that storytelling angle down quite yet."

"No. It's been a great lesson and reminder for me actually. Our number one job is to provide communities impacted by wildfires with the information they need to make the best decisions for them and their families. I realize I get caught up in those feel-good stories a bit too much myself. I'm an old-school journalist after all."

"Well, thanks, I guess. For me, I just know how angry members of the public feel. I don't try to minimize those feelings. It doesn't seem to help anyway. If I owned land that was being threatened by wildfires, I'd be scared and angry if I thought people didn't care enough about it too."

"That's perfect. I wish I'd recorded that, and then I'd play it for every S-203 PIO-training I taught."

Andy beamed at that. He was clearly an outsider in the PIO world. Most of the people he was working with were public-affairs types for their regular jobs. Hearing Glen say things like that confirmed his desire to do more PIO work moving forward.

"Let's call it a day. We can leave the info board here. Just find a rock to put on top of those flyers on the table. We'll have someone come back to check on it later or in the morning."

Andy found a rock and dropped it on the stack of info sheets and followed Glen to their rig. The two men mostly enjoyed the silence as they made their way back to the Incident Command Post, which was fully operational and occupied nearly every square foot of a couple of grassy fields surrounding Salmon City Park. After a twelve-hour shift of interacting with the public, Andy was ready for some quiet—rather *silent*—time. But as they entered the ICP and Glen gave a wave to the security guard, he cocked his head toward Andy. "So you have three days of R and R. Are you going home or resting up here? And please don't tell me that we've scared you off from PIO work?"

"I'll be back. I don't scare that easily. These last fourteen days have really been great. Different from fire-line work, that's for sure. But I think I could get used to it."

Glen just nodded thoughtfully, so Andy continued.

"And I think I'll probably just do laundry. Try to catch a bit of extra sleep. Those sorts of things."

"Sounds very sensible," Glen said as they wound their way past the area of the camp where morning briefings were held.

Andy noticed the board up front still held several maps showing the current fire perimeter with different quadrants labeled by letters like A, Alpha; D, Delta; L, Lima.

"I haven't noticed it for years, but fire operations like to pretend they're military, don't they? I mean, with all the 'Build anchor points within Lima and Alpha quadrants.' We don't need to talk like that, but we do."

"What do you mean we don't need to? Come to think of it, why does anybody talk the way they do?" Glen asked, backing into a spot between two hotshot engines.

"I'd imagine it's for convenience and efficiency. But I think there's maybe some cultural elements there too. These last couple of weeks with you PIO folks have made me realize that we require the public to understand us when maybe it should be the other way around."

"Whoa!" Glen stopped the rig but held still with closed eyes and a very satisfied look on his face.

"What?"

"I'm glad you're taking those R and R days because, a few more days of PIO work, and you'd have my job." Glen opened his eyes and nodded seriously toward Andy, who got a thrill out of what Glen had said. Glen didn't flatter others.

Then Andy remembered something he'd wanted to ask Glen a number of times before but had always ended up distracted. "Thanks, Glen. I appreciate that. I still have a long way to go, but thanks." He cleared his throat. "Say, total change of subject, but how do we notify all the rafting-tour folks?"

"How do you mean?"

"I mean, do we have a plan to send some folks down the river or to any of the lodges along the Salmon River? There're probably hundreds of people going down the different forks of the river on any given week."

"They typically have their orientations in Stanley or McCall, so we give out information to the main inns and lodges. That way, we can hit the rafters as well as all the other recreating public. And we sometimes have volunteer river guides at key boat launches."

"Got it. And at what point will we close the river to rafting access? The fire is burning in the direction of the Middle Fork right now, right? Didn't Ops. say, this morning, that they anticipate the fire reaching the river within the next forty-eight to seventy-two hours?"

"We don't close the river access. That's a political hot potato that we don't want to handle."

"Of course, but eventually we'll have to, right? The potential threat to rafting groups has got to be worked into risk assessments somehow, right?" Andy fidgeted in his seat and turned to face Glen more directly.

"Yeah, but we don't close river access. The nearby forests might decide to communicate about obstructions on the river. That might close some of the river access and cause groups to cancel a rafting trip for a week or two. But so long as the river isn't blocked, we don't close it."

Andy stared at Glen, trying to process what Glen was telling him. Wildfire operations worked with county sheriff's offices all the time to declare mandatory evacuations. They worked with local Forest Service offices to put in temporary closures to campgrounds, cabin rentals, and the like. Why wouldn't they close river access?

Glen and Andy climbed out of the rig, grabbed their backpacks, and headed toward the dining hall for some dinner.

"You look confused or upset or maybe both," Glen said, observing Andy.

"Mainly confused but moving in the upset direction."

"There are lots of factors at play when it comes to the Frank. You know that we almost never actively suppress fire in that wilderness because it evolved with fire and its ecosystems need fire to be healthy. Besides that, we're losing runways and helipad locations all the time because environmental groups are buying the grandfathered-in homesteaders' land and private lodges that are allowed to operate in the wilderness."

"I know all of that, Glen."

"I know you know all of that, Andy. I'm getting there."

"Sorry. Please continue," Andy said, holding open the door to the dining hall tent for Glen to enter first.

"Thanks." Glen grabbed two trays and handed one to Andy. "So we have wilderness ethics on the one hand, playing an important factor in our decision space. We don't actively suppress fire in the Frank. We do in other wildernesses, as I'm sure you're fully aware."

"Yeah. I've fought dozens of fires in protected wildernesses."

"Exactly. So the Frank is unique that way. It's big enough that unless a fire is really threatening some of the major lodges or homesteads along the river or likely to threaten some important values on the outside perimeter of the wilderness, we usually don't apply active suppression. But there are other factors too."

Glen loaded up on a spinach salad and tomatoes that actually looked quite good to Andy. The urge to load up on high carbs and meat and potatoes still lingered in his brain, but he followed Glen's example and filled a plate with salad, adding some extra cheese and pecans as a compromise.

When they sat down at the table, Glen took a few slow bites without continuing the conversation.

"So you were saying there are other factors," Andy said, trying to prompt Glen.

"Hold on just a second. I won't enjoy the rest of this food nearly as much as the first couple of bites."

Andy took a couple of bites in the awkward silence. He had to admit that Glen had a point. He did enjoy those first bites a lot more than he remembered ever enjoying a salad.

"Okay. Other factors. Now we're getting into the more delicate matters. The political situation. A lot of wealthy, well-connected people spend a lot of money getting flown around the wilderness.

The Frank is also unique because it's the only wilderness that allows planes. I think there was some kind of compromise that Frank Church himself made to win over some Congress people who didn't like the idea of protecting so much public land any stricter than they generally needed to. And I think folks also wanted to maintain all of the runways for fire suppression. We don't really suppress fire, so we don't use the runways much. But a ton of privately charted flights come and go all the time. I'm talking about people who spend hundreds of thousands of dollars to be flown into the heart of the Frank to kill a moose or a bear."

"Now I get it. It's all about money. Like always."

"It is about money. But it's also about politics and giving up some things so we can get other things."

"So in a nutshell, we don't suppress fires in the Frank, and since tons of money is being made by flying billionaires around to give them a wilderness-frontiersman experience, we don't interfere in the politicking either. Do I have it right?"

"Essentially, yes. Our formal stance is that the river is in wilderness, therefore natural processes, including fire on the landscape is allowed to function the way nature intends and people who choose to enter the wilderness do so at their own risk."

"So we don't get sued, you mean?"

"There are legal reasons, for sure. Here's another way of looking at it. I have family in England, so I try to fly over there every couple of years. In England, there are lots of spectacular views of the ocean from amazing cliff faces. But at first, it's a bit jarring to see that there aren't fences at the edge of those cliffs. At the main viewing decks of the Grand Canyon, there are fences. But there's nothing to stop someone from falling to their deaths along those cliffs in England. So the question is, is it the government's responsibility to put up fences?"

"Yes. Absolutely. Let's say a child was throwing around a Frisbee and wasn't looking?"

"Sounds logical. But how do you explain that to the many people who want an unobstructed view of the ocean from the cliffs?"

"They have to sacrifice that for safety."

"Very logical, again. I love London. The museums. The shows. The history. Anyway, it's interesting to see that at almost every pedestrian crossing there are painted signs saying 'look right.' It's probably for all the tourists who look left first because cars come from the wrong direction in England. But why do you think the government would go through all the bother of warning the public about traffic patterns in the city? Wouldn't it make more sense to be consistent with their warnings and just let people know that cars are dangerous and that they run the risk of being hit if they're not paying attention? That's their tactic with the cliffs."

"Glen, I can tell you're nearing the moral of your story, so don't let me stand in your way."

"You're too accommodating for an old man. I think England gets it right. They warn people where it's appropriate. And they don't take away from the ocean view by putting up fences. People should know that the cliff is there and if they fall, they will most certainly die. I think our agency tries to take a similar stance with the Frank. We don't put up fences. People should know that going into wilderness areas is inherently more dangerous than walking around town. But controlling access, putting out fires, and closing rivers would take away from their experience."

Andy slowly and thoughtfully chewed his spinach salad, again aware of the bright and noisy chatter around him and Glen. "I think England's wrong. Nice analogy though, Glen. Enjoy your salad. I need to get some air," Andy said with a smirk and a squeeze to Glen's shoulder.

"There's a lot of great air to be had here. Partly because we don't put up filters," Glen shouted toward Andy just before he disappeared out the door.

"All those poor Frisbee-throwing kids, though, Glen. Think about the children." Andy put two fingers to his brow in a casual solute and stepped out of the dining hall.

Glen was right about one thing—every decision was built around a series of tradeoffs. As Andy walked away from the dining hall, the sound of firefighters laughing, the constant low hum of the generators that kept the lights on all night long, the distant night-time sounds of birds he didn't know the names of, and the smell of smoke were so familiar, but in that moment, he witnessed them through a new lens, and nothing fit quite right anymore.

Without conscious thought, Andy found himself standing in front of the map board in the briefing area of camp and staring at the fire perimeter, the growth of which was steadily bearing down on the river. He imagined that, at night, from certain bends of the river, rafters could see the red glow of flames, and they certainly could smell the smoke. Forty-eight to seventy-two hours until it reached the river. Give the fire a good wind, though, and it could be there much faster. And what exactly would the rafting guides tell the tourists to do when the fire reached them? Probably what anybody else would try to do—wait things out in the river. That was the logical thing to do. Except windblown wildfires could have walls of flame taller than the river was wide. And by the time that wall of flame reached the river, it would be shooting off large embers and other fiery debris thousands of yards in front of the main fire.

Andy started walking away from the map board and the stark vision of those trapped rafters caused a memory to flash in his mind unbidden.

Duck Valley, Utah
August 2005

THEY WERE BOXED IN. NO WAY OF MAKING IT UP THE ROAD NOW. No other escape route. Andy had instructed Jenny and her Grandma Carol to turn on any sprinklers and to start spraying down the roof with hoses. It couldn't hurt anything, and they urgently wanted to do something, anything, to help.

The fire's wall of flame could be distinctly seen through the trees, and the darkened sky took on a sinister red hue that was deeper than it had been at any other point during the day. Andy surveyed the yard to see if there were any last-minute flammables he could move away from the house. Thankfully, he'd been working with a couple of other crew members to make the property and others nearby more defensible. Limbing up trees to remove ladder fuels, trimming bushes back, teaching proper techniques for cutting over-hanging branches away from roofs, and instructing homeowners to clear out leafy debris from rain gutters—though he wasn't exactly sure if he was allowed to do that. It just made sense to him.

Some fires became unpredictable, following their own laws. Maybe someday computers would be powerful enough to draw real-time analytics that would feed into huge-scale models that could tell the exact trajectory of a fire.

For now, though, there was a reason insurance companies rightly called such losses acts of God, and even for him—who'd interacted with fire for a couple of seasons and completed several assignments on smaller wildfires that year—the reason why some homes were reduced to ash and others were left unscathed was a complete mystery to him. All he could do at that moment was reduce the fuel load near the home he was trying to protect and cool it down with water. He pulled himself out of his thoughts and remembered he wasn't alone in that fight.

"Great, Jenny! Keep that water going!"

Andy needed to focus on the task at hand—preparing the home for wildfire impacts the best he possibly could in these last minutes. But his focus kept getting pulled to other stark realities. If the fire burned over the home, as it was close to doing, he might not survive. As a firefighter with at least a couple of seasons under his belt, he'd come to terms with his own human frailty. But in those last moments of cutting the few branches that were within reach; checking to ensure all sprinklers were on full blast; tossing anything particularly flammable, like deck chairs, as far away from the home as he could; and turning off the gas lines to the house, Andy realized he had never been afraid of wildfire before, but he felt it then—raw, ragged fear. It made his hands and arms shake with abounding nervousness, like he'd drunk a few too many energy drinks. And though that energy sharpened his thoughts, he had a hard time focusing on any one thought at a time.

Then the fire was there, bearing down on the house like a tidal wave. As it bore down on the house, Andy was glad to see that the section of the fire threatening them was an offshoot of the main thrust. That section of fire was farther north. Still, the section that was quickly consuming all the vegetation in front of the house was spread wide enough to easily envelope the structure.

"Carol, Jenny, come here, now!" Andy shouted over the crashing sound of wind that whipped the trees in eerie circles. He pulled out the fire shelter that he always carried in his pack. It was packaged in the shape of a small rectangular box and covered in bright-blue canvas. He ripped the seal of the box and forced out its tightly packed contents. He grabbed hold of the two pull straps and fanned the shelter open, using the wind to blow it out quickly and completely.

"Get on the ground with me. Jenny, you lie down first. Face down. Carol, wrap your arms around Jenny, but make sure both of you have some air space between you. These shelters are designed to hold one person, but it can help the three of us if you two will make sure that the shelter stays tucked under us. Okay? Jenny, now!"

Jenny jumped down.

"We want to face away from the fire. So turn around so your head is toward the house. Great! Carol, your turn." Andy helped Carol down. "Start digging at the ground around you. We want to get down to the mineral soil. It'll also be a little bit cooler."

Andy tucked his foot in the bottom strap, raised the upper straps above his head to tuck the top of the heat-reflective shelter over him, and lay down, cradling both Carol and Jenny. He held the straps down tight and looked around to ensure the shelter was fully deployed without any openings.

"Hold on tight! It's going to get really loud and hot. Keep your face down against the cooler soil! Here it comes!"

Andy braced his arms and legs to hold the shelter firmly against the maelstrom that beat against it. Hurricane survivors sometimes talked about the strange peace and calm they witnessed as the eye of a storm passed over them. The epicenter of a wildfire was not that. Wildfires burned at temperatures reaching 2,000-degrees Fahrenheit and could have winds that approached tornado velocities.

The din of trees crashing to the ground and exploding in the heat were deafening. The heat bore down on Andy with its immense, nearly overpowering presence. But in those moments, when time seemed to slow to frozen frames, when he felt like he had always been and always would be in that shelter, holding down the protective sheeting with furious intensity, a strange peace washed over him.

He remembered learning in his high school biology class how animals that were caught by predators had one last mechanism to ease the pain. When their deaths were inevitable, chemicals released to ease their passing. Maybe that was what Andy felt. The recognition of his own death—nature's last gift. But he felt something else, which, under the circumstances, seemed misplaced.

Pride.

Even in those prolonged seconds, when the three of them failed to escape, he felt an exhilarating sense of accomplishment. He'd done his best. He'd used all of his training and skills and physical ability and preparation that led up to the exact situation he was in. And there was peace in that.

Andy woke from that moment when he heard a major shift in the wind's direction. It was a dramatic and complete shift from the south to the west and the effects were immediate. The temperatures dropped, and the thundering booms and crashes they had experienced eased. Andy held the shelter around them against the ground, knowing that the urge to get out of the shelter too soon was one rookie mistake he wouldn't make. Even if the main intensity of the fire had moved, there was still a good chance that things would be burning around them and the temperatures could still kill them. "I know it's miserable in here, but let's make sure it's safe before we lift the shelter, okay?"

Carol and Jenny didn't reply. He didn't expect them to. He was sure they were both in shock. He was probably in shock too, running on adrenaline more than anything else. But he found Carol's hand and gave it a firm and fervent squeeze. After what seemed to be whole lifetimes in some ways but no time at all in others and after the din of the wildfire had rolled off to the west, Andy cautiously lifted the shelter and took his first glance at the ground surrounding them.

Blackened, burning tree fragments that looked like they had been chewed off by some fire-breathing animal lay scattered all around them. Whole tree trunks lay along the perimeter of the grassy front yard. A few burning embers threatened the roof, and his rig was stripped to a melted metal frame. He pulled the shelter the rest of the way off and helped Carol and Jenny to their feet.

"We made it through. I hardly believe it. But we made it," Carol said in utter disbelief. "You saved our lives."

Andy didn't have words to explain what he was feeling. Instead, he pulled Carol into a fierce hug. Carol clung to Andy and started to break down into visceral sobs as the weight of the fear and anxiety and desperation started to lift and made it possible for the three survivors' logical brains to contemplate just how close they had come to the end of their lives. Jenny hugged her grandma from behind, visibly shaking. After a long moment, Andy gently moved Carol away from him, keeping his hands on her shoulders to steady her slight frame. "We still have some work to do. Will you two help me?"

Both Carol and Jenny nodded resolutely, wiping at their eyes.

"Okay. Jenny, could you grab a hose and make sure that all of those burning embers around the yard are good and dead out?"

Jenny jumped to it, obviously grateful for something useful to do.

"Carol, could you double-check you have all you need in your go bags since we're fortunate enough to be able to get back in the house?"

She nodded with wide blank eyes.

"I'll run a hose up on the roof to put out the embers that are burning up there. It's going to be okay."

Andy's encouraging smile stirred Carol to action. She headed into the house that was, by some miracle, still standing nearly untouched, while all the surrounding forest trees lay smoldering in shattered heaps or as bare, charred poles.

After saturating the roof embers and those found around the yard until they were cold to the touch, Andy took a breath and surveyed the area from the roof. He had heard of fire behavior like this before. Whole neighborhoods could be completely incinerated except for a single house that, for some unexplainable reason, was left untouched. The grassy lawn of the front yard was still green. Years later, that was the thing he could almost laugh about. The lawn was still in an excellent manicured condition.

Andy knew then what he needed to do. He didn't stop to check with Glen before he set his plans. Anybody he talked to from the fire management team would tell him not to go. So he headed to his tent straightway, planning for a very early start the next morning. He would hitch a ride on a charter plane that would land on one of the runways near one of the main lodges where the rafters stopped for a night or for ice cream, and then he'd fly back in time for his next workday in three-days' time. It wasn't rebellion that drove him, he decided as he tried to clear his mind enough to get a few hours of sleep. It was pure necessity—the kind of necessity that only people who had experienced ultimate helplessness could under-stand—people who had seen nature's raw and horrifying power and been blown into awareness by their total lack of control. He would do whatever it took, use up his energy and time—even his last breath—urging others to avoid such an experience. And if no one changed their plans, at least he would know he had done what he could. He hoped that would be enough.

Middle Fork of the Salmon River, Frank Church Wilderness

August 2024

 *Certain elements of the pine's life took on more importance than others, and after having overseen the Middle Fork all its life, it understood that the river had a greater influence on the environment than it could ever hope to have. But it also recognized that everything had its proper place in the order of things. The tree provided an important habitat for animals that interacted with the river. And when it reached the end of its life, it assumed it would fall into the river and mingle with many other trees to shift the water's flow in small but significant ways.*

VALERIE ADJUSTED TO THE RHYTHM THE RAFTING TRIP DICTATED. Each morning, the participants were assigned to a boat. There were seats enough for eight people in larger paddleboats where people were guaranteed to get closer to the action and wet. There was also a much higher risk of falling out of a paddleboat, and that added risk seemed to appeal to most of the participants. Valerie had tested that out, and though it'd been exciting, the temperatures dropped considerably midway through the trip and the prospect of being wet most of the afternoon didn't carry quite the appeal that it had that first warmer day.

Evie and David, on the other hand, were completely sold on the paddleboats. So, Valerie planned to tag along that day and prepared herself the best she could for a cold ride. Just then, Evie came around the corner, wearing her two-piece swimsuit and sandals.

"Hey honey, where's your wetsuit? And don't forget your splashguard. Here you go," Valerie said to Evie, holding the bright-blue splashguard in Evie's direction.

"I'm not wearing a splashguard today."

"Oh, Evie, you'll freeze. Here let me help you." Valerie held the splashguard ready to slip over Evie's head. But Evie darted away from her.

"No! Do you have to control everything I do?" Evie blurted loud enough for the entire rafting group to hear.

Valerie nodded in the direction of the kitchen crew and smiled apologetically. No one looked her way or stiffened in judgment over her parenting, but embarrassment flared up her neck and flushed through her face.

"I'm not wearing that thing today. It was hot and sweaty, so I'm not wearing it."

"Evie, you need to—"

David appeared behind Valerie and took the splashguard from her hands. He whispered softly in Valerie's ear. "We're trying to save our daughter from herself, remember? Maybe we could let her be cold today and learn how smart you are for wearing your splashguard tomorrow?"

His words latched onto Valerie's attention, and she focused on her body language for a second. Heavy breathing. And her arms were tightly folded around her chest. David dropped the splashguard and slowly pulled Valerie's arms apart, then kissed the top of her hands. Valerie sighed. "You're right. But I don't think it's a good idea for me to ride in your paddleboat today. Evie's clothes, or I guess lack of clothes, are going to bug me all day. I'll see if there's room on an oar boat." Valerie picked up the discarded splashguard and took a couple of quick steps to where the oar boats were tied up at shore.

"Hold up!" David raced to catch up with her. She turned.

"We still have a lot of trip left. Things will get better. I promise."

"I'll believe that when I see it. But keep track of our daughter, okay? Don't let her fall out. Or at least make sure you get her back into the boat if she does." Valerie gave David a mischievous grin that he reciprocated, then she headed toward the river.

"I'll see you at lunch then," David shouted after her.

"I'll be fine. I get to spend the day with Bob and Heidi!" Spending a good part of the day with that delightful couple didn't bother her one bit.

Throughout the day on the river, Valerie learned a lot about Bob and Heidi. Bob was a retired plumbing wholesaler who'd been born and raised in Vermont on the land his grandfather had bought. He was the kind of guy who showed he cared by helping put a rainfly up or helped a person on or off the raft without even a single thought. That was simply who he was.

Heidi was a correctional nurse who loved the work variety a prison provided. She was clearly quite smitten by Bob and was thrilled to be on this adventure with him. She proudly told Valerie about their connection through online dating as if she were telling it for the first time. Though, Valerie had already picked up snippets of the story from Heidi's various tellings to other group members. "When I saw on his profile, *paramotoring*, I was like, 'Wow, I wonder what that is?' And then I saw rafting, which I love. The great thing about online dating is you can weed out people pretty easily. Like on the site, you can check a bunch of boxes and there is one for whether or not the person believes animals have souls. I mean, that's clearly a deciding factor for me."

Valerie decided not to seek clarification on where Heidi stood on the matter, but she assumed the affirmative.

Time on the river was a funny thing, especially on the oar boats. So many micro victories filled the hours. Ryan, the oar boat captain that Valerie rode with that day, would steer the boat smoothly downstream. But then she suspected that he purposefully led them to choppy water, which pleased everyone she was riding with on the oar boat, and she didn't mind getting wet. Ryan would read or tell a little bit about the rapids—like how they got their name or information about the historic landmarks or homesteads they passed along the river. They'd make it through the rapids with appropriate hoots and shouts as the frigid water splashed over the boat, and then they would recover and laugh about how it was Heidi's turn to be splashed or about Bob's glasses almost falling out of the boat or Bob's hat, which read *I am Bob and I'm doing Bob things.* He claimed it was his name tag. And then the four passengers of the boat would prepare for the next set of rapids or point of interest.

Valerie loved that cycle of chatting with Bob and Heidi, the occasional rapid, and then chatting about the rapids for the next half hour or so. About rapids Bob had gone on before. Or Heidi willingly filled gaps with intriguing anecdotes from her past.

Valerie was so thrilled to connect with Bob and Heidi in such an immediate and powerful way that she was encouraged to make friends with others from the rafting group. She remembered how easy it was to make friends with just about anybody growing up. But since getting married and especially after having kids, she didn't practice the intentional effort of making friends with people who weren't assigned as a consequence of the work she did in the community or at her kids' schools.

Her curiosity turned to the family she affectionately started to call the PF—short for Perfect Family. The dad, Michael, was a critical care doctor working in downtown Philadelphia. He was passionate about a new device that Valerie didn't fully understand, but as he described it, it basically took over the essential functions of the body so the body could heal itself rather than deal with trauma directly. And his wife, Amy, was a seasoned physical therapist who'd practiced internationally as well as in pediatric hospitals but now ran a private practice that offered in-home care. Valerie decided that Amy was who she wanted to be when she grew up. Well, maybe some combination between Amy and Sylvia.

One of the things Valerie had picked up on earlier was that the river dictated their progress a lot more than any human visitor did. Some thrilling glimmers she'd launched on the trip with still remained, but most lost their luster after two hours of sitting awkwardly in a raft designed for either incredibly short, stocky people or expert yogis with greater flexibility than she had. Her knees developed a nagging pain that, by the time they pulled off the river for lunch, had invariably invaded her calves and hips. She was glad to stand and stretch her legs fully, and the sand, warmed by the morning sun, felt fantastic between her toes. During that day's lunch, the only thing that kept her mind from focusing entirely on her stiff legs was Maggie.

Maggie had been true to her word about having a lot of questions about Valerie's work life. She plopped down in a camp chair next to Valerie and peppered her with eager questions. But Valerie had played enough rounds of Twenty Questions with her kids to know there was a huge difference between knowing how to frame a question and how to engage in conversations spurred by those questions. Maggie knew how to engage in rich conversation. Talking to Valerie about her professional attainment with someone so interested in it created something Valerie didn't realize she'd lost—pride in her work.

Ever since she'd left the full-time job with her last firm, her skills as a technical writer were nothing more than a way to keep herself competitive and pay for a few extras. Things like surprise stays at upscale lodges for anniversaries or kids' braces. She worked for many reasons, but since she had shifted to freelance work, her focus had been on pleasing clients well enough that they wouldn't abandon her for the any number of cheaper options. Like the growing artificial intelligence route. Once AI text generators picked up a little more nuance in style and variety, her work would have to shift a lot.

But the conversation with Maggie didn't feel like an informational interview. She'd done those at the high school. The difference was, Valerie decided as she stretched down toward her toes to ease her sore hamstrings, that Maggie showed as much interest in her as she did in the information Valerie gave her. As engrossed as they were in conversation, it didn't take long for Maggie to thank Valerie for the great chat and leave to work on lunch, leaving Valerie to look for her family.

"That rock could basically have floated across the river, it was so flat. And you just got two skips? Seriously?" Valerie overheard Evie tease David.

Valerie picked up a smooth stone from the quiet shallow water by the bank and trotted over to them. "Who wants to bet I can't skip this six times?" She asked bending her knees and getting some practice swings with her arm.

"Yeah, right. If you count skips at the bottom of the river," Evie teased her, getting an impressive run with the rock she'd just skipped.

"Prepare to be amazed!" Valerie let the rock fly, which made an impressive first skip but disappeared below the surface once it hit the river the second time. "Okay, so I count that as three, and did you see how far it skipped? That's got to count for something right?"

"That sounds more like changing what success looks like. Isn't that some managerial technique you business types throw around?" David said, sidling behind Valerie with his own rock to skip. He wrapped his arms over Valerie's shoulders and grabbed her throwing hand. "I think you need to loosen up a bit. Sway with me." David moved with Valerie, shifting their weight backward and forward while he moved her arm in slow practice sweeps.

"Gosh, get a room you two," Evie said, acting disgusted but fighting a grin all the same.

"Consider yourself lucky to have parents who actually like each other. Okay. One, two, three, now!" David said.

Valerie let go of the rock, and it sank without skipping once.

"Yeah, much better that time, Dad. Excellent training," Evie shouted at David.

"Well, your dad didn't have much to work with anyway. Thanks for trying, honey. My knees are pretty sore. I'm going back to my camp chair for a while. See you later," she said, giving David a quick hug.

Valerie knew that if Evie was going to warm up to either of her parents, it was much more likely to be her dad. She shivered involuntarily and wrapped her arms across her chest—the thought an uncomfortable one. Some of the strands of worry and shame remained too tightly wound across her chest to be unraveled by a simple morning spent in a raft. She'd read about daughters feeling there was a competition with their mothers until later in life. Valerie hoped she'd last long enough for Evie to come around.

That afternoon, the cooking crew whipped up a surprisingly elaborate lunch—elaborate, considering all the cooking and food supplies had to fit in a few coolers and be stowed on the rafts. Spinach salad with fresh melon slices was exactly what the warming summer day called for. They even had iced coffee. She almost felt guilty about eating better on the river than she did with her family at home—meals prepared using every appliance and convenience she could ever need or want. She made a mental note to add this particular meal to her regular routine, especially because it would be so easy to add chicken separately for her, David, and Thomas. Evie could enjoy it vegetarian style.

After the chatting that morning and the questions with Maggie, Valerie was grateful for the long, leisurely lunch breaks the trip built into the schedule. She needed some downtime to cool off her introverted, overstimulated brain. She walked a few dozen yards away from the group and found a spot partially screened by tall grasses and reeds with a nice large sun patch that she stretched out in.

Direct sunlight was something hard to come by within the deep canyon, and Valerie imagined that many areas along their course over the next couple of days would be shaded most of the day, staying cool even late into the summer. She rolled up her shirt sleeves and pants hems and took off her hiking sandals. Inside her hidden, sunny stretch of beach, sunlight radiated through her skin and warmed her chilled arms.

A bird sounded up the canyon. The river's gentle gurgle soothed her, and she let go of the tension held around her eyebrows and in the deepening creases separating her lips and cheeks. For an anxious moment, she remembered deciding to leave her heavy retinol-rich facial cream in the car. Yet another way she could rough it, she redetermined. And maybe a subtle act of rebellion too. Evie and David would be forced to see her. Wrinkles and all.

But in that moment, as she took in the vast canyon walls that'd been chiseled over hundreds of millions of days like this one, she almost laughed out loud at the absurdity of caring about the slight crevices in her face—the absurdity of worrying about much of anything at all. A cool breeze hit her arm. With genuine fascination, she watched the way the breeze played with the hairs on her arm and was amazed to see goosebumps appear, caused by the shock of cold in the presence of the otherwise warming sun. She paid silent tribute to her body's amazing ability to regulate itself without her needing to do anything. Day in and day out, her lungs inflated and deflated in their regular course with hardly any notice from her conscious awareness. She flexed her legs and wriggled her toes. Her feet were ready for her any time she needed them. What an interesting thing—to realize her own insignificance while also recognizing what an incredible machine she was.

And for once, she didn't cling to the moment. Maybe it was her presence amid such clear evidence of geological time that drove her to realize that even if she could hold on to memories, her time on the planet was minuscule. Whether she lived to be a hundred or she died tomorrow, the space of time wouldn't even register as a mark on the canyon walls, which dealt in millennial timelines. Even the trees standing prominently on ridgetops would take in many human lifetimes during theirs. So she didn't matter in the grand natural saga she saw at play. The one that had been at play for millions of years before her and would outlive her for billions more. Why, then, did she feel more connected to the scene, not less? How was it possible that she didn't resent the natural order that dictated her own insignificance and called for her moment on that stage to be so tragically brief? Yet she didn't resent that fact. Not at that moment at least. Reverence was what she felt most, mixed with a beautiful excitement brimming with possibility. She would live her brief and insignificant life to the fullest, come what may.

She lay in the filtered sunlight now provided underneath a massive ponderosa pine that smelled deliciously like vanilla. As she gazed out over the wide bend in the river from the corner of her eye, she caught the slightest movement. She turned and found a small black spider sprinting in spurts along the crust of a rock. Again, she realized what a small piece of the entire worldly experience she was—even though she was a thousand times larger than that spider. She knew, perhaps more powerfully than ever before, how many other living things were moving and striving and dying around her, all in the same moments that she breathed in and out, looking at the beautiful expanse of mountain and rock and water and trees.

"Okay, folks, let's get back on the river. Our next stop will be our camping spot for the night, and I guarantee you, it'll blow your mind," Valerie heard Nate say from near the rafts, about a hundred yards or so away.

She stood up and dusted the sand off her body, keeping her arms and legs exposed to take in more sun as they continued down river. Barefoot, she slowly made her way back to the rafts, swinging each sandal by a strap. She caught David's eye, and he waved and gave her a boyish and excited smile. How was it possible that he was still so innately excited to see her after so many years? She waved back and read the curious look on his face. It reminded her of the look he wore when he tackled the Sunday *New York Times* crossword puzzle. Living with someone for so many years and genuinely enjoying nearly all of that time would do that to someone—make it possible to pick up on changes in their loved one's presence. Not requiring changes in their tone of voice or haircut to signal a significant shift in mindset.

Valerie walked right up to David who stood at the edge of the bank, waiting for things to be loaded into the rafts, and wrapped her arms around his waist, nestling her face against his chest.

"Well, hello. I guess that lunch break was good for you?" David said suggestively, wrapping his arms around Valerie's back and rubbing her shoulders with a thumb.

"Definitely good for me. And maybe good for you later tonight. Who knows."

David craned his neck to bring his face against the crest of Valerie's ear lobe. "Scandalous," he whispered, his breath tickling the nape of her neck.

She nodded, grinning. "Let's get this boat ride done first," she said, reaching up to plant a kiss.

Later that afternoon, they pulled off at a long bend where the river widened substantially, providing a broad beach with a wide-angle view of the russet canyon walls and a few layers beyond those tucked into the purple mist hanging over the distant mountains.

Evie spent the time before dinner drawing in a notebook. Having finished storing her belongings in their tent, Valerie started toward her, then stopped. What point was there in being thrown aside again? It was better not to seem too eager to see Evie's work. Maybe one day she would show it to Valerie on her own, and Valerie could share her past love of drawing—her considerable skill at it, come to think about it—with her daughter.

Why is it that kids are so reluctant to take advantage of their parents' expertise? Maybe it is unavoidable. Refusing expertise. A sad artifact of the human species. Pushing so hard to prove one's own worth that we undervalue the people closest to us.

But in that setting, where the low-crashing sounds of the river slipped past the towering canyon walls just before the sun tucked behind them for the night, leaving just the reflected warmth and indirect light behind, Valerie was tired of being undervalued. She couldn't control the way others valued her, not even her own daughter, but she could control the value she had for herself. And a part of that, she was learning, came from asking for things she wanted. She turned back toward her daughter.

"Hey, Evie! Show me what you've got so far." Valerie approached Evie from a respectful distance but without any of the regular tiptoeing.

Evie automatically reverted to tightly holding her notebook against her chest. She spun around on the flat boulder she was sitting on that looked out to a small hidden side channel of the river that squeezed into the canyon. A shaft of light illuminated what was tucked behind the front row of the canyon walls. Valerie was instantly intrigued by the setting and some part of her longed to explore the other side of that canyon.

As she stood near Evie, she saw how the river wound its way around the near ridge. Beyond that, three other ridges hid with only the upper portions visible. While she watched, the puffs of clouds gained new color and the sky brightened. She saw the top of those ridges and thought about the adventures she would have with her daughter and her husband as they wound their way around those hidden depths and ridges. She would be exploring those adventures with her favorite people on the planet. Despite the pain Evie caused her, that was definitely still true. Her love for her daughter was still iron clad. That same thrill that had activated when she went down those first rapids rose inside her again. "You have an amazing eye for subjects. That hidden canyon makes even me want to be an adventurer and mountain climber, to explore what's beyond these canyon walls."

Valerie fought the urge to laugh at seeing the clear dilemma Evie went through as she determining her response. There was the immediate brightening of her eyes and an engaged tilt to her head, but also a stiffening of her lips and some activation of her lower eyelids that spoke of her suspicion. Still, after all of that, there was a curiosity and maybe a bit of hope. Valerie could work with that.

"I really liked the light," Evie said. "I didn't know if I could show the shift in light while also showing the shadows against the river. Water is hard to draw, especially in pencil."

"I absolutely agree. My art professor in college always got after me for showing too many details and not the right ones to portray the flow of the water. I'm not sure if I ever got it quite right."

Evie gave a slight nod and looked down at her notebook as if she were only just aware that she was holding it so hard against her chest. She loosened her grip.

"Then again, my professor would've also gotten after me for assuming there is a right way with art. So who knows. Anyway, glad you found a challenge. That's the best way to get better." Valerie turned to leave.

"It's not finished yet. But you can look at it if you want."

A chill ran down Valerie's back that electrified her at the invitation. She walked the few yards between her and Evie—a distance that was so easily crossed. A few seconds of directed steps. The only difficult part of taking those steps was being invited closer. Only humans had the delicacy of emotional attunement to offer that invitation, or sense its rejection, in the nuanced way it was proffered to Valerie. She hoped that her eagerness didn't show in her legs as she crossed over the invisible barrier that Evie kept up so firmly. She rested on the edge of Evie's boulder and waited to be invited closer.

Evie held out her leatherbound notebook, opened to the page she was working on. With her first glance at the sketch, Valerie knew she wasn't the only person being undervalued. "Wow, Evie. How on earth did you capture the light so well using just pencil? Seriously." Valerie's response was the only response she knew how to give as she looked at the sophisticated way Evie had used negative space to create the appearance of light in contrast to the dark water. And what thrilled Valerie most was that the praise she felt was genuine, unfiltered and unconstrained.

Evie smiled and impulsively started rubbing the back of her neck with her free hand. "It's not all that, Mom. Still a lot of work to do."

"I know that. You've had what? Thirty minutes to work on it so far? So obviously you're not done. But you haven't answered my question. How did you go about deciding on the negative space to bring out the light?"

Evie pulled the notebook into her lap and scrutinized it for a few moments before responding. "I guess I saw that light is just the absence of darkness, right? So if I wanted to show a beam of light, I just needed to fill in everything except for the light. If that makes any sense? It made more sense in my head," Evie said with a nervous laugh.

Valerie smiled, holding back the laughter that built up inside of her at seeing Evie laugh around her for the first time in so long. What made it even richer was that she had been the reason why. "I think you're on to something there. Strong work." Valerie shifted her weight as she started to stand. Out of the side of her eye, she picked up a slight movement from her daughter and watched Evie stiffen.

"I didn't remember that you had art classes in college."

It was just a statement. A true statement. A fact. Such a simple one at that. It implied the idea that someone hadn't given conscious awareness to statements given in the past. It dawned on Valerie that statements are the scaffolding of relationships. Their health or distance, depth or lack of gravity, warmth or longing to be understood were based on simple statements like the one her daughter had just said. Even seconds later, that freeze frame's full intensity was gone, the memory catalogued and sorted in each woman's mind for ongoing interpretation and possible recall.

It was also another offering for Valerie to gratefully embrace. She turned her full weight toward Evelyn and gladly gave her attention too. "A couple of them. Yeah, it was a part of my communications program. At the time, I didn't understand why technical writers would have to take figure-drawing classes, with all of the awkwardness of nude art models to deal with and everything, but those classes ended up being some of my favorites."

"Why were they your favorite. Shouldn't your major courses be your favorites?"

"Hmm... insightful question. I'm sure my twentysomething self wouldn't express it this way, but having twenty years to think it over, I guess they were my favorites because they challenged me, which was exciting. I mean, consider learning about perspective and color theory versus the rules for commas. Both important, one *way* more stimulating."

Evie laughed again. This time it appeared to have come more naturally too.

"And I think another part of it was that I felt like I was learning a craft. You know how much I used to love watching that woodworking show on PBS?"

"Yeah. I assumed you had a thing for the host. What was his name again? Norm Abrahms or something?"

"I dug his beard, that's for sure. But there's something about being able to step back and see what you've created."

Valerie looked down at her daughter, close enough now to pick up on the nearly imperceptible sheen of short golden brown hairs that graced Evie's cheek and shone warm and bright in the cacophony of ripples from the river. They sat silent for a good while, enjoying together the background music of river and wind within trees and the distant murmurs from the rafting groups as they got excited for what smelled like a marvelous meal. Valerie took a risk then. It was another element necessary to shore up the relationship scaffolding. To throw her offering at the feet of her daughter in hopes that the structure they were building would someday be strong enough. Because of risks like these.

Valerie brushed a few stray strands of Evie's summer bleach-blond highlights back beneath her ear and bent down to give her a gentle kiss on the forehead, right where a scar remained from some emergency long forgotten.

Evie leaned toward her, Valerie ready to receive her into the embrace she had been hoping would come for so long. Valerie's neck perfectly accommodated the side of Evie's face, allowing her to drop her chin in her daughter's wild and full mess of hair and smell the sunlight that emanated from it.

"Dinner is ready folks! Come and get it while it's hot!" Nate called out from where the rest of the group sat in camp chairs.

The moment couldn't last forever. Moments never could, nor should they, Valerie decided as she helped Evie to her feet and then started to walk with her arm still around Evie's shoulder. Another freeze frame. A few more statements exchanged. A bit of reinforcement to the scaffolding. A memory to store and to recall, for whatever might come.

That night, Evie headed to their tent as soon as it got dark, in order to, as she put it, spill her thoughts about the day into her journal. Valerie had gotten to know a few of the members of the other rafting groups that night, and to help her remember what story was attached to which person, she reviewed what she'd learned with David.

"So there was Cassie—a.k.a. Cassandra but don't call her that because it's way too formal. She's the Finance VP, right?" Valerie rattled off while poking a stick into the fire's coals, sending off bright sparks into the dark sky.

"I think so. I kind of get her and Terre mixed up. Terre is the HR manager though, right?"

"Right. And Terre grew up in Taos, New Mexico, and is disgusted by how posh and touristy the town has gotten."

"That's what stuck about her? For me, it was her telling us that she had a home in Taos, another in Aspen, and still another in Italy," David mused, throwing the segments of a stick he'd been methodically breaking into progressively smaller pieces into the fire. A few flames rose out of the ruddy coals.

"Oh, right. That too," Valerie smiled, giving David a playful shove that almost knocked him over in his camp chair.

"Whoa! Careful! I think my legs have finally recovered from sitting in that raft for so long."

"Sorry! I didn't mean to push you that hard."

"Don't know your own superstrength. It's common enough with superheroes, I've heard," David said, adjusting his chair in the several inches of sand, supposedly to make his chair more stable.

It also brought him close enough to Valerie that his tanned, hairy leg bumped right up against her leg, which could probably use a shave. *Yet another way of roughing it*, she thought.

Valerie and David let the night's stillness settle over them, and by the time she looked up from the mesmerizing smoldering coals, she found that she and David were the last people on the beach. She looked up at the shaft of visible sky that rose above the dark canyon walls and let out a deep and rewarding sigh. As she took in her next breath, it was as if she took in a renewal of the vitality she'd felt earlier that day. A current of energy rippled down her back and legs, and she shivered even though the air was still warm from the sunlight-baked rocks and sand. She slipped on her sandals and braced herself to jump out of her chair in a moment of delicious spontaneity. She kicked a wave of sand on the coals.

"Hey I was enjoying that—"

Valerie leaped from her chair and onto David's lap with an agility that surprised her. In the lush air, moist with rising river mist, she felt timeless and real and heathy and eager. She knocked the chair over, and David fell backward, seemingly in slow motion, as the chair lost the fight against gravity slowly in the sand. David's breathing was hot and urgent as Valerie brought her face close, her chest pressing down on his, making it hard for her to tell whose excited heartbeats were whose. She found his lips for a moment, then whispered into his ear, "Catch me if you can."

Valerie sprang away from the chair and sprinted away from him, throwing off her shirt before disappearing into the darkened tree cover. At first, David lay startled with his head resting in the beach sand, then he made an awkward backward-somersault move, rolling to his side and standing, shaking the sand out of his hair.

He dashed after Valerie.

Valerie stifled giggles at seeing David's struggle to escape his chair from her hiding spot—a soft, spongy bowl that had formed when a tree had fallen years before, the remnants of which had broken back down to enrich the soil she rested her toes against, naked and expectant.

The moon pierced the dark with cool light that shifted through the layers of shadows. When David was close enough for her to see the determination in his eyes, she silently lifted herself out of the negative space and crept forward, goosebumps flooding her body as a cool breeze brushed against her exposed skin.

Valerie walked to the opposite side of the clearing where David still searched for her, his eyes flashing. She stepped forward into a pool of moonlight that made her already pale skin look alabaster. The moon's gaze down on her, gave an iridescent glow to all of her curves. The curve of her chest, the rise of her shoulders and calves, and the imperceptible divot under her nose that separated the ridges of her lips. Her bare legs shivered slightly, and she swayed, shifting her weight from side to side nervously, realizing this was the first time she had ever been so exposed or felt so vulnerable—or needed such a deeply rooted connection.

A thrill ran through her when she caught her husband's eyes—those eyes that could look past her stubborn love handles and the proportions of her hips. In that precious suspended fraction of time, she realized this was the reward that came from paying the price for emotional connection. She and her husband had built that. Together. They looked past roads not taken, even other lovers who might have seemed appealing from time to time. They could never have provided the security she felt in that moment. She was seen. She was known. She was loved. She was adored by a good man.

David approached her with a determined but deliberate step. Beads of sweat stood out on his forehead and arms as he strode toward her in the same cool light silhouetting the tips of her breasts that rose and fell with each catch of breath. He wrapped his arms around the small of her back, drawing her toward him. His tenderness and care for her satisfaction was something she had always appreciated about him. But strangely, that night, she didn't want to explain or even express through subtle body language what she wanted or needed. And the only way she could be satisfied in that primal moment was if David was in sync and desired the same heightened sensations. Sensations that she had never known to hope to feel before.

Valerie drew her face to David's chest, feeling the familiar brush of his chest hair. But then, with her arms around his waist, she playfully pulled down his shorts, and before he had any time to react, her body was against his, matching the alcoves of elbows and chins and pressing against anything that didn't fit perfectly. She pulled away and led David by the hand down to the hollow where she had hidden moments before, baffled at how a few seconds could extend forever when she let go of time and shed her future worries with savage disregard, rejuvenating a new sense of life and possibility.

David must have caught the spell or signal because, when they had climbed down into the bowl, perfectly designed to hold two people, he lifted Valerie off her feet by tucking one arm under her knees and the other behind her back. She had draped her arm around his neck, thinking she'd need to brace herself to help him lift her, self-conscious for just a second about her weight, but pleasantly surprised by how completely he carried her to the loamy forest floor.

He crawled his fingertips across Valerie's exposed back and shoulders and the slight slant that transitioned from her back to the rise of her hip. She was startled and thrilled to think that David's meticulous accounting-brain probably stored figures like the number of moles and scars and gentle imperfections the backside of her body offered him to analyze. He knew that part of her better than she would ever know it. That realization touched a deep nerve-ending that tickled her spine and brought her back completely to the moment. That beautiful, desperate, frantic moment of visceral pleasure and connection.

They moved in a synchrony that mirrored the sigh and sway of the pines that stood on the cliffs far above them. A deer padded past, paying little attention to the most natural thing two humans ever did in the short timeline of the human species, their genetic code designed over hundreds of thousands of years to arrive at an instant just like the one Valerie was experiencing. The triumph of the human body richly rewarding nature's experiment with a rush of its most generous chemical reactions and released neurotransmitters, filling Valerie with a flood of warmth, closeness, and deep abiding joy.

After that stretch of fervent searching and longing, Valerie rested with David, leaning against the gentle incline of the hollow's walls, both looking to the sliver of sky they could make out among the trees and canyon walls and feeling the afterglow of intense physical exertion and the endorphins that lingered within their tired, satisfied bodies.

Most people don't get this far. She knew that for sure. She had surmounted Maslow's hierarchy and given a primordial shout from the precipice. Whatever might happen from then on out, her ledger for life was clearly and gratefully in the black. It was enough.

Middle Fork of the Salmon River

August, 2024

 *Seedlings that were overly optimistic about the future, who shot up from the poor soil in hopes of embracing the sunlight, didn't last long, the pine had observed. It attributed its own longevity to its measured existence. It didn't get excited when things worked out better than it hoped, but it was also rarely disappointed. It let the small sphere of the world around it come as the physics of nature dictated.*

MAGGIE WOKE UP WELL BEFORE THE FIRST INCONSISTENT GRAY light shone down on the canyon, and the first thing she noticed was the smell of burning trees. She'd smelled wood smoke plenty of times. They'd had a campfire the night before, and some of that smoke had made her hair thick, as if she'd used some earthy hair-volumizing cream.

But she'd spent enough time in the wilderness to know that wildfire smoke carried with it a menagerie of smells. Plants let out different smells when consumed by fire. Some bushes, like sagebrush, smelled amazing when burned, while others let out the acridest of odors.

She tried to run her fingers through her hair, and when she could only get a few inches in without serious snags, she decided it would be a good day for a river bath. Sitting up in her small tent, she pulled on her jacket and struggled to put on her boots. She peered out her tent when she first unzipped the door part way. It was already warm enough that she could leave the jacket behind, but since she already had it on, she kept it on.

The smoke was carried by a warm westerly wind. It struck her as odd, having wind in the morning in the canyon. Usually, gusts only kicked up in the afternoon. Fire was a common occurrence in the Frank Church Wilderness, partly because of the wilderness's size, which meant a portion of it almost always burned during the summer. The way the Forest Service had chosen to manage the landscape also increased fire's existence in the area.

Maggie was always a fan of letting the forest do its thing rather than pretending modern science knew how to take better care of it than Mother Nature. But it was easier to champion fire's natural role on Western landscapes when she wasn't on that burning landscape. She ordinarily resented the fact that one night of the rafting trip was spent at the lodge along the river, but with the distinct smell of burning trees so close at hand, she was glad she'd be around other people and have at least some perception of protection against the wildfire. She pushed aside the reality that no amount of people or the lodge's quaint farming fields could stand against a large fast-moving fire.

She climbed out of her tent and zipped the tent door behind herself. She was pleased to see she was up well before any crew members. Crouching to do up the d-ring hooks of her boots but not bothering to tie the laces, she felt the cold, dry sand against the palms of her hands as she braced herself to stand.

Then she found a discarded T-shirt. *Wasn't Valerie wearing this yesterday?* Valerie really didn't strike her as the kind of person who would leave clothes lying around. Not to say that she really knew who Valerie was. But Maggie felt like she knew her better than the amount of time they had spent together would normally allow.

Her boots crunched softly on the sand, and doing her best to not think about the possible scenarios that would lead to Valerie discarding her T-shirt, she draped it over a branch near Valerie's tent, where Maggie was certain she would see it. Maggie smiled as she realized she was getting a similar feeling to the one she used to have as a teenager when, from time to time, the odd recognition struck that her parents had sex sometimes too. Wandering upstream, she searched for a small inlet she'd come across the day before, just as they'd pulled off the main current.

She followed a roughly defined game trail that skirted along the river about a mile, her mind in that muffled headspace where it was easier to just focus on the path ahead of her. Once she plunged into the frigid river inlet, that cozy, muffled openness that was free from worry or to-do lists for the day would be gone. So she enjoyed it as much as she could. Now that her body was moving, the warmth of her jacket was more than she needed, but that too, was a nice thing. The river would be cold. Later in the day, when she was soaked by the river spray and in the shadowy areas so common in the canyon, some part of her would long for the feeling of warmth, the kind her jacket brought her right then.

The inlet she was searching for appeared off to the right. The small tributary curved to the left after a hundred yards or so, and Maggie followed it as it rose—the water tumbling down dozens of meager cataracts surrounded by green willow trees that enjoyed the perpetual access to water. As she climbed above the river, following a path that hugged the foot of the rugged mountain that jutted up on both sides of the stream, she discovered standing, dead trees left over from a fire that must have whipped through the river drainage. But underneath the skeletal snags, the canyon floor was flush with a green understory of grasses and a flurry of lodgepole pines that crowded the gray trunks of burned-out sentinels with blackened gouges carved out of them like some bronze public-art sculptures Maggie remembered seeing when she'd visited Chicago as a kid.

Eventually, she came to a place where the river was calmer with several deep pools scattered around an open area covered in scree and lush grasses. She took off her jacket, and unhooked her boots, kicking them off in front of a startlingly clear pool tucked away from the main tributary's cheery gurgling sound. Her lungs constricted with a shocked intake of breath as she took her first step into the icy water. She slipped out of her other clothes and hesitated. The water would be utterly unbearable at first. Maybe for the first minute or two even. Some part of her would scream for her to get out and seek comfortable, easier temperatures.

But she also knew that as she took a couple more steps into the pool, if she had the courage to stick it out, she'd experience, what she sought when taking early morning dips into unnamed tributaries—a ritual she stuck to each time she wandered down the river to find some hidden offshoot and then plunged into its cool and clarifying depths. That heightened awareness of living in that exact place and time—stripped of everything else. Rent, relationships, expectations, and that lurching awareness of her inadequacies. She could rest in the cold present, naked and complete.

So she leaned forward into just enough predawn gray to provide an opaque reflection of her face as she let gravity fully submerge her. The pool was deeper than it appeared—the refraction of light squeezing the distance of the pool from top to bottom. She sank to the bottom, and her toes caressed the smooth firmness of the stones wedged securely in the river mud. Finding a spot unburdened by rock, she dug her big toes a couple of inches into the mud and was surprised to feel pockets of warmth brush past her ankles as air was released.

She burst to the surface of the water and welcomed air to her lungs—air which was much warmer than the pool. She flipped to her back, gently flicking her fingers to scull across the water, her arms fully outstretched to her sides. She gazed up at the varying shades of gray with the slightest beginnings of blue as the morning sky warmed the day and goosebumps overspread her body.

This was it. The sensation she looked forward to the most on these river-guiding trips. The time when she could be alone and have the extreme coldness and beauty of the river beat down her misgivings of the life she had built for herself. Deep down, she knew her life was her own making. No petty excuses about a lack of parental care or support fit the immensity of space and feeling she got from places like these.

She basked in her full awareness, somehow paying more attention to everything—her breath, once again falling into a comfortable rhythm after braving those first minutes of extreme chill; the way the quivering ripples danced against her skin and flowed between her legs and under her arms; the low rumble of the river. Yet not giving a name to or weighing the significance of every thought or feeling that came and went as easily as water molecules flowing downstream.

A new thought started to pervade her consciousness. An awareness that she wouldn't return to this place. She'd felt similar feelings before, and had come to terms with the fact that she would probably never visit the same tributary. But this felt different. It had more finality to it. It was time to leave the river, as a guide at least. She hoped to visit sometime down the road. Maybe as a tourist. Wouldn't that be a thrill? To see people like Nathan, how she used to be, guiding her for a change.

How she used to be.

There was some layer of sadness that came with the thought of moving on to other things. But as Maggie rose out of the pool, feet stable, knowing how to walk in rivers, each step forward brought conviction to her new path. She rested on the bank with legs outstretched and elbows supporting the weight of her torso. She let the air dry her skin and bring her body temperature back up. She put on her clothes and boots and draped her jacket over her arm. With a soft breath, she took one last look at the serene scene where she had spent the best part of her day, grateful that such places existed even if she wouldn't return, grateful to know there were many other beautiful places she would see because of her willingness to leave this one behind.

By the time Maggie got back to camp, a couple of staff members were warming up skillets and pulling out food supplies for breakfast. She jumped into the familiar breakfast-making routine. She cracked a dozen eggs into a skillet and swished the yellow contents around.

"Hey, Mags. Beat me to the start, yet again," Nathan said, reaching around Maggie to grab a basket of mushrooms and effortlessly putting a hand on the side of her waist as if it were the most natural thing in the world.

"Hey, Nathan. Why don't we grab lunch when we get back to Boise. You live there, right? Isn't it crazy that we've been down the river a dozen times and I don't even know where you live?"

"That is kind of crazy. I'd love to get lunch. Why don't you let a staff member drive your rig back to Boise, and we can ride together?"

"Sounds great. Thanks. Sure thing," Maggie said, hoping that her eagerness didn't play out as clearly on her face as it was shouting inside her mind.

"Eggs..."

"What?"

"Your eggs are burning." Nathan pointed, moving to pull the skillet off the propane burner.

Maggie grabbed the skillet off the heat before Nathan had the chance to and laughed nervously. Nathan smiled and left to move some food to the waiting card tables , Maggie feeling quite foolish. *I still have a lot to figure out about adulting.* She sighed.

Maggie brought the partially crispy eggs to the table and set out some mugs for coffee.

"Morning!"

Maggie looked up at Evelyn, who was sipping her mug and trying to play cool. She knew Evelyn was keen on impressing her, but she realized for the first time that she would have behaved exactly the same way Evelyn was if she were still her age—unsure of who she was or what she cared about, assuming a particular older person had what she wanted: confidence, comfort in her own skin, an adventurous lifestyle away from family ties. If only Evelyn knew how many times Maggie had questioned her path within the last week or how nicc it would feel to have a closer connection to her family, especially to her mom.

"Morning! How'd you sleep?"

"Okay, I guess. I think I'm finally getting used to sleeping in a tent."

"That's fast work. We've only been on the river four nights now. Nicely done. Would you like some eggs?"

"Sure. Back at home, I'm kind of trying the vegan thing, but when in Rome, right?"

"Yeah, you'll need that protein to power some strong paddle strokes today." Maggie gave Evie a warm smile and a spatula full of scrambled eggs and then turned to get some other breakfast items.

When Maggie saw Valerie climb out of her tent, she stood still, watching as Valerie scrutinized her shirt's placement on the branch. Maggie almost laughed out loud at the confused look on her face, as she clearly tried to remember why her shirt was resting on a branch outside her tent. She swallowed a chuckle at the furtive sideway glances and embarrassed giggle as her recollection came. Valerie had had a good night, Maggie guessed.

"Okay, folks. Dig in. We'll be shoving off in about an hour," Nathan announced. "We'll be staying the night at the lodge, as you know, so feel free to stay smoky and maybe a bit stinky for one more day because you'll have hot running water tonight."

And that hot water was most gratefully used by Maggie after they had finished the long day of navigating the river. She pulled on some yoga pants and a T-shirt and slipped on her running shoes without bothering to put on socks, then wandered out of her room to the outdoor dining area with her hair still dripping. A dozen picnic tables stood underneath hanging white lights. She knew her dark-brown hair that was frizz-prone would be completely unmanageable the next morning, but that was one nice thing about rafting in a wilderness. Few people expected her hair to be done up after going through rapids. She let the sound of the river and cool breeze lull her to a soft place of unawareness, thankful that, for the moment, she didn't have to be in charge of anything or anyone.

A peal of laughter brought her back to the scene around her. She glanced behind her shoulder at the remodeled lodge, which spoke of rustic living in façade only. In her room, terry cloth towels and robes, electricity and internet, were all standard fare. It was an odd thing to be in a place designed to cater to people of wealth when she couldn't afford to fix her car, and the purchase of Honeycrisp apples, rather than the plain old Red Delicious, was a splurge.

The laughter was coming from a group congregating around a man wearing the firefighter's yellow Nomex shirt and dark-green pants and scarred, heavy leather boots. She strolled toward the group, going for casual, fully aware, however, of her lack of grace that most of the wealthy people she knew carried. As she got closer, she picked up on fragments of the conversation.

"So this guy is totally a city slicker to the core. I mean, he wouldn't know a cow from a goat. That meant he had no clue how to back up a truck with a trailer..."

Maggie sank onto the bench of a picnic table near the back of the group and rested her head in her hands, propped up by her elbows.

"But his response when I asked if he'd ever done it before? He was like, 'Well, yeah. I mean, of course, right?' So I had to decide how much damage he might do to the truck or trailer and whether making him into an example would be worth the cost. Guess which way I went with that?"

Several people shouted responses at the same time.

"You let him have it!"

"Teach him a lesson."

"I'm sure it was good for him!"

"That's right. I took him at his word. And do you know what happened?" This firefighter had the whole group in the palm of his hand by then.

Like the crowd, Maggie was soon drawn into the story and this guy's charisma.

"He couldn't even get the rig out of the warehouse! After he'd banged it against multiple walls, I rescued him from his embarrassment. I doubt he'll ever forget that driving lesson."

The crowd cheered and laughed appreciatively at the end of the story, and many individuals went up to talk to the firefighter individually, once the group broke into more isolated pairings. Maggie watched the firefighter interact with each person as if he had known them for years. She could see how drawn to him they were. And she understood the appeal. The firefighter had that rugged rogue look down perfectly, with his beard that only fit on his face even though she was certain he had done nothing to maintain it for weeks. The dark bushy eyebrows that overshadowed his eyes brought a sense of mystery to them in a very intriguing way. But his eyes remained sharp and clear. When he listened to the many people who approached him, she got the sense that he was engaging with them in an active and intense way, as if they were the only people on earth at that moment.

Keep it together! He's got to be old enough to be your dad! Maggie shook her head and cleared her throat and was just about to escape back to her room, when the firefighter saw her staring at him. She had nothing in her hands and no reason to be sitting there watching him, so she gave up trying to appear busy. Instead, she gave him a sheepish smile, and in return, he gave her a slight nod, which was accented by those piercing eyes.

She watched him say good night to the couple he was chatting with and give them both parting arm squeezes, and then he strode toward Maggie. She contemplated running but thought better of it. She tried to stay casual.

"Hello."

"Hi," she said.

"I'm Andy. Who are you?"

"I'm Maggie. I mean, my name is Maggie." Maggie shot out her hand awkwardly. "Nice to meet you."

"Whoa. I'm just a firefighter, not a CEO or trust-fund billionaire like most of these folks. Let's cut the formality, shall we?" Andy smiled warmly.

Maggie felt her guard slip, whether she wanted it to or not.

Andy still shook her extended hand, wrapped in both of his, then plopped down on the bench next to her. Seeming to let go of some invisible weight, he leaned back against the top of the table and let out a long sigh. "Can I be real with you?"

"That depends, I guess."

"That's fair. It's just I can play the part of the life of the cocktail party for about a half hour. Beyond that, my energy starts dying. I guess I'm a well-functioning introvert. So you can guess where I'm at after a full day of this sort of thing here."

Maggie let out a snort for a laugh, which made both of them laugh even harder.

"How long have you been, what? Stationed? Is that the word? How long have you been staying here?" she asked.

"Got here yesterday morning. Just trying to update the guests and river guides about the Greenfield Ranch Fire. What brings you to this rich-man's-attempt-at-the-rustic-life?"

Maggie was a bit startled that Andy had picked up the very thread she had been musing about when she'd first seen him.

"I'm a river guide, coincidentally. My group is spending a night here to connect with some modern conveniences, like running hot water and Wi-Fi."

"I hear that. A week is way too long to go without a connection to Instagram. I mean, what's the point of the wilderness if you can't livestream it?"

Andy had said it so matter-of-factly that Maggie wasn't sure if he was joking, and not wanting to take the wrong turn in the conversation, she just smiled and nodded.

"I'm totally joking. Boy, sometimes there really are generational differences. Mine is famous for playground bullies and horrible nicknames. Yours is more known for considering offense as the cardinal sin."

Maggie bristled a bit at the characterization. "I think it's fair to say that neither of us knows what the other is like. So maybe it's not wise to generalize."

"Excellent! You do have some opinions then. I like it! And your statement even rhymed. Nice! Have you ever tried rapping?" This time Andy raised his eyebrows and grinned to help Maggie know he wasn't serious. "I bet river guiding is fun. Really tiring though. And I'd imagine you deal with a lot of entitled folks trying to teach their kids character and integrity overnight. How far off am I?"

"Pretty close, actually. Impressive. Have you ever been a river guide?" Maggie asked, leaning forward and toward Andy.

"No. But I've tagged along with our forest's river ranger a few times. I think I've picked up on the vibe."

"You're with the Forest Service, then?"

"Yeah, this is my twenty-first season. It's been a pretty good gig, all in all."

"And you've been fighting fire this whole time?"

"Yeah. Well, I guess up until this assignment. I'm doing PIO work right now."

"PIO?" Maggie asked with a blank look.

"Sorry. Fire and the Forest Service love their acronyms. Public Information Officer. Basically, I do my best to share information about fires with the public."

"I figured that, with a title like public information," she said, giving him a wry smile.

Andy was a bit slow to the draw but caught up and laughed. "I need a good night's sleep. Correction. Several good nights' sleep. My tired old brain isn't what it used to be, I guess."

Andy rubbed at his temples, and Maggie felt awkward sitting there. She'd almost decided to say good night and let Andy be alone, but then she caught the whiff of smoke again. It'd been such a constant presence all day that she'd almost gotten used to it.

"Can you tell me about this fire? I hope your job includes more than just entertaining wealthy resort patrons."

"Strike two for me. I should have gone through my spiel from the get-go. Gosh, I'm really not firing on all cylinders. Good thing I'm flying out tomorrow morning as are most of these guests, I think."

Andy pulled a worn map out of his cargo pants pocket and laid it out on the picnic table, grabbing a couple pieces of gravel to weigh it down against the breeze. He pointed to the map.

"This is our current location on the Middle Fork. I imagine you're heading toward the Salmon takeout, right?"

Maggie nodded as Andy dragged his finger along the blue squiggly line representing the river and made a circle around the town where her group would end up.

"That means you're a little over halfway there, right?"

Maggie nodded. Two more full days of rafting and then a short day to end things, she thought as she ran through their itinerary.

Andy pulled out a different map. This one was just a printout on legal-sized paper and much less detailed—it identified a few major landmarks and cities. But the most prominent portions of the map were big blocks of irregular shapes in bright red. Andy drew an X on a blue line that she recognized as their current location on the river. Andy didn't explain or mark anything else on the map, allowing her to figure things out on her own. It took her only a few seconds, but when the realization came, her heart rate picked up and her breathing instantly shallowed.

The blue line was so insignificant compared to the bleeding red splashed across the map that it looked as if the red were trying to devour the blue. Surveying the map, her first reaction was driven by fear and her biological desire for safety. But then logic started to seep back in. The fire extended easily twenty miles ahead of the course she would lead her tour group along.

"What direction is the fire heading?" she asked, standing up and grabbing Andy's pencil, ready to do some quick calculations.

"What way is the wind blowing?" Andy said, folding his arms and giving her a half-smile that made her feel like she was back in middle school and her teacher had just asked her a question to show how smart he was rather than to teach her anything.

She played along. "It looks like the wind is blowing in a northwest direction."

"Correct! And the wind's been blowing in that general direction for at least a week. In some cases, with serious velocity. The fire is going to head the same direction as the wind so long as there is fuel and no major barriers."

Maggie waited for Andy to say what she had already figured out, feeling like she needed to hear him say it.

"There's plenty of fuel between here and the fire perimeter. And the next barrier the fire is going to face will be the river," he said.

"But they wouldn't allow rafting tours to continue if the fire was heading right in their direction, right? I mean, they'd close the river if it was that much of a threat."

"Who's they?"

"The Forest Service. You guys. I don't know. The sheriff's office. Somebody!" Maggie's agitation was growing. "And, I've got to say, you have a horrible bedside manner. Is this how you do all your public information stuff?"

Andy tried to hide the smug look he was giving Maggie. "I'm sorry. It's kind of tough to transition from a firefighter's way of looking at a fire to the way people who don't get a thrill fighting it see it." Andy folded both maps and put them back in his pockets, then slowly sat back down at the picnic table. "That's one of the biggest things I'm realizing about this assignment. Everybody cheers on the firefighters. Towns put up posters and make food donations. They call us heroes. And running toward a fire is heroic. No doubt." Andy leaned back and closed his eyes thoughtfully. "But it's exciting too. You get that adrenaline pumping, and you grip your Pulaski or chainsaw with a gloved hand, ready to save the day, and you feel capable because you've gone through so many trainings and scenarios, readiness reviews and physical trainings. This is what you train for. It's like being tapped to make the winning three-pointer and feeling completely sure you can make that shot."

Andy looked up and gave Maggie a tired smile. "Which of course has nothing to do with what you asked. Sorry. The Forest Service doesn't close river access very often these days, for a couple of reasons. One is the river is in wilderness, and years ago, the agency decided that natural processes like fire should be allowed to run their course in wilderness areas. Especially in the Frank because it's probably the best known and, by some measures, the biggest wilderness in the country. At least in the lower forty-eight."

Andy pulled out a water bottle from yet another pocket in his pants. *How many pockets does this guy have?* Maggie thought.

"The other reason is a lot less admirable, I'm afraid. There's a ton of political pressure to keep the Frank open. The liberals push the agency to keep it natural, whatever that means, and the conservatives fight for the free enterprise and tax base that guided tours bring to the state. Oh, and of course, there is a lot of influence from the well-connected ranchers with homesteads along the river. How many issues do you know of that both sides of the political divide actually agree on?" Andy asked with raised eyebrows.

Maggie didn't say anything, but she nodded.

"Exactly. So, the policy is we don't put closure orders. We advise the public to make the best decision for their individual circumstances. I call it passing the buck, but there it is. Under other conditions, when we aren't at Preparedness Level 5—the highest level, which means we basically have no spare resources—we'd most likely help protect resources like this lodge and threatened landing strips. But, at this point, there aren't any extra resources available."

Andy waited to get some kind of response from Maggie, but she was still shocked to find herself in this situation. She was employed by a respected rafting company. Thousands of groups had gone down the Middle Fork before. And thousands of people with zero rafting experience had gone through such tours without so much as a scraped knee. Was she honestly in the path of a major inferno? It just didn't add up.

"So what are you going to do? I bet I can figure out a way to fly your rafting folks out with the other resort people tomorrow."

Maggie took a long time to respond. And when she did, she tried her best to keep a measured tone. She was tired. She needed time to sleep before making a decision. "We'll see in the morning. Thanks Mister PIO," Maggie said, standing and extending her hand again, this time in a less awkward way.

"That's a good answer. But please consider leaving. I don't care what kind of life-changing experiences those rafting groups are hoping for, it's not worth it—in my book anyway. The fire has slowed down a little these last two days, but remember, all it takes is for the wind to pick back up. There's plenty of fuel. Good night, Maggie." Andy shook Maggie's hand and gave her a genuine smile that spilled into the smile lines the many years of sweat and sun and exposure to the wind had etched in his expression.

"Good night." Maggie said, desperately hoping she'd have more clarity after sleeping in a bed much nicer than she could ever afford at home.

Luxuries were rare and appreciated on the windswept ridge—the animal remains at the pine's feet brought extra nutrients and nitrogen as the once-alive deer or squirrel or coyote slowly faded into the soil and into its roots. The occasional seedling that had survived long enough to connect its root system helped itself and others bolster against the wind and constant earthflows. These special things were never expected but always accepted with gratitude.

VALERIE HAD MIXED FEELINGS ABOUT SPENDING THE NIGHT AT the lodge. It felt like a step back from her attempt at closeness with Evie, and though she would never have said it to Evie, it always felt strange having a child share a hotel room with her and David. Not to say she had any desire to attempt anything intimate again, so soon after yesterday morning's surprise discovery—her discarded shirt, left for someone else to find. She was sure that person had put two and two together. Maybe that didn't matter. What was she really trying to hide anyway? She was a married adult. *Normal people have sex, right?* There wasn't anything unusual about that.

But even as the thought came to her, she knew it wasn't completely true. There had been something unusual about that night. It had been unusual in the best possible way. All day, she had felt the afterglow of being that connected to David, and he felt the same way. The simple look or smile he gave her throughout the day told her as much. Definitely worth dealing with a small dose of embarrassment, she decided.

What she needed now was some way to connect again, this time with her daughter. And as Valerie got up that morning and saw the bed next to hers already vacated, which probably meant that Evie was near the main lobby, relishing in a different kind of connection—to friends—through the indulgent Wi-Fi running right along the river in the middle of the largest contiguous wilderness in the lower forty-eight, she wondered how to do that.

Valerie had held concerns about the way social media simulated connection without real substance for years. Looking back, she was a part of the in-between generation—definitely not a Gen Xer, but not quite comfortable being called a millennial either. She'd grown up as computers and the internet rose to dominate life. She set up her Facebook account in college, back when it was only available for college students, and when all you could do on the site was post text and give so-called gifts like clipart PB&J sandwiches to friends. Facebook had been around for over twenty years now though.

Her kids would never live in a world knowing what a dramatic change these technologies had on human connection, and that caused a sadness inside Valerie that gnawed and festered. But being in the forest, falling asleep to the sounds of the river, feeling a primal connection to the wilderness and a deepening bond with the people she loved made that wound flare to a fierce degree. She wanted to give her kids the choice at least—to make up their own minds whether they wanted to "connect" in superficial ways that ate up their emotional stores or know what it was to be *seen*.

She wasn't opposed to technology. Goodness knows, her whole profession was based on technology. She was as "with it" as any Gen Z could be. She just wished Evelyn had lived a day without knowing she could get a slight pick-me-up from a like on a post— just enough dopamine and weak euphoria to get by.

That was one of the biggest problems in the world that her generation had built and her kids' generation had eagerly inherited. There were so many ways of making weak ties to people and things that those ties often felt like enough. People were addicted to likes and follows. She understood how easy it was to defend that addiction. She, too, had memories of rare-but-deep conversations with long-lost friends. Friends she would never have found or reconnected with if it weren't for social media.

As she sat up and gently caressed her toes against the plush carpet in her room, gazing blankly at the empty bed beside hers, she realized how much she missed going to the video-rental place to pick out a new release or ask the somewhat seedy-looking employee about her new favorites. She missed feeling lonely enough that when she got back to school in the fall, a jolt of happiness rolled through her as she hugged a friend who had been gone all summer. She longed for those summer days when she could safely assume that she'd find her daughter in a tree, reading a book. She wanted her daughter back. And perhaps the only hard thing about feeling so deeply seen—as she had been by her husband—was that it opened the door to gaping holes in other relationships that should have already been filled by deep ties that were rich in love and shared experiences.

She'd filled a few cracks with Evie the day before. Maybe she'd inch closer and fill a few more today. And sleeping on a memory foam mattress with goose down pillows meant she could stand up with no more than the regular annoying back pains that were a familiar part of being forty. And, before her was another day for her to work within her small sphere of influence and let the people around her know that she cared. That's what she would try to do.

"Morning." She heard David, who was clearly still half-asleep, say.

"Morning. I'm going for a short walk."

"I can get ready real fast and go with you."

"No. Just sleep." Valerie walked over to David's side of the bed, brushed the mussed hair out of his eyes and gave him a kiss, trying not to grimace at their morning breath. "I'll meet up with you at the picnic area for breakfast."

David smiled and raised a hand to wave, then rolled over, falling back to sleep. Valerie shut the door carefully so as not to wake him more, then zipped her jacket. She padded down the wooden steps and across the lawn that was saturated with enough dew for moisture to seep into her shoes. It was almost like having the pleasure of walking barefoot without the worry of stepping on something she shouldn't.

"What the hell are you doing there, Andy!"

Andy was very used to being yelled at by supervisors. But it hit him harder coming from the normally gentle Glen. He put the phone back to his ear, having pulled it away so he didn't impulsively say any of the things he wanted to say.

"Just my job, Glen."

"What job is that, exactly? Because I seem to remember distinctly telling you that we wouldn't discourage people from using the river or the lodges along it. Do you remember that conversation?"

"A-firm." Andy bit his lip to keep from following up with *Where you were too much of a coward to care about real people.*

"And you went ahead and did it anyway?"

"Yes."

"Do you care to explain?"

How could he explain how desperately he needed to warn people? To get them to safety. How he couldn't escape the memories of the fire that should have killed him; the girl, Jenny; and her grandmother, Carol. About how little tolerance he had for political expediency and weighing pros and cons when it came to people's lives.

"No. Not really."

"Well, that's really helpful because I've been trying to explain it to the IC, who is making it his new mission to see that you never serve another fire assignment for the rest of your life. What are you thinking, Andy? You're smarter than this."

"Glen, how can I not warn them? How could I live with myself, knowing what kind of danger they're in and only swapping out some maps at a grocery store? I'm sorry, but that just doesn't feel like enough."

There was silence on the other end of the line for a long time. So long that Andy worried his connection might have dropped, but when he checked, the call was still connected.

"Glen—"

"I get how you feel and what you're doing. I do. I was where you are now maybe twenty years ago. You feel responsible and like you're the only person on earth who really gets the way things are. Like you're the only person who can help these people."

"Yeah, that's part of it—"

"Let me finish. The problem with that approach is you don't ever consider the consequences of driving full-bore ahead without thinking. Consider this: Let's say you're wildly successful. You save maybe a couple of people from being caught in the fire on the river. But one of those well-connected people I'm sure you're hobnobbing with at the lodge mentions to his senator buddy, over a golf game, that a firefighter told them to leave the lodge. Right or wrong, that senator might get a bad taste in his mouth toward our firefighters. He might decide to fight against our budget the next go-around. And then, the next fire season, we'd be short-staffed even more than usual, maybe even during another record-breaking fire season. A crew could work their asses off, refuse to admit they should take R and R, and get trapped in a burnover. A dozen of them could die."

"That's hardly a fair comparison—"

"There's nothing fair about it. But it's the world we're living in. One where a single vote could mean the difference between getting fully funded or dealing with continuing resolution after continuing resolution. That's why we need our PIO team. So that when we see no other solution, our teammates can talk us off the ledge before we do something stupid. Just get back here, and we'll see if we can pick up the pieces, understood?"

"Copy."

Andy tossed his phone on the bed in his room that the lodge had offered him free of charge due so many cancellations because of the fire. He understood where Glen was coming from. Why, then, couldn't he feel like Glen was right? Andy wasn't being impulsive. Not really. He'd even anticipated that his actions would lead to this very end. He let out a slow sigh, grabbed his pack, and wrote a quick thanks to whomever would come in to clean his room after he left. Then he wandered downstairs, heading toward the picnic area.

After a few days of soaked shoes ravaging her heels and toes, Valerie had learned to take advantage of any chance she got to warm up her feet. So she took off her shoes and selected a seat on a wicker couch with robin's-egg-blue cushions that invited her to put her feet up next to a gas fireplace.

"Do you mind if I join you?"

Valerie glanced up at a tall man with a scruffy beard who wore dark-green cargo pants and a T-shirt with the Forest Service logo and some custom logo of a mountain and a fire-crew number. "Sure thing. Go right ahead."

Holding a plate of eggs and oatmeal in one hand and a beat-up backpack in his other, the man sat down in one of the two wicker armchairs that matched the couch. Valerie did her best to avoid eye contact, knowing she'd have to say something, and with the clear enjoyment the man was getting out of the food, she didn't want him to stop eating unnecessarily to respond to anything she might say. Though, she had at least a dozen questions she wanted to ask. Foremost in her mind was what a single firefighter was doing at a resort in the middle of the Frank Church Wilderness? Even though she didn't understand why he was there, the fact that he was made her nervous.

At last, he put down his plate and took a long drink of water, nearly draining the tall glass in one draft.

"I'll never get used to it, I guess," the man said, leaning back and stretching his legs out to their full length, nearly having to brace his torso up on his chair to fit them under the coffee table between him and Valerie.

"What's that?"

"Hmmm?" The man said, looking up.

"Sorry. I guess you weren't talking to me."

"No. How rude of me. Sorry. I meant that I haven't gotten used to eating my food and enjoying it. After twenty years on the fire line, you get used to eating what's in front of you as fast and as much as you can. You burn through calories like crazy."

"And you're not on the fire line anymore?"

"Not this assignment. No. I'm just ending a public information assignment. First and probably last, actually."

Valerie had to weigh whether she had the time or the presence of mind to follow the new conversation threads and questions that had sparked in her head at the man's last statement. She decided to cut to the meat of where she needed things to go.

"Okay. As a parting gift to the public good, then, could you tell me what's going on with this fire? We've been smelling it for a day or two. There it is again. Just talking about it brings back the smell that I've almost gotten used to."

"Do you want my true assessment or the message I'm supposed to give?"

"Which one is closer to the truth?"

The man took longer to respond than she had anticipated, but she waited.

"I don't know anymore. I guess from my way of looking at things, the fire will reach the river by this afternoon, maybe in lots of places. The river isn't really a barrier for a fire like this one. It's been shooting off embers and sparks a mile ahead, so it'll pick up on the other side of the river. The fire itself probably isn't the biggest danger, though, if you're right in the middle of the river. There, it's the things that might fall on you that pose the greatest threat."

"What do you mean? What sort of things?"

"This area has a ton of landslides, which you can expect with the steep canyon walls. So boulders and trees." Andy gestured toward the river, and Valerie saw what he meant. Not only were the canyon walls steep, the rocks and trees seemed to be constantly fighting gravity and were mostly in some phase of losing.

"So what should we do?"

"That's where what I think and the agreed-upon talking point from the fire-command folks differ. They'd tell you to make your own decision and that the river remains open and accessible for rafting groups and other forms of recreation."

"Why wouldn't they close access if they know it's a threat?"

"That's talking point number two. We let natural processes occur in wilderness areas. And that includes wildfire."

"So you're saying that if you were in my soggy, cold shoes, you'd find a way to get out now?"

"I don't really know what to tell you, except—"

"Morning, Valerie. Ready for another day on the river?" Maggie came up from behind Valerie and sat down in the second and only available armchair near the fire. "It's amazing how chilly it can get here in August, isn't it?"

Maggie took a good drink of coffee before she noticed Andy. "Oh, I'm sorry! I didn't mean to interrupt. I'm sure my pal Andy was regaling you with one of his fabulous stories. Did you tell her the one about the poor new guy who didn't know how to back up a trailer? That one seemed to be a crowd pleaser."

"You know him? Andy?" Valerie asked, horribly confused and trying to decipher the obvious friction between Maggie and this guy named Andy who she'd just met.

Andy leaned forward. "Just since last night. We chatted a bit after I talked to a group of hotel guests."

"So we're all friends here, then. Excellent," Valerie said, stifling a chuckle when Maggie let the coffee run down the wrong tube and erupted into a coughing fit.

"Okay. So what gives? You and I were on decent terms last night? I didn't haunt your dreams or anything did I?" Andy directed the question to Maggie, who seemed hesitant to explain her chilliness toward him, or maybe she was trying to catch her breath after all the coughing.

Is this how girls show they like a guy now? Valerie thought. She could understand the rugged appeal in some ways, though she quickly thought better of that. Andy had to be nearly old enough to be Maggie's father.

Finally, Maggie spoke up. "Sorry, Andy. It's not really fair, but I've been turning it over in my head ever since we chatted last night. You know how you can mull things over in your mind so much that people take on a bad taste by association?"

Both Andy and Valerie responded at the same time.

"No."

"Absolutely."

Valerie knew exactly what Maggie was trying to describe, and Andy didn't get it at all. Maggie looked from Valerie to Andy and shook her head.

"It was like that, for me anyway. You got lumped in with a really tough decision. And I lost sleep over it, so now seeing you puts me on edge."

"You're right about one thing," Andy said, then waited to explain—Valerie assumed for dramatic effect—"that's completely unfair. I was totally charming last night. I didn't even try to tell you what to do. Not directly anyway."

"Okay. Time-out." Valerie said, making a time-out symbol with her hands. "I feel like I'm missing a central thread in this narrative. What big decision are we talking about here? Maggie?"

Maggie wrapped her arms tightly around her chest. "The decision on whether we finish the rafting tour or figure out a way to get evacuated today."

Valerie was taken off guard entirely. She'd had misgivings practically every time she caught a whiff of the smoke, which came to her in full force now that she was focused on the wildfire. "And you'd recommend we leave, Andy?"

"What I was going to say right when Maggie joined us was that if I were in your shoes, it would be a very tough decision. I don't think I got the chance to even ask if you're here with a corporate group or family or something?"

"I'm here with my husband and teenage daughter."

Andy let this new information settle in his head for a few seconds before continuing. And when he continued, his words came slowly, with consideration. "If I were here in your shoes, with my husband and daughter, and if I didn't have twenty years of fire behavior experience, I'd probably assume that everything would work out just fine and move forward according to plan."

Valerie's surprise was obvious to both Maggie and Andy. But Andy held up his hand so he could finish his thought. "But I'm not you. I do have twenty years of fire experience. And everything inside me says to tell you to get out now."

An awkward silence collected after Andy's last statement. Valerie didn't know what to say even though Maggie was perched on the very edge of her seat, obviously hoping she would make the decision easier for her. But Valerie couldn't make that decision. Not for the whole group, anyway, and she'd have to run it past David before she even thought about canceling the rest of the trip.

"I know these rafting trips aren't cheap—" Andy started to say.

"It's not about the money at all." Valerie stopped Andy mid-sentence. "And I know you'll think it silly, but I took this trip to get closer to my daughter, and it's working. At least I think it is. Maybe? I'm feeling like I'm getting through to her in ways I've never been able to before. If we end the trip now, I'm afraid it will all have been for nothing."

Valerie fell silent, still trying to work through the new developments in her mind, but she jumped in quickly when she saw Maggie's clear disappointment at the words she had chosen. "The trip has been fantastic! The trip hasn't been a waste for me. Even if we were to evacuate today, my life will never be the same because of it. And you've been such a fabulous guide, Maggie." Even though Valerie knew she was placating, it seemed to please Maggie a bit. "It's my daughter though."

"Evie."

Valerie nodded when Maggie said her daughter's name. Hearing the name out loud in that moment and in that context—rather than the way it had been gnawing at the back of her mind the whole trip and was often at the forefront of her mind, shouting for attention—changed the focus of how she thought about things with her daughter in mind. It was like Maggie had changed the radio frequency and Valerie suddenly realized there were lyrics being sung to the muffled static. Lyrics she had barely interpreted as music before. "I'll talk it over with my family. But it's not my decision to make. I'm sure you and Nate and the rest of the crew will talk things over and make a good decision for the whole group."

Valerie stood, and Maggie and Andy followed suit. It felt strangely comforting to realize that Andy and Maggie probably had more to say. Reasons for her to stay longer. How long had it been since anybody had wanted more of her company? That thought wasn't fair to her husband. He never seemed to mind her company. But he was stuck with her. Maggie and Andy had no obligation to like her or value her opinion. But she sensed that they did anyway.

By the time she got back to her room, she had all but made up her mind.

"You're back. Good," Valerie said at seeing Evie mindlessly scrolling on her phone and fidgeting a bit to let Valerie know she had heard her to some degree.

"I need you to put your phone away now, please." Valerie had said it with a confidence that surprised herself. It sounded as if she had zero doubt of being heard and obeyed. And more surprising still, Evie put down her phone without argument, and propping herself up more on some pillows, asked, "What's up, Mom? Are you okay?"

Valerie took a measured breath before diving into a conversation she didn't really know how to start.

"It's the wildfire. I've been talking to some people... a firefighter and our guide, Maggie. They told me it could be dangerous to try to finish the rafting trip."

"Dangerous, how? Like the fire is going to burn over the river? We'll be safe in the river, right? I mean it's a big river."

"I asked the same question. The firefighter told me that this wildfire is so big and moving so fast that the fire could blow embers across the river and start burning on both sides of it and that things might fall down into the water."

"Like ash and stuff like that?"

"No. Like trees and boulders. The fire can make the ground unstable. And I guess we'd be trapped if the fire started burning on both sides of the river. We wouldn't be able to go to shore."

"You guess? You guess we'd be trapped? What'd Maggie say?"

"She said we should make our own decision. The firefighter told me that he'd probably be able to fly us out if we left now." Valerie let the silence hang in the air for a few moments before asking her final question. "So what do you want to do?"

"What do you want to do about what?" David asked, stepping out of the bathroom, his hair still dripping from the shower.

Valerie wondered if it would be worth explaining everything again, but Evie gave him the quick version.

"Whoa. Hold on. How sure are they that the fire will reach us?"

"They haven't given us a set probability," Valerie said, trying to keep eyes on both David and Evie to gauge the slightest indication of what they might be thinking or feeling. "But the firefighter, Andy, seemed to think the fire would almost certainly reach the river. It's just a matter of when. We might be able to avoid it. Or, he said he would probably be able to evacuate us by helicopter or something."

"And staying here isn't an option? This place seems safer than the river maybe," David offered.

Valerie had thought about that as an option, and as she mulled that over again, she saw some definite merit to the idea that she hadn't seen before. "That might work so long as they aren't planning on evacuating this place too. I mean the lodge is made out of wood, and I'm sure the fire could burn through it just as easily as a tree but that's something we could ask."

"No. I think we should keep going."

David and Valerie looked at Evie with raised eyebrows. Then they looked at each other and back at Evie.

"Really, honey? I didn't get the sense that you were thrilled about this trip," David asked.

"I know. At first, I wasn't."

"And you seemed pretty happy with Wi-Fi just a moment ago," Valerie hinted.

"You got me. If I have access to a phone and an internet connection, I'm going to use it."

"And it doesn't bother you, at all? The risk of the fire and everything?"

"Of course it does! But so does driving or being at school where a kid might bring a gun, or flying on an airplane with possible terrorists while on our way to see Grandma. Aren't there always risks?"

"I don't think those are quite the same—"

"You're right." Valerie cut David off with a simple two-word declarative. "There will always be risks." She sat down on the edge of the bed next to Evie.

"You'll be taking a risk if you start dating anybody or decide on one college over another or if you take a break from college to do something else. You'll most definitely be taking a risk if you decide to get married or have a child or two. It might seem like just the thing to do, like you aren't really weighing those risks. But you are."

"Are we still talking about the fire, or something else?" David said with a concerned look toward Valerie.

"I don't know what I'm talking about really. The fire is a risk we could totally avoid. But we'll be missing out on what could be great memories and other beautiful things too."

"Exactly!" Evelyn swung her legs over the edge of the bed so she sat shoulder to shoulder with Valerie.

Valerie felt the warmth of her daughter's skin against hers and the wisps of wind that came when her hair settled close enough for her to see the sun-bleached strands of her brown hair, glistening in the light that filtered through the window. She so wanted to bury her face in her daughter's beautiful hair and just hold her close. As if on cue, Evie leaned her head against Valerie's shoulder and tucked her face under Valerie's chin.

Valerie's eyes glistened as unabated tears pooled in her eyelids.

"I don't want this trip to end yet," Evie said, almost as if she were saying it more for herself, but Valerie understood.

And so did David. "So we take the risk then?"

"Yeah, if the trip leads say they're going on, we're going on too. All agreed?"

"Agreed," David and Evie said in unison.

After Valerie left the seating area by the gas fireplace, Andy got the word that his helicopter would be arriving soon, so he left Maggie alone, saying good luck and goodbye. That gave her a few moments to process some things. Was Andy right? She didn't know. The protocol was to complete the tour unless safety concerns were agreed upon by trip staff. She figured Nate would want to push on. But she also got the sense that he would be amenable to her thoughts.

The problem was, though, she wasn't sure what to pitch. Leading a tour into a dangerous situation didn't make any sense, but river rafting always carried risk, small as it was. That was part of the appeal, she realized as she chose an apple from an overflowing bowl of fruit that sat on the raised fireplace hearth her feet were on.

She'd gotten so used to not having cell coverage that she almost forgot she was still carrying her phone. She pulled it out and logged onto the lodge's Wi-Fi, then flipped through her contacts to find the person she needed advice from the most. Unsure of the signal strength, she started a video call, and when Jay popped up on screen, crisp and clear and smiling, she was pleasantly surprised.

"Hey, Maggie! Small wilderness. I was just sending some extra good vibes your way. How are you?" Maggie smiled back, and seeing Jay in his workshop where she felt so comfortable and was seen for who she was made a tickle run down her spine. But then there was longing too. A longing to be there for one of Jay's legendary hugs. Longing for him to make the decision for her. To not be in the situation in the first place.

"Hey, Jay. It is seriously so great to see you. Technology these days, right? There's almost no place where I can't bug you from."

"Hey, you can bug me all you want, just don't expect me to connect to those interwebs while I'm in the backcountry. What's up? You don't usually reach out until you're done with your tour. Is everything okay?"

Maggie tried to put into words the complex mess of emotions contingent on the decision she had to make. *No, things aren't okay*, she thought. *But maybe things aren't so bad.* "You've been following the Sheep Mountain Complex fire, right? Or you might know it as the Greenfield Ranch Fire. I guess the Greenfield fire combined with some other smaller ones. It's kind of tough to keep track sometimes."

"Of course. You know how obsessed I am with wildfire science but especially when our crew is near one of them. Is it getting bad out there?" Jay asked with the normally imperceptible wrinkles popping up around his eyes and forehead.

"It hasn't been too bad, honestly. We've been smelling a bit of smoke for the last day or so but you forget about it after a while. But we're here at the lodge"—Maggie held up her phone and made a slow sweep of her surroundings for Jay—"hence the Wi-Fi connection. But I'm really struggling to decide if we should take advantage of the possible evacuation we were offered while there are some helicopters and things available. Or we could just take our chances. What do you think?"

"Boy, that's a tough one." Jay propped up his phone, then interlaced his fingers and leaned back with his hands behind his head. "The fire does seem to be heading in your direction. But we've dealt with wildfire a ton in the past too. We both know the 'right' answer," he said with air quotes around *right* and dramatically rolled eyes.

"Yeah, decide if it's an immediate safety risk. If we're unsure, report it to corporate and let them decide what's best," Maggie said, putting down her feet, suddenly aware that they had gotten a bit too warm, being so close to the gas fireplace. She winced. It was a bit strange to talk about a threatening wildfire while taking advantage of a contained fire to keep her toes toasty.

"That's it. But we both know that either way corporate decided, you wouldn't be satisfied. I wouldn't be either. So that means it's up to you, Nate, and other staff."

"That's what worries me."

"How do you mean?"

"There's a couple with a teenage daughter here."

"Ah, the entitled redemption-from-horrible-parenting-through-wilderness type? Valerie wasn't that her name?"

"Yeah. You got it. No, they're great people. Their daughter is, well, a teenager, I guess. But the parents are really great. I just don't want to let them down."

"There it is right there."

Maggie turned back to her phone with a puzzled look.

"You've already made up your mind. You just want me to tell you you're not wrong for feeling the way you do."

Maggie had to admit that Jay was spot on. She wanted to finish the rafting trip, now that was clear. It also became clear that she needed to finish the trip, not just for Valerie, David, and Evie, but for herself. To make the final stamp on the experience so she could make a clean break to whatever was next—college, career, family…

"You're right, as usual. I think I'm going to suggest we keep going."

"That sounds like a fine decision."

"It does?"

"Because there are good arguments either way. You just have to make a choice. And you're committing. *And* you're brilliant when you commit to something."

That would usually be the point where Jay would give Maggie a bear hug and then go back to tinkering with some broken-down machinery, leaving her to think about what he meant.

A morning ray struck her face. The sun had finally climbed over the tall cliff walls.

"Thanks, Jay. This really helped a lot."

"Remember me when you're a millionaire," Jay said with a wry smile. "I know you'll make a good choice. Keep those paddles moving though. See you, Mags." She waved and put down her phone.

Maggie could get a raft out of nearly any jam if everyone in the raft kept paddling. Direction of the raft mattered, too, but she'd always been able to deal with that once she got the raft to more consistent currents. Despite the seriousness of the fire and what Andy had said, she and the group would be okay. Maggie was sure of it. And Valerie and Evie needed to finish the trip. *She* needed to finish the trip.

The rafting guides made the decision to keep going easier than Maggie had anticipated. After making it clear to all of the participants that the rafting crew would make every effort to get them evacuated if they decided that was best, everyone decided to push forward as well. Maggie set her mind to navigating the remaining couple of days' on the river and making the experience as positive and impactful as she could for the three people under her special care. Like Jay had explained, she had made a choice based on some good information and some uncertain variables. She might have regrets down the road, but at least she would know that she had made the best decision she knew how to make at the time. And that had to stand for something.

Middle Fork of the Salmon River
August 2024

It would never do for the pine to feel picked on or selected as if by some grand design when unforeseen setbacks struck. Any day with lightning could spell its end. Any windstorm with just the right velocity and direction could send it skidding downhill. Insects could decide to take interest in it and attract enough of their companions to overwhelm its massive structure in the matter of a season. The pine had learned it was best to live for now—enjoy enough sun while it lasted. Take drinks when it could. And do what it could today to be prepared for tomorrow.

MAGGIE THOUGHT IT WOULD BE BEST TO LAUNCH BEFORE THE lodge emptied completely. She wasn't sure why, but the thought of being left behind at the abandoned lodge gave her a lonely feeling, even though she had two-dozen participants and a half-dozen crew members that she would mingle with closely either way. Maybe a deeper reason for her urgency to push off on the waiting river was so she wouldn't have to contemplate the alternative path she could have taken.

The choice she'd made was the harder choice in a lot of ways. She'd already determined that this guided tour would be her last before starting college again, so to hell with protocols or best management practices. What would they do to her? Fire her? As ridiculous as it felt, even as she checked the bags one by one to ensure they were properly stowed and secured in the rafts—even as she ran through the last security checklists—her strongest pull toward staying the course with the trip was Valerie and her family. A family she had met five days before and didn't really know. All the projecting that had taken place as Maggie prepared for the trip with nothing more than a couple of photos and a two-paragraph description of each family member.

The hard part was, though, Valerie had lived up to her hopes. She was traditional in the right ways and spontaneous and adventurous in endearing ways. She was who Maggie wanted to become in the next decade or two—down to the brand of water shoes Valerie wore and the two memoirs *and* a novel she had packed for a six-day trip *just in case she was in the right mood for a different read.*

Maggie had let the two decision tracks run in her mind a hundred times by now. If she had pushed for the evacuation, the other raft crew members would've gone along with her. She knew how she would've sold that decision to the client groups too. She could see their nodding, approving heads as they were reassured that the crew was doing what was in their best interest. She visualized the validation in Andy's eyes when she caught him just in time for coordination with evacuations. And in all the bustle, there would be no room for real conversation about anything other than getting people out and back to Boise or wherever they were dropped off.

And that would be it. The trip would be over. The immediate shift back to regular life for all participants as soon as they touched down. Her decision wasn't entirely based on selfish motives. Mostly, maybe. But not entirely. She really wanted to see Evie carve out a space in her life to recognize the important role her mom could play in it. A role Maggie felt begging to be filled in herself, constituting a gnawing hole that she'd tried to fill with staying busy or pretending she didn't care. As if maternal affection was a state of mind she could shift and shape with her own jaded point of view.

Maggie stood up, fully straightening her spine and putting both hands on the small of her back, enjoying a satisfying pop. She made one more visual survey of the rafts while her thoughts continued to drift. She knew for certain something that she had always suspected but had tried to deny before—the uncomfortable distance she made for herself by pushing that maternal care away was like the dark shadows in an Ansel Adams photograph. The lack of light was just as important and as clear as the discernible parts, shining with glaring clarity in the immensity of contrast.

She never put anything in the spaces where her mom should be anymore. She just gouged out what she could, leaving empty cavities, hollow and unfulfilled. But now that she was feeling a resurgence of life with new possibilities—giving college another try, leaving her thrilling-but-dead-end job—other new things seemed possible. Maybe even giving her a way to connect to her family again. A chance to rebuild the relationship with her mom that she'd let drift away.

Maggie rolled her shoulders back and gave her neck a quick roll from side to side, then clapped her hands above her head. "Are we all set?" she shouted over the happy babbling of the shallow river water and the pleasant chatter of the participants who waited to load onto the boats.

"We've got this, Maggie!" David shouted back, raising his paddle to make an air high-five as he, Evelyn, and Valerie settled into their small paddleboat. Maggie put up her hands to accept that high five and took a running start to kick her raft off its moorings. It was the smaller four-seater raft she had stuck a sticky note to just a few days before in the raft-repair shop. Days that now seemed almost a lifetime ago. Maggie saw the other groups just untying from their raft's moorings and a couple of paddleboats up ahead of her raft, quickly losing sight of them around the bend in the river.

The course led toward a natural tightening of the riverbank where the same volume of water got squeezed into a funnel, increasing the flow's intensity. They passed under towering batholiths that shimmered in the morning sunlight that was amplified by the reflection of the water below. The shock of the first couple of splashes on her legs and arms were icy but the sun soon warmed her, and she remembered what a great appeal the river-guide gig had been when she'd first applied for it. What a gift to be in the heart of such beautiful and wild places and to feel confident in her ability to guide the raft to its final destination. She no longer required conscious thought to see the direction the raft would go, and she effortlessly called out directions to Valerie's family.

"Left side, forward paddle!" The raft righted its direction, entering some mild rapids.

"Lean in!" The group prepared for a jolt, which ended up being nothing but a little scoop down and back up, but it kicked up a fair amount of spray. Evie and David, who were up front, both cried out in surprise that turned into laughter. Evie leaned across the raft to give her dad a friendly shove. And David splashed Evie with a sly slap with a backward paddle that mostly missed her.

"Okay. So now we're awake, let's see what we can really do with those paddles, shall we? Paddle Forward!"

As the rafts continued along in the wilderness, Maggie picked up the anticipated change in tree species. The mountains were closer around the river now, and the pine trees clung to the ridges more fervently.

All four people in the raft paddled in near-perfect unison, their raft skimming across the surface of the water as if it were a hockey puck on an ice rink. Maggie had never considered herself a sentimental person, but as she paddled alongside Valerie's family, her muscles engaging with the work but reserving enough energy to paddle all day if needed, she watched the magical effect that always seemed to come when a group worked together. To see such obvious and thrilling results nearly brought her to tears. At least, she felt emotional. Her face was too wet with spray to know for certain if tears mingled with the river water.

The morning sailed past, but as they steered off the river and pulled their raft onto shore for lunch, the sky took on an alarming red hue. Clouds scrolled across the stretch of sky that they could see above the granite and quartzite walls, and from the east, a hot, dry wind drove through the canyon. Maggie prepared lunch, assisted by the other crew members who pulled up their rafts a couple of minutes after Maggie did hers.

She tried to keep the mood light, but conversations were whispered and most participants ended up sitting silently with a hand tapping or a leg bobbing nervously. She brought out a dessert they had planned to save for the last night of the trip— the next day—deciding they could use it more to brighten the mood right then. "I know wildfire can be scary, but let me tell you, the smoke makes for some amazing sunsets, so we're in for a treat tonight."

A couple of people responded with kind chuckles but most just nodded and smiled with uneasy looks.

"We'll relax here for about an hour, and then we'll take off again," she said, looking back to ensure everything was set for the meal.

Valerie knew the smoke and red sky beyond the first ridges of the mountains were dangerous. That was probably the reason the group gathering around the lunch table was so subdued, but she didn't feel any fear. Not really. In a strange way, the fire threat felt like the next thing she needed to face in a long series of challenges, many of which she had navigated pretty well.

Figure out a big adventure that might give her opportunities to connect with her previously unreachable teenage daughter.

Check.

Explore new forms of intimacy with her husband.

Check.

Draw new meaning from her professional life.

Check.

Dealing with a wildfire seemed manageable in comparison. Wildfire was something she'd never faced directly, though, so maybe she wasn't giving it enough weight.

Evelyn and David connected with Valerie in the lunch line.

"Where did you two get to?" Valerie asked David as she grabbed a plate and fork only to realize their lunch consisted of sandwiches. But she felt foolish about putting them back. She was glad to see that there were also items like hummus and carrots that would at least do well with the plate. She still needed to figure out what to do with the fork.

David pointed to a bowl of salad, reading her mind. "One of the guides, I think his name is Ethan? He was talking about some marble deposits that give this area its name—Marblehead. It was nice to stretch my legs, even if the marble was somewhat lackluster," he said, spreading mustard on his sandwich.

"I'm sure it was nice to go for a little hike anyway. I could probably use a walk, myself, before we get back on the raft. And how about you?"

Valerie waited for Evie to say anything, but when she didn't, Valerie prompted her.

"Are you working on any new sketches today?"

"Yeah, I guess so. Just now, though, I was just sitting by the river. It's kind of soothing, isn't it?"

Valerie nodded and did her best to hide her pleasure. She had raised a child who could appreciate the stillness and soothing of a river. Put that in the win column, for sure.

"I know what you mean. I was doing sort of the same thing."

"Let's make sure there are enough vegetarian protein options before everyone else eats them, okay?" Valerie overheard one of the crewmembers saying, so she decided on a turkey sandwich on wheat. As she spread mayonnaise on one of the slices of bread and laid out tomatoes and lettuce on top of her sliced turkey, she remembered some lunchtimes just like this one when her mom worked full-time and she and her siblings had hours of free rein to amuse themselves during the summer. The amount of mayonnaise might have been a bit less than she would've put on her sandwich as a ten-year-old, but the fact was strikingly similar—there was a simple pleasure that came with eating good familiar foods.

Valerie followed David and Evie to sit on a long log overlooking the river. She dipped a carrot stick in a generous portion of hummus and chomped down on it, enjoying the tangy bite the mix of flavors brought.

She overheard snatches of conversation around her.

"Can I join the smoker's lounge?" Maggie asked when sitting down to eat with the college buddies.

"Of course. Grab a beer and sit with us." One of them said.

The friends had been nearly inseparable for the entire trip, and Valerie quickly searched her memory. *His name is Joe, and he is the one with the almost-mohawk hair.* Two of the other college buddies, Nick and Dean, she thought their names were, appeared to be in a pretty intense conversation.

"His stories are more anecdotes—" Dean started to say.

"Those two words mean the same thing," Nick interjected.

"No they don't. One is more like little sound-bite type stories. Right? Maggie, you studied English, right?" Maggie looked in their direction.

"Yeah, but what makes you think I was taught that?"

"I don't know. Just seems like the meanings of words would be important to an English major."

"They are, but the point you're arguing is definitely not important. At all," Maggie said with a smile, which got all three buddies laughing.

Valerie lost focus on that conversation and settled into a feeling she had experienced several times since launching on the raft that first day. It was a feeling of being away from it all, a reminder of how easy it would be to do anything or go anywhere if she had enough money. Since she and her family had been on the river, planes had flown overhead several times a day. They'd already floated past at least a dozen private ranches over the last couple of days. One of the ranches was nearing the completion of a remodel, with several brand-new buildings—including a yurt. She remembered that yurts were a Mongolian invention. Somehow, though she loved staying in yurts at the beach, seeing one in the Frank Church felt out of place. What would it be like to drop into places like this whenever she wanted, by simply hopping in her private plane and landing at her private ranch in the middle of the wilderness?

Later that night, after they had set up camp, the rafting crew devised a game that required teams to throw a Frisbee into a bucket. A couple of women who were perhaps old enough to be Evie's grandmothers encouraged Evie to play on the team with the boy a couple of years older than she was and who went shirtless most of the day and flexed his chest anytime he stood still. By the second round, Evie and the boy had things down so well that they went undefeated for six rounds.

Valerie cheered with the rest of the group when Evie won yet another round, this time taking the game in one turn, never even giving the other team a shot at beating them. But Valerie soon left the group and wandered down a path, past the tents and along the river. The roughly marked trail led to a secluded riverbank, and she sat on a boulder to watch the clouds filter across the sunlight beyond the far ridge to the west, showing up in a white-and-pale-blue glow.

She almost lost herself to the rhythmic sound of the river but woke when the sound of a breaking branch broke the peace. Only then did she see another rafting camp directly across the river. It was easily as big as the one she was a part of. Maybe bigger. With dozens of people focused on what appeared to be a similar game. There was something sad about that. She supposed it was nice that so many people could have the experience she was having, but the thought got confused as she considered the strangeness of having so many people run the river. When she headed back to the camp, the crew was serving dessert. Biscotti with fresh raspberries and strawberries topped with whipped cream.

"Hi, Valerie. I saved you some dessert," Maggie said, handing her a small ceramic plate with a larger helping than those she saw others eating. "Whipped the cream myself. I was like"—Maggie mimed the action of whisking cream in an imaginary bowl complete with whirring sound effects.

"Well, gosh! I'm honored to taste the fruit of your hard labor." Valerie took a bite and responded with a very satisfied smile. "Delicious! Well done, you!"

Maggie seemed pleased, and Valerie wished her a good night. She did eat the dessert, and it did taste good, but she couldn't quite escape the feeling of something with the experience being slightly askew. Eating freshly whipped cream on the banks of a river in the heart of one of the biggest wilderness areas in the country seemed off. At the same time, she knew how much the trip cost them. So, it was probably worth it and was what she would expect from the heavy price tag. At the same time, though, maybe it wouldn't be so bad if the accommodations were a bit more rustic, given the rugged environment they were traveling in.

She set her plate and fork on the table designated for dirty dishes and wandered toward a campfire where David and Dean were chatting. Valerie dreaded the intense look on David's face. She knew that look. He was totally relishing the chance to talk about some obscure thought that only he would find worth the time it took to explore. She settled in a camp chair next to him and took his hand.

"If you think about it, none of us on this trip has any real fear of *not* getting to our destination safely."

"Come on, David, let's not give people a reason to fear that while still on the river," Valerie said, trying to lighten things up with the conversation.

"No, I'm not portending anything happening to us. What I'm getting at is that the reason we don't fear anymore is because our lives have become so predictable."

"And that's a bad thing," Valerie heard someone nearby ask. Bill was his name. *A retired veterinarian who is here with his son Ian,* Valerie rattled off in her head, trying to keep all the participants straight.

"That's a very good thing. A hundred years ago, people venturing into this area wouldn't have been nearly as certain. They had to face their own mortality anytime they went down the river or climbed these ridges. Their whole focus had to be on survival. Where would they sleep? What would they eat? What would they do if they encountered a pack of wolves, which there were a lot more of back then too."

"I see," Bill said with a waning interest that Valerie picked up on from his vacant look.

"Really, Dave, let it go. Now Bill, you worked for Pfizer right—"

"I'm sorry, I don't mean to go on and on. I just think it's interesting how much of our attention can be focused on so many other things because we're all but certain to make it home in near-perfect shape. It's just something I don't think we should take for granted."

"Great point," Dean, *the mechanical engineer*, said, inviting David into a continued conversation.

Valerie made a mental note to thank him later for that.

The most annoying part about David's somewhat-inappropriate comment, at least from Valerie's perspective, was that there was definite truth to it. She wondered how many modern American citizens really worried about their survival day-to-day. Then again, there were millions of houseless people all over the country who lived very much how David described people living a hundred years ago, worrying about predators of a sort and scrounging for food.

It almost made it seem absurd that her dinner that night had included appetizers like chilled brie cheese and fileted salmon not caught fresh from the river but pre-prepared by a grocery store in Salmon, Idaho. She wasn't a particularly philosophical person by nature. That was more David's forte. But as she watched the sun slip behind the western ridges, and as the wind picked up, chilling the night air considerably, the parallels between the houseless of modern America and those struggling to survive in the wilderness a century before stuck in her head that night and didn't leave her when she tried to go to sleep.

The houseless even sleep in tents, she thought as she drifted off to sleep.

The next morning as Valerie left her tent to sit by the river, the sun rose in as unassuming a way as it had set the night before. The few fleecy clouds drifting above the ridges, turned golden. The light in the canyon brightened gradually. The profiles of pine trees on the ridge became more defined—making it possible for Valerie to first discern branches and then needles.

Temperatures remained low with a cool breeze following the river. A solitary crewmember, *Trevor,* she thought was his name, started to set out breakfast items, an à la cart breakfast table with instant oatmeal, Greek yogurt, and coffee.

Valerie sat facing the sunrise, waiting for the first actual sunbeams to reach her face. She saw, for the first time, that the bases of the towering ponderosa pines in the camp had been scarred by long-past fires. She remembered learning somewhere that lots of trees in Western landscapes required fire to rejuvenate, and she bet the ponderosa pines were no exception. The surprisingly straight trees in front of her had lost their lower branches long before any fire had come. Their blackened, bare trunks easily lacked any needles or branches below fifty feet.

The constant wash of sound coming from the river was so easy to forget about, but from time to time, her focus was taken back to that comforting background noise. Why was it that certain words carry bad connotations? *Noise* conjured thoughts of honking horns, falling buildings, almost any toddler toy. But the noise from a river was a different mettle entirely. Yet there was no other way of describing the sound of a river—its consistency, its rise and fall in regular intervals, its frequency—then, to call it background noise—because no matter how hard she tried, she lost focus on its existence within a matter of minutes, even when trying to stay focused on it…

All the trees that stuck out from the steep scraggy hillsides seem to be in some state of falling. Some younger trees were still quite upright, but she could see the sequence in perfect display. The ones nearest the river had roots that ran exposed down to the waterline. Those not fortunate enough to be close to the water, must have needed extra resources and time to dig their roots deeper.

She remembered reading a nice analogy about trees that needed to dig their roots deeper. They were better able to stand than those with shallow roots. Especially when windstorms struck. All because water wasn't so available to them. She didn't know enough about botany to confirm any of that, but she liked the lesson.

One thing was certain, however, fire was often the deciding factor in whether a tree remained standing. The trees that found themselves in the line of fire, usually up steep drainages and canyons, were mostly lying in a state of blackened or grayish branchlessness.

The eastern ridges that the river flowed toward were definitely brighter now. The sky was a more perceptible blue, but whether the sun would come above the ridge in five minutes or an hour was impossible for her to tell. The depths of the canyon meant that none of the far ridges in any other direction showed any sign of being warmed by the sun yet.

Then the dusty-hued western ridges were touched by sunlight still higher up, but the light swept down the hillside with graceful speed in a beautiful symmetry—the physics matching the light and shadow, building the three-dimensional panorama.

The tops of the trees near her were lit up next, sun filtering through the ponderosa pines' bursts of needles. She could almost see the trees embracing it as it inched down their trunks, warming and energizing.

At last, through a nearby pine tree's needles, the warming and brightening kind of sunlight struck her face. She sat as still as she could with her eyes closed, trying her best to witness something that had happened every day for millions of years, whether or not she was there to enjoy the grand effects, like it was unfolding for the first time.

Nearby in the camp-chair circle, several of her rafting mates who had gotten up by then, were chatting about self-driving trucks. She had half a mind to signal to them. To make them see things the way she saw them. The immensity of time and significance of space on such clear display. But she thought better of it, deciding that her way of enjoying a sunrise was her way, not necessarily the right way or the only good way. Instead, she moved into a general sense of gratitude for the decisions she had made—those that never seemed important but ended up being pivotal to drive her on her path— that had led to this very moment. Then an unknown bird chirped its morning song, and Valerie knew another day had officially begun.

It was fascinating to her to see how little she actually needed to be content with life on such a trip. While packing, She'd been worried she wasn't packing enough clothes, but she soon realized that with no one taking showers, no one cared how she smelled. In camp, most people wore baseball caps to hide their messy hair, so no one cared about her normally blown-out and curled hairstyle. It had taken her a good day on the river to get more comfortable with that situation, but by this stage of the trip, she found it liberating.

She glanced back at the circle of camp chairs and saw her daughter, who still looked stunning without makeup or styled hair—just a braid tied with a rubber band. It wasn't too long ago that Valerie was able to do nothing with her hair or makeup—that she could skip hours on the elliptical—and still maintain such a physique. *Youth is wasted on the young*, she thought. She hoped her daughter enjoyed it as much as she could while she still had that luxury. But after spending a couple of evenings with the retired women on the trip, Valerie was learning to be a lot more accepting of her own figure too. All of them had stripped down to swimsuit bottoms and sports bras multiple times during the day with zero shame. She sensed that they wanted to feel the sun on their skin and, after wearing a wetsuit for hours, the opportunity to give their bodies a chance to breathe was delicious to them. That had become so obvious. Valerie had yet to follow their example, exactly, but she didn't feel self-conscious when walking around camp in Lycra shorts and a tank top anymore. The wilderness didn't care one way or another who was passing through it, and these people didn't mind sharing it with less-than-perfect fellow humans.

The sweep boat, which carried most of the supplies, always sailed off first, so Valerie had gotten into a routine of getting up before dawn, packing her sleeping bag, taking down her cot, and putting the things she wouldn't need during the day, like extra clothes, journals, and books, into her go bag, which would be loaded onto the sweep boat. It was always a bit of a struggle because she had to change clothes before rafting and her tent was usually down by that point and her remaining self-consciousness ordinarily meant that she had to hide in the trees to change into rafting attire.

But not that morning. She stripped down to her underwear right next to where her tent had been and changed into her rafting clothes within view of several participants who were taking down their tents. She stuffed her camp clothes in her go bag and was proud to see that her yellow bag marked with the number five was the first loaded onto the sweep boat.

I think I may be getting the hang of this, she decided.

Maggie was taking her turn driving the sweep boat, so Valerie didn't see her until that evening when they came into camp for the night.

"So, how did it go?" Valerie asked Maggie with concerned looks at seeing how exhausted Maggie was. "Oh my goodness! You look so tired."

"Yeah, it's been a good day."

"That's it? That's all I'm gonna get?"

Maggie grinned. "You got me. It was so hard. I had to be on my game all day. The sweep boat doesn't ride anything like the oar boats or the paddleboats, so I was adjusting and fighting the current all day. The hardest part was landing it at camp. I only have one shot because there's no way we would ever be able to make it upstream if I missed the landing spot. And we didn't tell you about it because it's not your concern or anything, but yesterday we did miss the camp, and we had to unload and carry the sweep boat back up to camp. But I made it today."

"Gosh! That sounds so hard. Nicely done, you!" Valerie said, giving Maggie's shoulder a gentle squeeze and an approving smile. "I sure hope you get some of the other duties or tasks off this evening so you can rest a bit."

"No. But that's okay. I wouldn't want to make the other crewmembers do extra work."

"That's awfully noble of you. But I hope you don't have to do the sweep boat tomorrow." Valerie's words were somewhere between a statement and a question, but she was very pleased by Maggie's answer.

"I think tomorrow I'm gonna be in one of the smaller paddleboats we tried out a couple of times before. Maybe we could convince Evie and David to take a break from the larger paddleboats and the three of you could ride together with me again?"

Valerie thought about trying to convince Evie of anything and David was as enthusiastic about riding in the bigger paddleboats as Evie was. Then again, they seemed to enjoy riding with her and Maggie the day before. Maggie seemed to understand Valerie's concerned, doubtful look and quickly continued. "I'll just tell them that they need to take a turn in the smaller boat so other people can have a chance to experience the larger paddleboat." Maggie gave Valerie a knowing smile.

"It's a bit scary how quickly you've picked up on my body language, Maggie. Soon, we won't have to talk at all, and we'll still know what we're both thinking."

Maggie chuckled. "You still have a lot to tell me about the joy of technical writing, though, so I'll look forward to that tomorrow. See you around, Valerie."

Maggie shuffled off toward the dinner preparation area and Valerie sat down on a camp chair facing the river. As she did, she heard one of the other guides say, "I just wish I were as cool as Maggie." Valerie leaned toward the sound of the voice, which she thought was Ryan's, a usually quiet, thoughtful late-twenties' guy who'd been rafting pretty much straight out of high school.

Ryan draped an arm around Maggie's shoulders in clear affection and support. Maggie wrapped her arm around Ryan, and they leaned into each other as they made it to the cooking area.

Valerie beamed at seeing such brotherly care and celebration being shown to Maggie, who was fast becoming very important to her too. *Human dynamics can be so complex sometimes*, she thought. But didn't it really come down to people wanting to be cared for by their tribe? *All we really want to say with our work and good deeds is "I have value. Please care about me. Please love me for who I am right now and help me feel safe."* The words bubbled into her mind as if someone else were speaking and she was simply taking dictation.

But wherever the thought had come from, from somewhere deep down, she knew that they were true.

She recognized what it was that kept her from being completely at ease among her rafting companions. They all seemed perfectly comfortable in their own skin. They had nothing else to prove. Even the doctor's kids had an effortless confidence that she assumed came from knowing and having reinforced the belief that they were more than enough, that things would work out how they expected them to, that they were not only capable of great things but that the universe would make it so just because of who and what they were.

She wasn't envious of that comfort level. She longed for her daughter to embrace it, though. It was the goal of every parent from her generation—to raise children who believed the world was their oyster, and more importantly, that the oyster was generous and would open at the right time and they would know what to do with the meat inside of it. Or, if they were particularly fortunate, find a pearl.

She had no such assurance in herself. She knew that starkly as she considered one of her raft mates who had made it big in real estate and now ran a hobby farm because he enjoyed staying busy and it was fun for the grand kids. In the way the three college buddies laughed with zero reserve—men who were probably misunderstood in high school but had found their tribe among the nerds that grew up to become brilliant engineers or analysts and could now afford to take trips like these while their cool-kid counterparts worked cash registers at their local convenience store.

She knew the simple choice to see the world differently could transform her point of view. But no matter how much interest these amazing people showed her, she couldn't quite let go like clinging to that piece of driftwood she'd collected as a child during a beach trip long since forgotten. She couldn't leave it behind. She kept taking it from one house to another, hiding in one closet, then another, clinging to it with emotion that she didn't understand.

The last night of the seven-day rafting trip, it rained heavily, and Valerie dreamed that she was back at her old office before she'd taken on freelance work ten years ago. The dream was a familiar one. She had made some mistake, and she was trying to fix it, but as hard as she tried, things just got messier and messier. It was the kind of dream that felt real—not visually but in emotion and tenor—so that she woke up multiple times throughout the night, trying to figure out how to explain how she had messed up by listing the wrong end-date of their trip on the company website.

She woke up to wet tents, wet trees, but gratefully no wet clothes. She had taken in what she had hung up to dry the night before and her shoes, which had been wet the night before, were thankfully under the rainfly too. The group would be leaving camp about a half hour early so that they could fit in the twelve miles before reaching Dagger Falls around noon that day. But Valerie was still the only participant up when she made a quick visit to the groover, the affectionate term the group gave to the modified latrine, which got its name from the older models with only bars for seats. Afterward, she planned to get her first blessed cup of coffee.

She was genuinely looking forward to her memory foam mattress, a hot shower, restroom facilities with privacy, and her own space with her own things. But she also recognized some grief hidden underneath the grit in her fingernails.

There was something simple in knowing that what she carried in a small yellow bag was all that was available to her. There was no room for things "just in case." She had brought three books, but she had only read about twenty pages of the only one she'd bothered to crack open through the week.

She'd learned what was important on rafting trips. Camp clothes in any condition could be worn all week. But good rafting shoes were vital. She could go without her regular face cream, but needed a lot more Vaseline and lip balm. Her bloody, chapped lips were a testament of that fact. The neoprene gloves she had bought on a whim in Stanley were one of the best purchases she'd made, but she should have also bought warm wool gloves, or brought some from among the dozens in a basket in the hall closet. They would have been useful in the chilly late evenings and early mornings.

The discoveries felt important, and she was certain there was some deeper meaning there, but after seven days of less-than-normal sleep and an abnormal diet, and after all the exertion of paddling the paddleboat most of the previous day, her brain was too tired to parse it all out right then. *That'll be a fun way of reliving some of the experiences of the trip*, she thought. Process thing when she got home.

"So, are you going to go in our boat with us today, Val?" Bob asked as he helped her take down her rainfly.

"Bob, you don't need to do that. Evie and David will be back as soon as they're done brushing their teeth."

"I've got to stay busy. I don't know what to do with myself if my hands aren't busy, so really, thank you for giving me something to do."

"You're welcome, I guess, but seriously, you are the kindest man. Thank you so much for all the help throughout this crazy week."

"You betcha! Happy to do it."

"And to your original question, I don't know for sure. I guess I'll leave it up to the two who are in charge of this operation." Valerie nodded toward David and Evie, who were using the camp's makeshift pump sink. They were joking about something, laughing and spewing toothpaste. Just then, Maggie walked past.

"Are you up for one more paddle with me, Evie, and David today, Valerie?"

I guess that answers that question, she thought. She smiled at Bob, and Bob gave Valerie a knowing nod.

"Yep. I am all in."

Despite the early launch time, there was still plenty of free time after packing up camp, loading the sweep boat, and eating breakfast. Valerie tried to help a couple of other participants with their tents to return the favor Bob had always shown her. But after several kind declines, she gave up and thought she'd find out what Evie was up to.

Valerie knew where to look.

"I thought I'd find you here."

Evie looking up from her sketchpad. She sat cross-legged, facing the downstream flow where an opening in the canyon provided a broader view of the darkening sky. As Valerie approached, she glanced at the pad and saw that Evie was using the same technique she had used the last time—focusing on the dark places first and leaving space for light to pop out from the contrast.

"You've captured those darker clouds wonderfully, Evie. Really. Nice!"

"Thanks. I've never seen anything like it, really. It's a bit apocalyptic, isn't it?"

"Yeah, now we'll all catch some horrible disease and turn into zombies. I can see the Netflix series now. They'll call it something like *What Happened Down River*. Something hokey like that."

"Don't give them any new ideas. There's already way too many zombie shows as it is." Evie smiled and adjusted her position a bit so there was more space on the large rock where she was sitting.

Valerie sat beside Evie, who kept her eyes focused on the sky in front of her. "I wonder if there's any way to learn that the things we think we care so much about, like the need to feel important or competent or good enough, don't matter very much at all," Valerie asked, mostly to herself.

Evie put down her pad and looked confused.

"Don't let me stop those creative juices." Valerie tenderly turned her daughters' face back toward the sky. Valerie had made some serious gains over the last couple of days with her daughter. Subtle changes, but significant. The fact that she could playfully turn Evie's face back to the river with confidence that Evie wouldn't bristle at her touch clearly showed that. So, Valerie sat enjoying the closeness. As she gazed out over the rhythm of the river, her mind strayed easily to moments from the past. Things she wished she'd said or hadn't said to her own mom who was now retired and alone in a house she was proud to have paid for herself but would need to sell soon to pay for assisted-living expenses.

What a sad thing it was to learn how to appreciate people just when they reached the point in their lives when they could no longer retain the full brightness of joy that could come from that kind of grateful relationship. Her own mom was slowly losing her memory and eventually her sense of self entirely. Valerie certainly had regrets about that relationship too. She would take back all the painful words and share the unspoken ones in a heartbeat if she could do life over again.

But maybe mother–daughter relationships are more like one of Evie's sketches, she thought. *The goal is never perfection.* The aim was just exploration and learning, and if she hit on some beautiful elements from time to time, then she'd be that much better prepared to bring out those elements into future sketching adventures. All relationships feeding and nurturing others.

"You know I love you, right?" Valerie said, reaching out her hand to brush the bangs out of Evie's face.

Evie glanced at Valerie with an unknowing expression, unsure of what to say or how to find the words to describe the feelings Valerie could clearly read on her face.

"You are beautiful and brilliant and talented and strong-willed, and you care so much about so many things. But that's not why I love you."

"Come on, Mom. I know you love me. Let's not make a scene or anything," Evie stammered.

"Sorry. Let me say this last thing, and then I'll let you draw in peace. I love you no matter what because you're my daughter and I'm your mom. And I am going to be on your side no matter what. Got it?"

Evie nodded, but Valerie knew full well that Evie didn't know what she meant. Not really. Evie wouldn't know about the mysterious way Valerie's love stayed firmly attached even when she felt attacked and stung by the most hurtful things or had her patience challenged to the brink of collapse, taking her emotions to places she didn't even know they could go. Evie couldn't know what it was like to love a child even when, sometimes, she didn't like that child much.

Valerie squeezed Evie's shoulder, and the two women locked eyes in one more rewarding moment of connection, then wandered back toward where the rest of the group was sitting. David was having an animated conversation with one of the college buddies. Valerie didn't want to bother either of them, and she didn't feel up for a conversation on what she imagined would be tax write-offs or wealth inequities or the carrying capacities of suspension bridges, or something like that.

She wandered her way to the cooking area where Maggie was finishing putting things away.

"Hey. Can I help with anything?" Valerie asked.

"No way. You're paying an awful lot to let me do the cleaning. Why don't you find a comfortable spot to read one of those great books you brought?"

Valerie picked up on the slight upturn of Maggie's eyebrows with her mention of books—as in plural.

"Yeah. I just never know what mood I might be in when I sit down to read. But right now, my mind is racing too much for me to focus on reading. I was hoping for some mindless task to distract me."

"Got it. Well, we have plenty of mindless tasks to take care of before we launch. Do you mind putting all the food on that card table over there into those two coolers?" Maggie pointed to the items off to her left.

"Gladly."

Valerie focused on the task at hand—putting mustard and mayonnaise and loaves of bread in sealed coolers.

"Should I take them down to the rafts?"

"That would be great. Thanks," Maggie said encouragingly.

Just before Valerie hefted her first cooler, Maggie called after her.

"Hey, Valerie, are you doing okay?"

"I think so. Why do you ask?" she said, standing slowly.

"You've just seemed quieter this morning. That's all. Just wanted to make sure."

"How sweet of you to ask. I guess I can't help but feel nervous with that red sky down river."

"You're right. It's pretty scary looking. I'm not going to insult your intelligence by telling you everything will be fine and all that crap because, frankly, I don't know. But we take a risk anytime we step outside our homes, right? And we'll watch out for that amazing sunset in Salmon tonight."

"Good perspective. We'll get through this, and then we'll be able to laugh about it later."

"Right." Maggie and Valerie both laughed quietly, then Valerie took the two coolers down to the rafts.

Valerie's comment of laughing together later was a throw away. Maggie knew she shouldn't read into it. But she felt the thrill of unrealistic connections flooding inside herself so fast that she took a load that was way too heavy for her down to the rafts just so she'd have to focus her full attention on that.

"Ready to shove off, Mags?" Nate asked from behind her.

She plopped down her heavy load onto the gravel beach.

"Whoa! We can make more than one trip. Save your back." Nate took one of the containers and hefted it onto the raft.

"Thanks. I knew it was too heavy about halfway down, but I was too stubborn to put one of the boxes down. You know me," Maggie said sheepishly.

"Yeah, I do. And I like you too much for you to deal with lower back pain. Way too young for that." Nate easily lifted the other box and put his hand on her back with a smile as he passed her to grab the last supplies.

She remembered their meetup plans and realized another reason to be nervous, but it kind of felt like excitement too.

With everything loaded, the groups filed onto the rafts. Maggie helped Valerie's family onto theirs and pushed the raft off from the beach and into the fast current, which set them off at a quick clip.

"Hey Mom. Do you want to trade places at all? It's kind of fun getting the spray hit you, and sitting next to Dad isn't all that bad either."

"That's a winning endorsement," David said, giving Evie a playful shove.

"Thanks for asking, Evie. But you two seem to be quite the team. We'll need you to pull together to get us past that red sky up there. And I'm getting plenty of splash from you guys back here anyway."

"Ouch. That burns," Maggie joked as she steered them into the deeper water. "It's almost a shame that there isn't another day so you could switch up seating. You'd notice the difference, for sure. In the back, you have a lot more influence on turns but less on speed. In the front, it's the opposite."

"So we're the forward momentum, and you're the ball and chain. Quite appropriate, eh?" David winked at Valerie.

Valerie made a messy paddle stroke that sent a small wave of water in David's direction. "Oops. Sorry. You'd think I'd have those paddle strokes down better by now," Valerie said.

David reacted too slowly and was soaked, but Maggie picked up on his relentlessly, warm smile. David reached behind his back, and Valerie leaned forward to give his hand a quick squeeze. The raft soon fell to a comfortable silence as the four people in it enjoyed their last views of the high craggy walls.

A squelching crack and roaring explosion split the stillness. Before anyone could identify where the sound had come from, a mature tree slid between the slanted rock of the reverberating canyon and struck the raft with terrifying force. The tremendous weight of its trunk yanked the raft downward and sent a wave upward that crested fifteen feet up the canyon walls.

Branches scraped across Maggie's face and legs as she tried to jump away from the massive tree, but the downward force of it pulled her underwater. She wriggled desperately at a loop in the raft that her foot had gotten entangled in. At last, forcing her shoe off and pushing off the river bottom, she broke the surface. David was already up and helping Evie toward the shore. She spun around, rubbing water out of her nose, her eyes darting in every direction for any sign of Valerie.

Not seeing her, Maggie dove under the surface several times, but the water was hopelessly cloudy with the dirt and debris kicked up by the tree. On top of that, the branches and needles were everywhere. After her fourth attempt, she had to make for shore if she was going to make it at all.

Valerie had a moment of consciousness right after the tree struck her squarely on the face and barreled into her chest. Time froze

exist in that bubble of space and existence. She felt no anger or ill-will toward the tree that dragged her down and ended her life. How could she? The tree certainly didn't do it out of malice.

No one living would ever get the benefit of her description of the experience though. It felt like a flash of all the paths she had taken—all the decisions she had made when confronting the proverbial fork in the road that had led her to that precise moment. And as she lost her sense of self and worry and the consciousness she had taken for granted her whole life—that sense of who she was in the universe—and after the momentary pain, she settled into a most profound and overwhelming feeling of gratitude. Gratitude that she had been hit instead of Evie or David or Maggie. Gratitude for the recent, albeit small, moments of connection she'd had with her daughter. Gratitude for the passionate and meaningful moments with her husband. Gratitude for what her life had meant and for the few lives she had shared it with during those brief years. She had done the best she could, and she drifted away in that comforting awareness until it too drifted away.

The pine knew it wouldn't live forever. Although compared to human life, it might seem as though trees could. Over the last decades of life, there had been more urgency in absorbing enough energy. More moments of, in its way, gasping for nutrients to withhold what it had gained and what it had become after centuries of fighting gravity. Less assurance that its roots would hold. And so now that the pine had become something else—a log slowly being pulled downstream, losing its remaining branches day by day—it felt content as its last living cells were incrementally snuffed out.

ANDY WAS THE FIRST TO ARGUE THAT THERE WAS A CLEAR CONnection between the fire and what was the only loss of life in the Payette National Forest that summer, though it was never determined whether the fire could be blamed. Though the fire never breached the Middle Fork, some speculated that the long duration of the fire killed off enough trees on the hillsides around the river that they fell despite the strange change in the wind's direction.

He tried to stay away from the speculation the best he could, but when he got back to his home office, he couldn't avoid overhearing discussions between botanists who pointed out that the massive scale of the fire had weakened root systems built and intertwined by the community of trees over several centuries. Most Forest Service employees agreed that climate change had been a significant factor too—that the fuels were drier and the temperatures well above average. And all of them shared stories of complaints by community members who were more than willing to give them an earful explaining why, *if the Forest Service would do this or that differently*, the forests would return to some magical, perfect state. Some claimed the agency should cut more timber. That, back in the day, when more logging trucks full of good-sized timber were rolling off hillsides, there weren't big fires like the Sheep Mountain Complex. But others refuted that, believing that if the forests were left to their own devices and systems, including letting fire play its natural role on the landscape, nature would correct the last century of mismanagement. Andy tried particularly hard to avoid hearing the laughter as employees laid on punchlines at the end of their stories.

Because he knew the person who had died.

Valerie.

He'd only met her once—the morning he was chewed out by Glen and told to return to fire camp where he was dismissed from serving any further assignments on that fire. Or at least, he assumed, any future assignment as a PIO. At first, he was nervous about losing his job as a front-desk person and an engine boss, but those fears were quickly dispelled. There was just too much need for firefighters and not nearly enough interest in firefighting jobs anymore. And his home district was struggling to fill positions, so he fell right back into his normal summer routine, glad to have had the PIO experience, which helped him appreciate the less nuanced role at the fire line. There were no political undercurrents driving his work when digging line with the hand crews, trying to prevent a wildfire from escaping containment lines, or with his engine searching for new fire starts in the woods.

But weeks after returning from his only PIO assignment, the image of Valerie sitting in her wicker chair lingered. He didn't think he could have persuaded her to evacuate in any other way than what he'd tried at the lodge. At least he'd tried, and she wouldn't have been any better off if he hadn't tried. He gave her the information she needed to make her own decision. There was some validation in that.

And, somehow, that validation spread in a broader sense than that one effort to make a difference. It completed a puzzle, helping him find the pieces he'd been searching for his whole working life. It made him feel more confident with his crew. It brought greater meaning to answering questions he was asked about past experiences like the Duck Valley Complex burnover incident.

And so when he left the office on a particularly fine Friday afternoon in mid-September, the air crisp and the start of a chill that reminded him that winter was around the corner, he was able to dedicate his full attention to adding a nice new coat of paint to the lookout tower's walls, to firm up the stairs, and even clear out some of the pervasive weeds so as to let the native plants have a better shot at growing strong.

Maggie wasn't able to process what had happened until she got back to Boise. Until that point, she did what she was told, focusing only on that. Get David and Evie on one of the other rafts. Get somewhere within range of a radio repeater so she could call emergency evacuation. Ride in the helicopter. Say something comforting to Evie. Anything. Knowing that it didn't really matter what she said. She understood why both David and Evie would disconnect from her as quickly as possible. She was tied to the most horrific event of their lives, though she was grateful that neither seemed to blame her.

She blamed herself enough for the three of them though. If she'd only left a bit earlier. Or later. If she hadn't insisted that the raft ride in the center of the river at that particular moment. There was no real reason why she needed the group to keep the raft centered on the river, other than it felt good to her obsessive-compulsive tendencies.

If she had advocated for evacuating like Andy had suggested…

She ran through plenty of alternative scenarios with that line of thinking. If she had advocated for a few seconds longer, then the raft would've been behind the falling tree and the large obstacle in the river would have only been a good primer for a quick life lesson about avoiding falling snags.

But after she had the space to process, and after she had given her landlord notice that she would be moving out—after reaching out to her parents, finally coming to terms with the reality that she would be spending the fall back at home—and after she had gone through a few therapy sessions, she came to a place that allowed her to begin to believe that if she had made any other choice, one of other rafts might have been hit. Or maybe the helicopter would have crashed on their way back to Boise. She hoped that, eventually, she could fully accept the truth that not all risks could be controlled. That there was inherent risk in everything she did day-to-day. And it usually wasn't her fault when things worked out poorly.

She enjoyed a wonderful "see you later not goodbye" dinner with Jay and his wife, which comforted her, knowing that she would see them again, not as fellow employees for a rafting company, but as friends while she finished her college degree in communications with an emphasis in technical writing the next spring.

And before leaving, she had that date with Nate as well. Sparks didn't exactly fly, maybe partly because of the shared pain they still felt after being so close to the tragedy on their last trip together. But when she gave him a hug as they were parting ways, she told him she'd stay in touch. And she meant it. Maybe being friends would work better.

She loaded up her car of her few things to take with her home to her parents' house back east. She nestled the pot planted with sunflower seeds snuggly so it would be safe during the journey. The seedlings were just starting to break above the soil line. The fact that the seeds could grow anywhere with sunlight, good soil, and water mattered to her. It was a nice reminder that she could do that too.

David and Evie returned home to their mountain town a couple of hours north of Boise. Everything felt wrong to David, and he had no idea how to help Evie or Thomas cope because he had no idea how he would ever learn to cope himself. Losing Valerie was like losing thousands of slices of her every day. A slice here and there, walking down the street, another couple of slices when looking at the ice cream shop or a half-dozen slices when looking for something in the garage. Dozens and dozens of slices in his home, which now felt like a place he had to get to know again—a place that comforted and repulsed him at the same time.

But time started to do its work for better or for worse. The visceral shock to his system slowly subsided into a constant ache. He and Evie and Thomas managed to scrape together something that resembled a routine just in time for school to start again. So many slices of loss at the school, but Evelyn seemed to relish the distraction, and for the first semester since her sixth-grade year, David didn't have to worry about her grades or her going to class. She just did it, and he was grateful.

As fall rolled into winter, snow came early, and with the cold and plowing and changing of the tires on his car to studded winter ones, he reached a point where he could manage a day without breaking down—in public at least—and take care of his clients' taxes. He was looking forward to tax season, to have his whole attention swallowed up.

Among all of the impacted players, the fallen pine transformed the most. After losing its moorings on the ridge, having occupied it for centuries, and after falling into the river below, it became a part of the natural means of recycling nutrients for reuse and new life. When Valerie's body was removed, the fallen tree was allowed to flow downstream. It was caught up with many other fallen trees that formed a logjam that provided shelter and places to hide and feed for fish migrating to and from the ocean—to spawn and to die and to have their nutrients recycled as well.

No one log ever made as much of a difference as when it was a free-standing tree, perhaps, but collectively, they nurtured generations of salmon that fed other animals who left parts of the fish along the forest floor, which, in turn, recycled nutrients from the ocean to the soil to grow future generations of trees.

Nothing was ever wasted in nature—not bodies, living or dead, animal or human; neither tree, standing or fallen. Trees became woody debris that the local environment had no way of remembering or paying tribute to, though each one made an important contribution. And, for now, regenerating their nutrients into new life was enough to keep that balance.

The End

About the Author

Chris Bentley is a District Ranger for the U.S. Forest Service. He received his Master's Degree from Indiana University's O'Neill School of Public and Environmental Affairs. Chris has written four books to date—*Running on Merit, Moments of Joy: Fifty-Two Ideas to Nurture Greater Meaning from Life, Soybean Revolution,* and now *When a Tree Falls in a Forest.* He lives in a small town in the mountains of Southern Idaho where he loves hiking and biking among the beautiful peaks and trees.

Start a conversation or ask a question on his website:
www.chrisbentleyinc.com
or email: connect@chrisbentleyinc.com.

You can also connect with Chris through social media:
Facebook: @cbentley1160
Instagram: @christoph.w.bentley